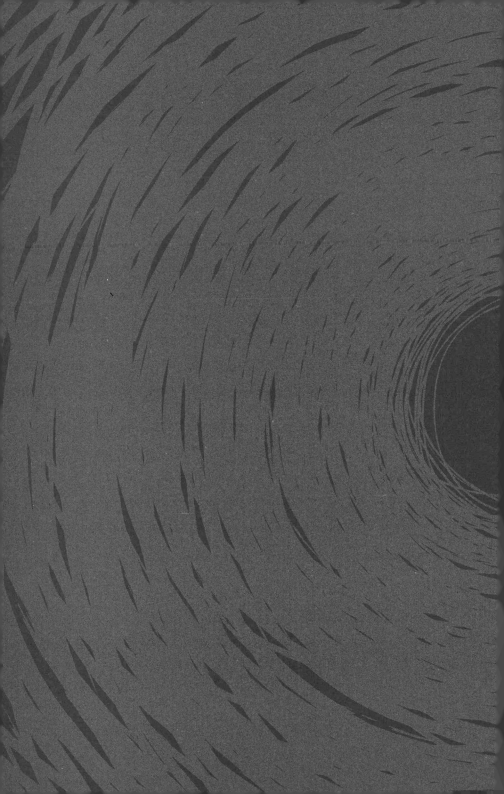

The CALL

PEADAR O'GUILIN

DAVID FICKLING BOOKS

SCHOLASTIC INC. · NEW YORK

Copyright © 2016 by Peadar O'Guilin

All rights reserved. Published by Scholastic Inc., *Publishers since 1920*, by arrangement
with David Fickling Books, Oxford, England. SCHOLASTIC and associated logos are trademarks
and/or registered trademarks of Scholastic Inc. DAVID FICKLING BOOKS and associated logos are
trademarks and/or registered trademarks of David Fickling Books.

First published in the United Kingdom in 2016 by
David Fickling Books, 31 Beaumont Street, Oxford OX1 2NP.

www.davidficklingbooks.com

The publisher does not have any control over and does not assume any responsibility for
author or third-party websites or their content.

Library of Congress Cataloging-in-Publication Data

Names: Ó Guilin, Peadar, author.
Title: The Call / Peadar Ó Guilin.
Description: First [American] edition. | New York : David Fickling Books/Scholastic Inc.,
2016. | "First published in the United Kingdom in 2016 by David Fickling Books." |
Summary: For the last twenty-five years every teenager in Ireland has been subject to
"the Call," which takes them away to the land of the Sidhe, where they are hunted for
twenty-four hours (though only three minutes pass in this world)—handicapped by her
twisted legs, Nessa Doherty knows that very few return alive, but she is determined
to be one of them.
Identifiers: LCCN 2016012970 | ISBN 9781338045611 (hardcover : alk. paper)
Subjects: LCSH: Fairies—Juvenile fiction. | Mythology, Celtic—Juvenile fiction. |
Survival—Juvenile fiction. | Good and evil—Juvenile fiction. | Ireland—Juvenile
fiction. | CYAC: Fairies—Fiction. | Mythology, Celtic—Fiction. | Survival—Fiction. |
Good and evil—Fiction. | People with disabilities—Fiction. | Ireland—Fiction.
Classification: LCC PZ7.O363 Cal 2016 | DDC 823.92 [Fic]—dc23
LC record available at https://lccn.loc.gov/2016012970

10 9 8 7 6 5 4 3 2 1   16 17 18 19 20

Printed in the U.S.A. 23

First edition, September 2016

Book design by Christopher Stengel

FOR MY SISTER, KLARA

Oh, my dearest friend!

I never thought you dead,

Until your horse came home,

Its reins along the ground,

Your heart's blood on its flanks.

FROM "CAOINEADH AIRT UÍ LAOGHAIRE"

BY EIBHLÍN DUBH NÍ CHONAILL (1773)

FOUR YEARS AGO:
THE THREE MINUTES

On her tenth birthday Nessa overhears an argument in her parents' bedroom. She knows nothing about the Three Minutes yet. How could she? The whole of society is working to keep its children innocent. She plays with dolls. She believes the lies about her brother, and when her parents tuck her into bed at night—her grinning dad, her fussy mam—they show her only love.

But now, with ten candles on a cake in the kitchen behind her, that's all supposed to change.

Dad can't know his daughter is right outside the door, and yet he whispers. "We don't need to tell her," he says. "She . . . she isn't able to run anyway. She's a special case. We could give her a few more years to be our baby."

Baby! Our baby! Nessa bristles at the thought. She's struggling to stand still, because with her twisted legs she makes quite a racket when she walks. However, once her mam, Agnes, starts sobbing, she decides she's had enough.

"Oh, for Crom's sake," she says, "I'm in the hall. I'm coming in and you'd better not be kissing!" She means that last part as a joke, but it falls flat.

"Come in then," Dad says. He still possesses enough greying hair to cover his scalp. Almost. He's even older than Mam, and on a bad day Nessa wonders if that's why she was born weak enough to catch polio. Her cousin told her that once, and Nessa often thinks of it.

"I know about Santa Claus," she says, walking in. "If that's what this is about. I've known for years already, but—"

Agnes starts heaving like she's been punched in the stomach. She shakes hard enough to rattle the bed beneath her. Dad wraps her tight with his long, skinny arms, and for a moment it's like this hug is the only thing stopping bits of her from flying off.

A chill steals up Nessa's spine. She can't know it, but this is the first hint of the fear that will never leave her again; that will ruin her life as it has ruined the life of everybody in the whole country.

Now Dad is crying too. His tears barely show: a hint of moisture about the eyes, his sobs thick, as though squeezed through a wad of cloth.

Nessa takes a ragged breath. "Whatever it is . . . ," she says—and deep inside a part of her is begging her to shut up, to stop, to turn around! "Whatever it is, I want to know."

So they tell her. About the Three Minutes and what has happened to her older brother. And she laughs, because that's her nature and the whole situation is absurd. It's one of her dad's stupid pranks! Of course it is.

But they keep the horrible story going and the fear builds up and up inside her until she screams at them, hysterical, horrified, "You're lying! You're lying!" She falls, her awkward left leg giving way.

For the next two days Nessa refuses to play or to talk. But she's too intelligent not to recognize the truth. The clues have surrounded her for a lifetime already, and only the monstrousness of it, allied to the trusting nature of her now-ended childhood, has allowed her not to see it before. She has never asked herself where all the teenagers were. Or why she has almost never spoken to anybody who is seventeen or eighteen or twenty.

But if she refuses to let the doctors put her to sleep, this is the future: Sometime during her adolescence, the Sídhe will come for her, as they come these days for everyone. They will hunt her down, and if she fails to outrun them, Nessa will die.

On the third day her twisted legs carry her out of her bedroom. Her eyes are dry. She says, "I'm going to live. And nobody's going to stop me." She believes every word of it.

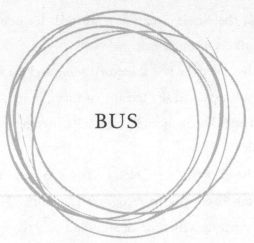

BUS

Four years have passed, and Nessa is standing in the sunshine at the bus station in Letterkenny. Everything is old and everybody is old too. Except for herself and the red-haired, red-cheeked Megan, openly smoking "greenhouse" tobacco and daring the adults around them to interfere.

Nessa wants to say something to her friend. Along the lines of: "We need to stay fit if we're to survive." Only one in ten children makes it through their teenage years as it is. But the warmth on her face is too nice to let her spoil the mood.

They buy their tickets from the granny in the office and head outside to get seats.

"Will you look at that bus!" says Megan. The tired engine burps fumes of recycled vegetable oil so that everything smells deep fried. "We'll be lucky if it can hold the weight of the rucksack you brought. It's gonna strand us halfway to nowhere."

A big, middle-aged police sergeant waits by the bus, brandishing an iron needle four inches long. Sweating under his cap, he swabs it with alcohol and jabs it into the arm of everybody getting on.

"Do I look like a Sidhe to you?" growls one old woman.

"I hear they can look any way they want, missus."

"In that case, they wouldn't want to look like me!"

"True enough," he says.

She curses as he stabs her anyway.

He grins. "My apologies! Iron's supposed to hurt them."

When it comes to Nessa's turn, the officer stares at her legs and can't keep the pity off his face. *Didn't your parents love you enough to kill you?*

Nessa's own expression stays bland. "Was there something else?" she asks.

Megan butts in. "Sorry, Sergeant." Her tone is polite and respectful. She has the sweetest face in creation: rosy cheeks and sparkling green eyes. "What my friend is trying to say is, Mind your own business, you goggle-eyed turd sniffer."

When Megan steps up to face the needle, the sergeant makes *extra* sure that she's no spy. She takes the iron well enough, but the second he withdraws it, she kicks his feet from under him and twists his arm up behind his back so that the adult, twice her size, is on his knees before her.

"Megan," cries Nessa, "enough!"

"They train us pretty well," Megan says with a wink. She releases him and gets onto the bus.

The coach rattles off toward Monaghan, with Megan chatting every step of the way, mostly in English. Nessa tries to keep her own responses in Sídhe, not because she loves it, but because her ability to speak the enemy's tongue may one day save her life.

She knows she should find a better friend: somebody who won't smoke or grow her hair dangerously long. But Nessa's not quite ready to sacrifice all the world's happiness and fun to the ancient enemies of her race. Not yet.

Shortly after Lifford, they roll over a bridge into what used to be Northern Ireland. Nobody cares about that sort of thing anymore. The only border recognized by the Sídhe is the sea that surrounds the island from which they were driven thousands of years before. No human can leave or enter. No medicines or vaccines or spare parts for the factories that once made them; nor messages of hope or friendship; nothing.

A veil of mist hangs off the coast, and all those within, whatever their passports used to say, now belong to the same endangered species.

The boy gets on at Omagh. He's fit-looking, of course, with the body of a runner. Most teenagers are the same, but it doesn't look awkward on him, despite the fact that he has more growing to do. He smiles at the sight of them. "Off to Dublin, girls?" The Sídhe words spring naturally from his tongue. Nessa likes the look of him, and his bright, friendly confidence. He likes her too, she thinks, but won't have seen her legs yet.

As usual it's Megan who answers. "Our survival college is in Roscommon."

"The one in Boyle? Aye, I heard of that one. Didn't one of their boys make it through two nights ago?"

The girls gasp. "Who?" says Nessa.

Twenty-five years ago, when the Sídhe began taking teenagers, less than one in a hundred survived. These days, with constant training, with fitness and study, with every spare cent in an impoverished country aimed at keeping them alive, the odds have improved tenfold. But they are still low enough that the thought that somebody she knows has made it through fills Nessa with excitement.

"Ponzy, I think. Is that even a real name?"

"No way!" squeals Megan. "Not Ponzy! Not that wee turd!" But she's laughing, because she likes Ponzy—everybody likes him. Nessa is smiling hard enough to hurt her own cheeks, and the strange boy lights up in response, but not as much as he should.

"It's just . . . ," he says. "It's just he came back a wee bit . . . *different*."

"Different how?" asks Nessa. Behind the boy's head they pass a neat little bungalow with trimmed hedges and a lawn full of lettuce. She'll never forget it, because rather than answering her, the boy disappears and his empty clothing falls to the floor.

Everybody else takes a second to gasp, but not Nessa; she's on her feet straight away. "Stop!" she screams. Then, realizing she has spoken in Sídhe, she repeats the command in English.

"We've had a Call," she cries. "Driver! You have to reverse! Reverse!"

Megan, proud owner of a windup watch, has already started the countdown. "Twenty seconds," she says. "I . . . I may have missed a few at the start there."

Half a panicky minute has already passed when the bus starts to go backward and Nessa has to hold on for dear life. A government car has come up behind them and the passengers at the back of the bus wave frantically to make it move. A whole sixty seconds are wasted in this way, but soon they are back beside the house with the lettuce garden and Nessa calls the halt.

Was it here? she wonders. *Or were we a little farther on?*

"How long?" she asks aloud.

"Two forty-five," Megan says, watching the murderous second hand. "It's three minutes now!"

That's when the boy returns. Strictly speaking, the famous "Three Minutes" are three minutes and four seconds. Everyone knows this, because many Calls were caught on security cameras in the first terrible year.

The boy's body reappears and thumps down hard onto the floor. Nessa is relieved to see that it's not one of the really awful ones. There's nothing to churn the stomach here, other than a little blood and a set of tiny antlers growing from the back of his head. The Sídhe can be a lot more imaginative than that, and they even have what experts refer to as a "sense of fun." Nessa shivers.

"They didn't catch him for a long time," Megan whispers. "Didn't get a chance to *really* work on him."

A few of the old people are crying and want to get off the bus, but it's not like the early days anymore. They might disturb the body as they try to step over it, and that's just not allowed. The antlered boy will lie there until the Recovery Bureau agents have examined him properly in Monaghan.

"These girls have to get to school," says the driver, and that's all there is to it.

Megan glares the weepers into silence, then sits looking straight ahead. Nessa too strives to appear calm, to gaze out at the passing countryside, trying not to think about all the murders committed by one faction or another in order to farm it.

She jumps as Megan grabs her by the shoulder and hisses, "Stop!"

"Stop? Stop what?"

"You were banging your head again. Against the window."

"Oh, yeah." Nessa can feel the bruise forming on her forehead. She finds that she's gasping for air like a hooked fish and more aware of the handsome boy's body than she has ever been of anything in her life.

The Sídhe stole him away for a little over three minutes, but in their world, the Grey Land, an entire day has passed, panic and pain in every second of it.

"Is it because he looks like Anto?" Megan asks.

Nessa suppresses a shudder. "He looks nothing like Anto."

The redhead shrugs. She doesn't care. And neither should Nessa. Not if she wants to live.

COLLEGE

They carry their own bags through the gate and go barefoot to toughen the soles of their feet. Nessa knows her friend is walking slower than she needs to, in order to spare her embarrassment. Neither speaks. It's a beautiful evening, coming up on autumn. The hooded crows, croaking as loud as they can, have filled the trees with grey and black feathers. Now and again a group of them will wheel out over the ivy-covered dorms and the monastic buildings that cower between them. Yes, Boyle Survival College is a clumsy hotchpotch of old and new, but Nessa is always relieved to see it. Much as she loves her parents, this is her real home, where everyone faces the same danger and fear, and shares the same hope too.

A few hundred feet away from the main entrance, and Anto comes out to join them. He grins, a little shyly, Nessa thinks, and she has to clamp down hard on the smile that threatens to take over her own face. They *can't* be together, and that's all there is to it. They can't.

"How's tricks?" he asks, his Dublin accent stretching the vowels in all the wrong directions. "Seen any nice puddles up in Donegal?"

It doesn't matter that he's handsome, that he has a face full of mischief—Megan rolls her eyes at him. "I have that Crom-twisted study to hand in to the Turkey," she says. "Can't be wasting my time on the likes of you, Anto, you filthy Dub." And off she strides, leaving the other two to fall back into embarrassed silence together.

Nessa likes that Anto doesn't offer to carry her bag, that never once has she seen pity in his eyes. Mostly he just likes to laugh, a viral happiness that spreads wherever he goes.

But he's not laughing right now. They are walking closer together than they are supposed to, their breathing synchronized, their gazes straight ahead, and both of them are remembering the same thing: the time she accidentally kissed him for ten full minutes.

It was the day Tommy was taken. The first time she ever witnessed what the Sídhe could really do to you, could do to her. And all the pointless longings broke free at once, shattering the dam she had built to keep them out. She has rebuilt it since then. Stronger than ever.

They have almost reached the main entrance when he says, "Why not?"

Nessa doesn't need to ask what he means. She stops, forcing him to stop too.

"You told me you liked my hair," she says.

"I did." His left hand is fiddling with the crucifix his mother gave him. He already knows he's not going to enjoy this.

"I shaved it off."

"Of course, Nessa. Nabil advised all of us to do so. I cut my braid."

"Right, Anto. And I liked having hair. When I go home, my mother cries to see me bald. But now, nothing . . . *nothing* can grab it, you understand? When the Sídhe Call me, that's one less thing to worry about."

"Of course." His face is pale. He hates this. Hates to talk about the inevitable day they will all be taken. But avoiding it is the problem everybody has here. They daydream. They sneak around forming bonds and distractions. Eating too much. Training too little. Speaking English instead of Sídhe.

She tells him the same thing she once told her parents: "I'm going to live." Her voice is as cold as she can make it, which is very cold indeed. "That was a one-off, that time with Tommy. I'm not interested anymore."

Anto is not allowed into the girls' dorm. She leaves him at the bottom of the stairs, and her face is as blank as a new sheet of paper. She doesn't look back; her hands don't tremble even slightly. She's getting so much better at this. Nessa knows Anto. She can trust him to leave her alone.

Miraculously she is still holding it together by the time she reaches the top of the stairs. There's a lump in her throat, but nobody can see that, and the speed of her breathing will be put down to dragging such a heavy bag after her.

The thing is that in spite of what she has said about distractions, Nessa is far more of a risk for Anto than the reverse. Of all the people she knows, his spirit is the most gentle. Stupidly so. Pointlessly. By Crom it makes her angry! Nobody who thinks as he does will last a minute in the other world. He's going to die, and it won't be quick.

Stop it! Stop it! She can't afford such thoughts. More than once they have made her . . . *reckless*, made her do that stupid Romeo thing.

She passes through the swing doors into a long, well-lit room of thirty beds. Twenty-six of them are still needed, but this is Year 5, the crucial year when most of the occupants will be Called. The proof of this can be found one floor farther up, where the girls' dorm for Year 6 boasts a mere ten beds, of which five are still in use. As for Year 7, it has lost all but two boys and one girl and none of these will see Christmas.

But nobody is acting like they believe any of that. Antoinette is even smoking out the window, grinning back at the rest of them with dark pudgy cheeks. At least fifteen of them are here already. Athletic girls from every part of Ireland, whose birthdays happen to fall in September or early October.

Nicole natters at Marya; Squeaky Emma fades into the background while Liz Sweeney scowls at everybody from the far corner.

They've all been home for two weeks and have plenty to chat about. Aoife holds up a bag of sugary treats baked by her Polish grandmother. She got her blonde hair and a ridiculous level of generosity from the same place, but her accent is just as much dirty Dub as Anto's. "You hear Ponzy made it?" she asks Nessa.

"I did!" And finally Nessa feels the tension easing from her shoulders. "Good old Ponzy! Will he come back as a veteran?"

"Dunno . . . He's staying home for now. Can't wait to read his account. Hey, you having a biscuit?"

Nessa, of course, never has a biscuit. She shakes her head.

As promised, Megan has gone to drop in her report to Ms. Breen, the school principal—aka the Turkey. So Nessa can dump her gear on her friend's bed until she gets organized.

First out of the bag is her *History of the Sídhe*: a mere hundred pages that contain all human knowledge of the species that has sworn to make the Irish extinct. There are larger books about them, of course, running to thousands of pages in some cases. But their writers have little more to offer than fear and speculation. Nessa prefers facts, and there isn't a paragraph in the *History* that she doesn't know by heart.

The next book is a heftier one. It consists of last year's Testimonies: the accounts of boys and girls who returned from the land of the Sídhe alive and with enough of their sanity intact to report on what they saw and heard.

The final book, a present from her mam when she first left home, is *Dánta Grádha*—a collection of love poetry. It's exactly the sort of thing she told Anto she has no truck with. She knows most of this one by heart too.

The double doors swing open again. Sarah Taaft stands there like a single block of muscle. The former US Marine must be in her late forties, weathered by wind and sun, but it hasn't softened her in the least. "We're going for a run," she shouts in English—she has never learned a word of Sídhe. "Tracksuits on."

Nessa feels a moment of dread as that pale gaze swings her way. "You coming, Nessa?"

"Of course I'm coming." She feels herself turning red, all the more so when Taaft rolls her eyes.

"We won't hold up for you."

"You never do."

Nessa doesn't need their charity. She is the first one changed. The first to reach the double doors. And *nobody* can catch her down a flight of stairs. She has developed a technique of locking her legs in place and sliding down from step to step on the tough soles of her feet. She is never more than a breath away from disaster, with only her arms on banister and wall to keep control.

Taaft shouts down after her. "No frickin' stairs in fairyland, kid! It's not gonna help you there!"

Nessa hits the ground floor at enormous speed, falling with precision to slide along the polished tiles almost as far as the main entrance.

Chuckwu is just arriving with his bags over his shoulder. "What're you doing on the floor?" he asks.

"Going for a run of course." She refuses a hand up. Already she can hear the rumble and laughter of the rest of the dorm charging down the stairs behind her. "Gotta go." From here to the trees she can only limp, and in no time at all the class passes her by. There's Antoinette, grinning and blowing her a tobacco-scented kiss, while Liz Sweeney tries to muscle past. Even Megan has arrived, one arm still out of her tracksuit. "That dirty wee bitch of a turkey! Tell you later, Ness . . ."

And finally here comes Taaft, jogging past her. "Seriously, kid . . ."

Then they're gone. Nessa's legs ache by the time she reaches the trees, but she doesn't allow herself to rest. "Stick to the rules," she mutters. "Stick to the rules."

She's an expert at this by now. She spots branches that are just the right size and knows too exactly how they should be broken, until, moments later, she has created a pair of springy crutches for herself.

Nessa has stronger arms than anyone she knows. Over short stretches she can keep up with most of the runners in her class, male and female alike. But not today. This is going to be a loop run, as they call it.

It takes her an hour, down into the dip between the hills, her crutches skidding dangerously on the first fallen leaves of the year; then curving up the switchback, along the ridge, until, as twilight falls, she reaches the formation known as "the Old Man"; the lone figure of Sergeant Taaft is sitting there, an illicit bottle of beer in her hand.

Nessa halts before reaching her. She trembles and sweats, panting far more than any of her classmates would have by this point.

"Just give it up, kid," Taaft says. "Go home."

Nessa bites back the first reply that comes to her. It's dangerous to antagonize Taaft. There's a reason she's the only member of staff without a nickname.

"Why are you out here, Sergeant?"

Taaft looks up. She has an angry face, made of toothaches and crab apples. But amid the pine smells and the forgiving rays of a dipping sun, she is as serene and lovely as the Madonna. "Maybe I'm hoping to catch a fairy."

"One of the Aes Sídhe?"

"Sure. You think I don't know that word, kid? The 'People of the Mounds'?" She takes a long swallow from the clay bottle. Several more lie at her feet. "I even know where they got the name. I read that Book of Conquests of yours. How you drove them out of their homes and forced that treaty on them—"

"I wasn't even born! Nobody was!"

"Your people sent them 'under the mounds.' Whatever the hell that means. And thousands of years later they turn up again and they're gonna wipe you out."

"They won't!" Nessa takes a deep breath. The sweat is starting to cool on her skin. She knows she should go, but will not give Taaft the satisfaction of rattling her. "More of us are surviving all the time," she says. "It's up to one in ten from one in a hundred twenty-five years ago."

"The fairies won't stand for it, kid. You can bet your life they're working on a plan right now to turn those odds back around. Whatever they come up with, I only hope it brings them here where I can snap their scrawny necks."

And that's exactly what she does to the clay bottle. It cracks as loud as a gunshot, spilling beer onto the soil.

Nessa swallows. "I have to get back, Sergeant."

Stopping to chat was a mistake. She's given her arms time to remember how tired they are. She skids down the slope, her legs catching on stray roots and stones. By the time she makes it into the refectory, everyone else has showered and their spoons are already scraping the bottom of their plates.

Anto looks relieved to see her and then pretends not to notice as she heads for one of the girls' tables and squeezes in between Megan and Antoinette. Conor Geary, on the other hand, has followed her with his eyes all the way from the door. He towers over everyone at the boys' tables. He could squash her with one blow of his fists and always looks at her as though that's exactly what he intends. She will find out why soon enough, but it won't be today.

"By Crom, but you stink!" says Megan. "Luckily this filthy stew is slowly killing all my senses. Look! I saved you just enough to keep you in the bathroom all night."

"Why should I go to the bathroom at all, Megan, when your bed is right beside mine?"

"You're calling me a turd, Nessa Doherty."

"I'm what?"

"If my bed is a toilet, and I'm in it, then—"

Antoinette interrupts them. Her plate is so clean it looks like it has just come out of the shop. She dips a fork into the rapidly cooling sludge. "Always happy to help, my darlings," she says.

There are eight to a table here in the massive hall, with each class in its own section, boys and girls separate. The biggest cohort consists of the Year 1s, the ten-year-olds. They look so tiny, so puny and sweet. They freeze like rabbits whenever the bell rings or when one of the burly instructors so much as looks at them.

At the top of the room lies the survivors' table, where three of those who have come back from the Sídhe eat in the company of the instructors. Nabil is there tonight, although he doesn't touch pork. His great dark eyes always seem so sad in such a gentle face. Maybe the scars running through his beard hold the reason for that. He doesn't impress Taaft, however, who scowls on discovering that the only free seat is on the Frenchman's left.

Then there are the teachers' tables, where Alanna Breen holds court. A famous scholar, she wrote *History of the Sídhe* and speaks their language like a native. She is joined this evening by the cadaverous Ms. Sheng, teacher of field medicine, and the portly, red-faced Mr. Hickey—another actual survivor, one of the early ones—who instructs in hunt theory. He's laughing about something, but whatever the joke, he's the only one who gets it.

Many of the remaining teachers prefer to eat alone or in the nearby town of Boyle.

Alanna Breen clinks her glass and silence spreads through the room. She stands, uncaring of the way the folds on her neck wobble when she moves, even though this particular feature has earned her the nickname of "the Turkey" among the students. Her appearance isn't helped by a tiny chin cowering in the shadow of a great ski jump of a nose. However, her voice is strong, and the words come easily, each one a perfect grammatical jewel of case and gender or tense and number.

"You'll all have heard by now that one of our own, that Ponzy, survived a Call."

She waits for the cheering to come to an end. "He won't be returning to join us here at Boyle, but his account will be published early next week. There'll be copies in my office, and Mr. Hickey"—she bows to the red-faced gentleman at her side—"Mr. Hickey will be sharing the relevant parts with you all."

"The relevant parts, miss?" This was from Bartley, one of Ponzy's two remaining classmates in Year 7.

"The relevant parts," she confirms, and so stunned are the audience that nobody else speaks for a while. Survivor accounts are always published in full. But the boy on the bus this morning, the one who was Called, said something about Ponzy, that he had been . . . *changed.*

"We all knew Ponzy," says Ms. Breen, "or Jack Ponsonby, as I suppose I should say. He has asked . . . he has asked that we remember him as he was. And having read his account, and in consultation with our master of hunt theory, I have agreed to leave out the final paragraph and any photographs of Ponzy's . . . um . . . *injuries.* Now, that's the end of the matter. We're glad to have him back. To have another living soul to keep the future alive for our dear country. We'll be serving dessert in a moment. But first the toast."

And she raises her glass, they all do, and cries, fervently, passionately, "The Nation must survive! The future is ours!"

Nessa sees that the ten-year-olds haven't joined in, but instead they are resting their heads on the tables.

"Poor darlings," says Antoinette. "They're sleeping. They've been given the Welcome Tea."

"It's pretty sick, if you ask me," says Megan, and Nessa nods, despite the fact that she disagrees with her friend. The Year 1s are about to get the most important lesson the survival college can teach. In a few hours, each of them will wake up naked and alone in the forest. It is an experience that will terrify them, that will mark them forever. It is meant to, because if it ever happens again, it means they've been Called by the Sídhe.

THE CLIMB

History class is a chance to doze right up until, out of the blue, the Turkey asks Antoinette, "Why do you think you're here?"

"Who? Me?" Antoinette practically jumps out of her seat. She hastily covers up the heroically proportioned male torso she's been scratching onto her desk. It's not really the sort of thing Ms. Breen appreciates, what with being the head of the college and all. "Um, why am I here, miss? Uh . . . the Sídhe want to kill me?"

"Oh, they mean to do more than kill you, child. They want to *twist* you. To crumple you up like an old sheet of paper. I'm here trying to save you, and you don't listen to a word I say!"

The principal doesn't normally teach class herself, but Chapman is having one of her "days" and won't recover until her stash of alcohol has been exhausted. Ms. Breen already has the paperwork ready to fire her. And several other teachers are on the list too.

But Ms. Breen is made of sterner stuff.

She herself is of the lucky generation that passed through adolescence just before teenagers started turning up with terrifying, impossible mutilations. She remembers airplanes leaving Irish airspace, only to fall empty from the skies. She recalls reading about the last ferry to leave Dublin, about how it ran aground on the Wicklow coast with no life on board apart from rats and lonely pets. And she had a younger sister, Antoinette's age, whose body she was never allowed to see after the Sídhe Called her.

Ms. Breen wants to scream at her students, but what would be the point?

"It's just, miss," says Antoinette, "I don't see what that man . . . Geng . . . Geng . . ."

"Genghis Khan."

"Yeah, him. I don't see what he has to do with us."

Ms. Breen grins. She holds up a picture of the man himself. "Antoinette, I'd like you to meet your ancestor."

"Him? He looks nothing like me! My dad's Nigerian! And my mother is—"

"I know exactly who your mother is, child!" *An incredible woman, though far less charming than her daughter.* "But you're right. He looks nothing like anybody in Year Five. Yet he is ancestor to all of us. Every single one. I know you don't believe that, and you don't see what this has to do with the Sídhe, but I will explain. Now, let me start by saying he had a great many mistresses."

"Like me, miss!" shouts Conor, and his status in the class has everybody laughing dutifully. Even Ms. Breen smiles tightly.

But Nessa freezes, because Anto, the compulsive joker, can't resist playing with fire. "Oh, not like you, Conor," he says. "I doubt the Khan's mistresses were anywhere near as pretty as you are."

Now the class is laughing for real. Even Conor joins in, in apparent good nature.

But after the lesson he turns his fury on Anto in the corridor.

The children have been trained to fight, to maim even, by the ex–special forces of half the world. And Conor has learned better than anybody. Anto is pretty good—fast enough to block the first blow or two—but before some of the others can bring his attacker down, while Nessa is struggling to push forward, Conor has already blackened an eye and broken a rib.

Nessa feels her gorge rise. All she can think is, *What if Anto is Called right now? In this weakened condition? What if the Sídhe Call him?*

He may be thinking the same thing, because he's shaking and blood is dripping from split lips. He's desperately trying not to cry in front of everybody. Nessa wants to go to him and lift him up. She wants to hold him close, and it's the right thing, the *only* human thing, to do.

She bottles it all down. It's his own fault. His own bloody fault—he was practically asking for it. Nessa is here to survive. She cares for nobody and her face is as serene as the statue of a saint.

Anto must see her there in the crowd, as his friends help him up, but he knows the rules too and his eyes sweep over her. He limps away, the beaten dog.

Nobody speaks up for him. Nobody goes with him. Many, in fact, snigger.

Conor, meanwhile, shakes off his own gang like so many fleas. "Sooner he learns respect, more of his blood stays on the inside."

"Don't worry," says Megan in Nessa's ear. "That dirty wee shite will spend days in the Cage for this."

Only if an instructor catches him in the act, because being a bully is somehow never as bad as being a snitch.

That night Nessa does the stupid thing again, the thing she swore she would never repeat. It has been building up in her since the boy from Omagh was Called on the bus, and the events of this day have made the pressure unbearable.

When the others fall into exhausted sleep, she slides out from under her quilt and puts the paper into the breast pocket of her pajamas.

"Where are you going?" Megan whispers. She has a godlike instinct for knowing when Nessa is doing something wrong.

"The bathroom?"

"You never go after lights-out."

"I do. You just sleep through it."

"No, I don't, you filthy whore. I warned you about this last time, didn't I?"

"Go back to sleep."

"How do you expect me to sleep now?" But Megan sighs and lies down.

As promised, Nessa heads for the bathroom, which is in a little annex at the end of the dorm. She meets Squeaky Emma on the way out. The girl only comes up to Nessa's shoulder, but she's one of the fastest runners in the year.

"The . . . uh . . . You might want to wait a bit, Nessa. And open a window. Sorry."

"Sure," says Nessa.

The smell isn't as bad as advertised, but she opens the window just the same. Then she removes her dressing gown and climbs outside in thin pajamas. She's three stories up. Down below, cracked old paving stones are waiting to welcome her should she fall. They nearly get their chance when a leg catches on the windowsill. But after that her powerful arms do most of the work.

The cheap construction of the dorm buildings provides Nessa with plenty of handholds. Even better is the ivy that has had a generation to grow strong. She climbs crabwise, full to the brim with joy. This is not the act of a survivor. It goes against everything she believes, everything she needs to be doing. None of that can keep the smile off her face.

Now she's at the corridor window. A yelp comes from inside and she spots some of the dogs wandering around. They're supposed to patrol for nonexistent Sídhe spies. But the students' theory is that the authorities just want to keep boys and girls apart. Nobody pregnant has ever survived a Call. Not once in twenty-five years. *But then why not just have us in separate schools?*

The animals are snarling, and Nessa has a horrible realization: *They know I'm here!* She panics, pulling herself past and away until the noise fades and she finds herself at the window of another bathroom.

She is exhausted, her own breath as loud as any animal's growl.

This is where she is most likely to be caught. Then she'll spend a full day in the Cage with no food and nothing to do but reflect on how weak she's getting and on how she could be Called at any moment.

But she calms her breathing and manages to force the window open. Minutes later, Nessa is in the boys' dorm. Here she stands among their snores. It would be worse than the Cage to be found here: It would mean disgrace and so much ridicule she might pray for the Sídhe to rescue her from it! Her muscles are trembling, her legs won't cooperate as she tries to move quietly. Count the beds: one . . . two . . . and three.

This shadow is Anto, who needs to forget her if either of them are to have a chance at life. Her nostrils twitch with the smell of the medicine they gave him for his injuries. She hears his soft breathing and strains to see the shape of him under his quilt. She thinks, as the sweat begins to chill on her skin, how warm it must be in there. But all she does is slip the paper under his pillow.

The climb back is so much harder.

"You're a fool," Megan told her after the last time.

"If I was a boy, you'd say it was romantic. Like Romeo on the balcony!"

Megan rolled her eyes. "I'd say no such thing! That was the stupidest film ever. It wasn't even in English. I don't know *what* that was."

Nessa loses her grip and whimpers like a child, but her other hand manages to hold on at the cost of a scraped knee. When she reaches the window where the dogs were patrolling she sees something strange: Five of the animals are lying down there together. All of them appear to be asleep, except . . . except their eyes are open. Is that normal? But she is too tired to worry about that now.

The first thing she does on making it back to the girls' bathroom is to lie on the floor for ten minutes. The linoleum feels like a carpet to her. She imagines Anto's face in the morning when he finds the note she has left for him:

> *And it's a long time since I've slept*
> *Awaiting the taste of his kisses*

He won't understand a word of it, for the lines are in Irish. But if he can track them down in a country that hasn't had internet access for twenty-five years, he'll find they belong to a poem by a long-dead girl: "Young Man with the Braided Hair." And maybe he'll remember that his own hair was braided once.

There's nothing else she can give him. Or herself. The giddiness threatens to bubble up again into laughter. But it's time to seal herself back into the bottle. She actually lost her grip at one point! She nearly fell! This has to be the last time. It was a one-off. A *second* one-off.

Back in the dorm, the shapes of her friends are all around her. One of them moves. Seems to settle. The bed is suddenly flat, and Antoinette, the generous, the lovely, the foolish, is gone.

ANTOINETTE

Antoinette was dreaming of home. Her father was one of the first people to survive the Call, but he has been eating ever since, and at the age of forty the doctors have told him he's well on the way to a heart attack. It's one of the reasons Mother, another survivor, doesn't live with him anymore. She moved in with another woman, but she always says, "I'm not gay. It's just that I'm in love with Gillian. I love your father too, pet, but he wants to die and I want to live. And you too. I want you to live most of all."

They've had this conversation more than once, and Antoinette always ends it with promises to stop smoking, to train harder. Above all she must study Sídhe—it was Mother after all, the famous Michelle McManus, who overheard enemy speech and remembered enough of it that when she came back, the scholars were able to figure out what it was . . .

For a second, Antoinette thinks she's still dreaming. She opens her eyes and the entire sky is filled with whirlpools of faint light. Silver spirals turn sluggishly in the sky, brighter than stars but weaker than the moon. Her nose is already running with a burning, bleach-like stench.

They've been warned about this from their first night in survival college, when they wake up naked and alone in the middle of the woods. As Mr. Hickey is always repeating in hunt-theory class: Even in your dreams, act as if your life depends on it, because one day it will.

She rises onto her knees. There's a ringing in her head. *I'm not ready. I'm not ready. Oh, please, God . . .*

She is in a slight dip in the ground. Around her lies a carpet of what must be slicegrass. It tears at the skin of any who walk on it. But plenty of stones break the surface, and less than a dozen paces farther on, the grass gives way to an ankle-high bonsai forest whose trees can't harm her much at all.

Years of training are coming back to her.

And then a terrible screech tears through the chill air, with a sound so sharp, so bitter, that every tooth in her head aches with it. The dogs. The dogs are coming, and the first lesson Antoinette was taught at her first class on her first day was this: MOVE!

She stands, naked and goose-pimpled. She hops from rock to rock, the toughened soles of her feet feeling nothing, not stumbling until the dog howls again. But by then she has made it into the bonsai forest and is already clambering up and over the top of the first of the small hills, spitting from the bitter taste of the air.

The silver landscape falls away in front of her like a scroll with a map drawn on it. Fairyland in its entirety: lakes of red fire, the only color here, spewing and bubbling in the distance; forests growing terrible fruits; tornadoes that look like a giant's fingers digging into the soil; scattered lightning; burning rains and murderous flora of every kind.

And Antoinette thinks, as a million have before her, *We banished them here. No wonder they hate us.*

It doesn't matter that the event happened thousands of years before Antoinette was born. To the Sídhe, it is very real.

And so is the dog.

It screeches again, causing the hairs on the back of her neck to stand up. Is it closer already? Is it onto her? Another cries out far away to her left.

Antoinette runs, plunging and sliding down the hillside. Each breath of the acrid air hurts her lungs. She ignores it. If she can avoid them for a day, or thereabouts, she will return home alive and never have to see this awful place again. She has been trained for it, to run that long in rough terrain. She skids, falls forward, and rolls perfectly to her feet. It's almost fun!

Halfway down, dark flecks of ash start falling from the sky, obscuring the view ahead and hopefully foiling the pursuit too. She is within ten steps of a stand of knobbly grey trees when something flies past her ear and thuds into a trunk. The whole tree shudders and Antoinette sees an arrow buried in the bark. A black liquid spurts from the wound.

At the top of the hill she has just left stands a Sídhe bow-woman, half-hidden by the falling ash. There is no doubt that she is young and beautiful—nobody has ever seen an elderly Sídhe. Nor is there any doubt as to her intentions, for she has already fitted another arrow.

Antoinette flees.

It is some time before she sees anybody else, but she does not stop. Her breath is rasping in her throat. *Why . . . why did I smoke? Why? Why? Why?*

In spite of her parents, in spite of the four Calls she has personally witnessed up to now, she has never really believed this day would come. Not for her. Not Antoinette!

Panic has made her run too fast and now her limbs are wobbly with fatigue. What if she finds somewhere to hide? A number of survivors have managed that. Keeping out of the way until their time was up, but that will only work if she can throw the dogs off the scent.

Lucky for her, her path soon crosses a stream. She steps into it, walking along its slippery bed, pausing to cup her hands and drink. The water here is safe enough in small quantities. Appalling parasites make their home in it, but she won't be here long enough for them to do her any real harm, and nothing that is not her own flesh can return home with her.

In the end, it is not the parasites that drive her from the water but the "fish," with their disturbingly familiar shapes. They are gathering in a . . . a *gang* near to one bank and swimming hard with tiny limbs to keep up with her. They seem to be mustering their courage for something, an attack maybe. So she staggers back onto dry land just in time to hear the dogs again, howling loud enough to make her jump with an involuntary cry of alarm. They're so close! How did that happen? Oh, God! Oh, Crom and Dagda and Lugh!

But they don't have her scent. They can't know where she is, and right beside her is a small pile of rocks surrounded by plants she thinks she recognizes as being mostly harmless. With no time to double-check, she slides in among the bushes.

Spider trees, she realizes now. They latch on to her, but they are young specimens and she should be able to break away easily when the time comes. The important thing now is to control her breathing to—

The first of the "dogs" comes into view. She wants to cry out when she sees it, or to weep.

The creature was once a human woman. Now she pads along on all fours. Her back legs bend the wrong way. Her jaws have grown thick and large with massive teeth that don't fit properly together so that the mouth can never fully close, and a constant stream of drool hangs down from her chin. Her paws are still recognizably human hands. Her all-too-human breasts hang down, catching on rocks and bushes so that Antoinette aches to see it and wishes she could do something to help.

The creature is panting and whining quietly to itself. "Catch," it says distinctly. "Catch and master will love me. Catch. Catch."

A nearby spider tree grabs hold of it and the monster explodes into a frenzy of savagery until its "paw" is once again free. Then it passes on by, leaving Antoinette to force back her feelings of pity and disgust. She dares not move, and soon enough two more dogs pass, both male, with tangled beards and lolling tongues.

Something stabs her in the leg. There it is again! Harder this time, and it is only with the greatest of self-control that she stifles a yelp. Tiny people are running around her feet. Like the dogs they move on all fours, but they rise now and again to poke at her with matchstick-sized spears. Their voices are too high for her to hear, but they are organized and they definitely think they can take her.

She jerks a hand free and sweeps them away as gently as she can, but that's foolish because already there are little numb patches around the wounds they have made. *Poison! They're using poison!*

She pushes away, more violently now, feeling the grip of the spider trees holding her in place as dozens and dozens of the tiny tribesmen gather for a charge. She has absolutely no choice in the matter; she lunges to her feet, ripping herself free. She staggers from her hiding place and something, or someone, splats sickeningly under her feet.

And just down the path, less than fifty feet away, is a gang of grinning Sídhe.

Their surprise gives her the chance she needs to run off the path and into the woods. But soon they're sprinting after her, crying delighted encouragement, one to the other. Never, never in her life has Antoinette heard so much innocent joy in a voice.

She runs completely without thinking, faster than she has ever run in her life. A horn sounds behind her, and then the handsomest man she has ever seen charges in from the right. He has glittering skin, huge eyes, and a spear that points right at her heart.

She slides under his attack. Turns perfectly—Nabil would be so proud—twists the shaft from his grasp. Don't let them touch you! Never let them touch you! But even as she is remembering the warnings, her body acts of its own accord and shoves the point of the weapon right into his belly. A mortal wound. She has killed someone, a Sídhe, but a person.

He cries out joyfully. "Oh, well played, thief!" He slides back against a tree as the blood comes. "A feisty one! I nearly caught her!" His face is already growing paler.

The shadows gather and again she flees. She has nearly reached the end of the trees and she can hear the dogs again.

Beyond the last of the trunks lies a sight that almost kills her. It looks like a field of cabbages, but these are human heads. Hundreds and hundreds of them, laid out in a grid. The bodies cannot be seen, but here and there a hand has broken the soil.

The eyes of a man right by her feet swivel toward her.

"Help me," he croaks in English. "Help me." And all the others hear and it becomes a chorus of desperate pleading, so loud that not even the howl of the dogs can break through it. But the Sídhe are coming and there's nothing Antoinette can do for these people, nothing.

She runs for her life, wasting precious time to avoid standing on the heads and hurting them. The Sídhe have no such qualms, and Antoinette cries out in pain as the first arrow clips her shoulder and a voice calls, "Be careful not to kill the thief! We have hours yet to enjoy her!"

Antoinette's limbs will not carry her much farther. She knows this, she knows it, but can't stop running. She looks for cover, for somewhere to hide or to make a fight of it. She's killed one Sídhe already; she might be able to take some others if the dogs will leave her alone. In the distance a tornado seems to be coming this way. Such events have saved survivors in the past. She swerves toward it, knowing it may rip her to shreds, but willing to take the gamble. She is only encouraged in her choice when the Sídhe behind her cry, "No, thief! Not there! Don't go there!"

Moments later, the heads are behind her and she is running into a bare stretch of mud.

A terrible wail of despair rises up from the hunters. This gives her the strength to surge forward, but the mud catches her, rising to her knees and then her hips.

The Sídhe are in a wide circle around her, hopping from foot to foot in their elaborately tooled leather clothing, their gold chains, and holding their carved bows. One of them throws her a rope out over the muck.

"Take it, thief," he begs. "We wish only to play with you. We promise not to hurt you as much as usual."

They mean it. The Testimonies show that the monsters always keep their promises, and so, as the chilly mud rises to her belly button, Antoinette is tempted and terrified enough to reach for the rope. But then she imagines her parents seeing the state of her twisted remains and manages to turn away.

She doesn't change her mind again until the mud has reached her mouth, but by then the Sídhe have lost their chance.

THREATS

Three days after the bells have rung for Antoinette, they're on a break from first-aid class. Squeaky Emma is sailing out the door. "I didn't even look at her!" she says, and Aoife, trailing after, "I'm not saying that! I'm saying—"

Their argument is drowned by laughter. Anto is entertaining Shawny, Aidan, and Cabbages with a story about his dog at home who will only drink from a baby's bottle and insists on being held when he does. Nessa, pretending not to hear, thinks he's got to be making it up. Like the tale he tells of the four-year-old sister who pees in her brothers' room after an argument, or the one about his doddery granny re-creating an erotic dance from a rap video of her youth.

"Nessa?" She represses the urge to jump. Mr. Hickey is at the door to the Year 5 break room. It is twice the size of the Year 6 break room and it has an ancient but working radio, so he has to shout. "You're wanted in Ms. Breen's office."

She wonders if there is a problem at home—her poor mam's health has never been great—and maybe everybody else wonders that too, because Megan gives her hand a quick squeeze on the way past, and Conor grins at her from the corner his gang has taken over.

She walks down the corridor and taps on the office door.

"Come." Ms. Breen raises her head. "You miss her, don't you? Antoinette?"

Of the many things Nessa might have been expecting to hear, this was not one of them. Her instinct is to deny her feelings, but how can she reject Antoinette? Of all people? In the end she freezes.

Ms. Breen sighs. "In any case, that's not why you're here. The thing is, you were the one who witnessed the Call. You were awake and in your dressing gown. Why was that?"

"The toilet, miss."

"The toilet?"

"What else would I have been doing?"

Ms. Breen nods appreciatively at Nessa's perfect Sídhe grammar, but it is not enough to distract her from her purpose. "The thing is, Ms. Doherty, somebody was seen climbing on the outside of the building and in through the window of that same bathroom. They must have come from the boys' dorm before it."

"The *outside*, miss? Somebody was outside the building?"

"No more messing, child. Was it you?"

"I stick to the rules, miss. You know I do."

And Ms. Breen does know that. Of course she does. The child least likely to survive the Call is also the first to shave her head; the most attentive in every class for every subject; the coldest of them all, refusing to show so much as a flicker of feeling. Nessa's behavior is impeccable. She has never spent a night in the Cage. But the timing of her "trip to the bathroom" is just too perfect.

"You wouldn't know anything about the dogs, would you?" Again no reaction. "Because, on the same night that Antoinette was Called, somebody poisoned them."

At last an emotion, and it is horror.

"Yes indeed, Ms. Doherty. Only one of them died, but the others couldn't be woken properly for over a day."

Nessa tries and tries to control herself. She's thinking of the way the animals were so quiet on her return journey. She is a witness to a crime against helpless innocent creatures, no doubt about it. Perhaps her testimony might trap the culprit, but again instinct freezes her tongue. Eventually Ms. Breen sends her away. Neither of them can know that at that precise moment one of the remaining two boys from Year 7 is being Called. Nobody is with him when it happens, and nobody will find out for hours yet.

As Nessa is coming out of the office, Squeaky Emma is on her way past. "The Turkey had me in there too." The smaller girl rolls her eyes. "Can't even go to the loo now, apparently!"

Nessa nods. She's wondering if the boys will be interrogated too. If Anto will reveal his puzzlement at the mysterious piece of paper written in Irish that turned up under his pillow. How many people here can speak that language, after all? And how many of them currently reside in the girls' dorm? Only two, as it happens. Only one of whom owns a book of poetry.

But Anto must have kept it to himself. She still catches him watching her at dinner later on, but she looks right through him, just another boy among many.

By now everyone is talking about the dogs, and speculating, as they always do, about Sídhe spies and other nonsense. They haven't noticed that the Year 7 table is empty—surprise training exercises are not uncommon.

What is uncommon is the arrival of Conor at a girls' table. He sets himself down beside Nessa in Antoinette's place. Nessa can feel the warmth of his body squeezing her off to the left. He's broad enough that the same must be happening to Aoife on the far side. He turns his great square head ostentatiously back toward the boys' tables and gives a thumbs-up. But some of the teachers at the top of the hall have spotted him and they are watching out for trouble with narrowed eyes.

He turns back now and smiles across Nessa at Megan.

"You've been bad-mouthing me again, you red-haired bogger"—although he himself is only from Tipp!—"so I'm just giving you fair warning now that I don't lose money on any deal. You understand me?"

"No," Megan replies around a lump of bread. "I wasn't bad-mouthing you at all. I was just wondering aloud if it was you poisoned the dogs so you could have your way with them?" She turns back to her plate, stifling a yawn.

Under the table, where no one sees, Nessa squeezes her friend's wrist. *Please, Megan*, she's thinking. *Please, just this once, pull your hand from the fire!*

Conor stiffens, but sensing the narrowed eyes of the teachers on his back, he calms himself. "When you least expect it, Megan," he says, "you'll find those little red cheeks of yours scarred with a razor."

"A pretty threat from a dirty animal rapist, but an amateur one." Megan grins, despite Nessa's tight, tight grip trying to make her shut up.

"Amateur?"

"Who do you think was in the boys' dorm that night? Who was standing over your bed while you dreamed of those deliciously seductive puppies? Here's a proper threat, shit-breath: You're always boasting how you can't wait for the Call, how good you think you're gonna do against the Sídhe . . . well, the next time I'm standing over your bed, I won't hold back. I'll take a knife to your tendons. We'll see how fast you run then, won't we?"

All the color drains from his face. Then he rallies. "I always win," he says. "I'll make you a promise and I'll keep it the way the Sídhe keep theirs; I'll—" He's interrupted by the big hand that lands on his shoulder. Nabil.

"You are lost, my friend," the Frenchman says.

The boy pastes a false grin on his face and goes back to his table. Nessa hears him saying, "The teachers don't want me seducing those girls . . . again! Not a whole tableful! Not at dinner!" Laughter explodes and his witticism has passed around the entire refectory by the time dessert has ended. Then the bells sound, and it is the first time they realize that one of the Year 7s has been Called.

FRANKENSTEIN

In the following week two boys are Called from Year 6, both with unhappy outcomes. That's three boys in a row, and the superstitious girls of the college are finding it hard to sleep.

But Nessa always sleeps. She has trained herself that way, learning to turn off her fears and fantasies like a light switch. And so she walks into the gym with her classmates more awake than most.

She refuses to quail when she hears that today's exercise is hand-to-hand combat. Those with firmer footing usually beat her, except for the ones who drop at the first touch of her hand, thinking to do her a favor. That's the last thing she wants, and she grinds her teeth at the very thought of it.

But it could be worse. Indeed it should be much worse, for today, once all the proper stretches are done, Nessa finds herself paired off against Rodney McNair. He's a sandy-haired boy of middling height with the body of Bruce Lee in his prime. He can hold his own with Conor sometimes and might do even better if he wasn't such a show-off. Rodney is *not* the sort to go easy. Instead he will drag out the fight, playing the matador for the benefit of the watching students.

Nessa has always pinned her hopes of survival on skills other than fighting. But she is tired of losing the one-on-ones to braggarts like Rodney; to cruel Conor; to apologetic friends. So while her opponent is still turning to grin at some of the other boys, she wakes him up with a tooth-loosening slap across the face. He's still rocking back on his heels, his stance all wrong, when she yanks him forward into a head-butt. Forehead to fore-head, it hurts her as much as it hurts him, except that she knows it's coming and has already prepared her next move in advance of the distracting pain.

A second later, Rodney is on the mat and his hands don't know whether to clutch at his groin or his face. Nessa keeps her arms by her sides, as if the clash of heads was little more than a bump. She prays that nobody can tell she is swaying.

Sergeant Taaft is over there in an instant. "How?" she cries, grabbing Rodney by the shoulders. "How did you mess this up? For Pete's sake, just tip her and she'll fall!"

"I was . . . looking away . . . She . . . she cheated, she—"

"If you can't beat the likes of her, how do you expect to—"

"Sarah!" It is Nabil, striding over. "Sergeant Taaft!" She follows him grudgingly into the corner.

Nessa feels her face growing hot because she likes the big Frenchman and knows what he must be saying. "Don't talk like that in front of the cripple . . ." although, being Nabil, he'll use a more polite word.

Still, there's a nice moment in the shower when Megan holds out her hand for a high five. Hidden by the steam, Nessa slaps her palm and allows herself a small grin that only her closest friend ever gets to see.

Her happiness is only increased on the way to the first class of the day. A crowd of boys is filtering through the door and Conor is furious with Rodney, his ally, his almost equal. As though it is a personal affront to him, to all of Year 5, that Rodney hit the mat so hard and so quickly.

"She's strong," Rodney whispers. "Those arms are like stone. You have no idea . . . And she didn't wait for the—"

Nessa misses the rest of it as chairs screech and she has to take her place near the back or be caught eavesdropping.

That's when Frankenstein enters. He is a tall man, stooped, and far closer to being a zombie these days than he is to Mary Shelley's creation. But his nickname was fated nearly sixty years ago when his parents baptized him Francis James O'Leary.

"Call me Frank," he used to say to the Year 1s. "Not sir or Mr. O'Leary. Honestly, Frank will do." He laughed easily in those days, a grinning giraffe of a man.

But that was before his wife died. Before the bureaucrats refused her treatment on the grounds that she was past childbearing age and not involved in educating the young or any other vital service such as . . . bureaucracy. She was an artist apparently. Good riddance, says the State.

That was only six months ago, and Frankenstein returned from the funeral dramatically changed. Visibly broken. It won't be long, Nessa thinks, before he joins his wife in the ground. The stench of alcohol fills the class, and when he leaves it will follow him down the corridor like a cloud of doom.

Yet Frankenstein has earned some tolerance. He knows each plant that grows in the Grey Land and can speak with authority on every monster that has ever been mentioned in the survivor accounts, the so-called Testimonies. He slumps into his seat, but Anto has a question for him.

"Sir," he says, and Nessa likes how formal he is with the teachers. She is just realizing now that even behind their backs, he calls them by their real names rather than "the Turkey," or "Frankenstein" or "Twinkleturd."

"You've told us that every single . . . uh, animal, in the Grey Land is made from human beings. But, uh, where do they get them all? I mean, the Testimonies make the place seem as full of life as our world is."

Frankenstein blinks slowly, but eventually he stirs himself to answer, his breath billowing out so that students in the front row recoil.

"You know where they come from, boy." His voice is distant, as though he is already speaking from beyond the grave. "All those thousands that disappeared trying to leave Ireland when the Sídhe blocked us off . . . And others from centuries ago who found ways into their world." He nods a few times, and his head begins to settle onto his chest. *I've done my bit now*, he seems to be saying.

But Anto persists. "Surely, sir . . . surely it can't have been more than a hundred thousand or so who disappeared? But it's like . . . like every niche in the Grey Land is occupied, you know what I mean? Tiny people instead of mice. Instead of birds and foxes and fish and . . . and even spiders! The Sídhe twist them into shape. I get that part. But how can there be so many? I mean—"

Frankenstein waves him into silence with long, knobbled fingers.

"Your daddy never explain the birds and the bees to you, boy? The Grey Land is full of life, because life breeds. The Sídhe have made themselves gods. The same deities you children all swear by—Crom and Lugh and Dagda—they were Sídhe! But more than gods, they have become like your Darwin. Winding the clock of evolution and letting it go its own way."

"What do you mean by '*your* Darwin,' sir?" Anto asks.

But Frankenstein is already fast asleep at his desk.

KNIGHTS

Later, after a day of lessons and grueling runs, after a spear-making workshop and a dinner of gossip and laughter in the refectory, Conor Geary sits himself at the head of the very same classroom where earlier Frankenstein fell asleep.

He is first to arrive—as a leader should be—and now he looks on indulgently as his Round Table assembles before him. Rodney, in disgrace, takes a chair in the second rank, keeping his face to the floor and showing only the blond stubble on the top of his head. Chuckwu is in next, grinning and chewing only Crom knows what. He's the tallest of them and can run for days without rest. He claims, openly, to be a coward, but Conor has never seen him flinch from anything.

Soon after, Fiver arrives along with chunky, dour Cahal. Tony is next, then Liz Sweeney, Bruggers, and Keith. They all grab chairs and swap stories of this morning's combat session. Most did well of course. They are here because they're the best. Some of them have even knocked Conor from his feet the odd time, and he likes that. He wants them to stand up to him, because if he can't prove himself the greatest of them, then why is he even sitting here?

The door opens one more time and Sherry glides in, winking at him over the heads of the others. She's only a Year 4, but she's his main consort these days. She's smart enough and fast enough that he has hopes for her survival. And as the leader, he needs to be seen to have a girlfriend. He trusts she's too wise to get herself knocked up. She doesn't deserve her place here if she does.

He waits for Sherry to sit at the back, then waits some more, daring them to get restless so that Chuckwu will say something stupid and earn another kicking. But their discipline has been growing over the year since he formed them and at last, slowly, he nods.

"I salute you, my fellow survivors," he says. No one from the Round Table has yet been Called, but this is how he always begins their sessions. Many of them will die, of course. Even these, the best of Year 5. But they are a seed for the future and, as he often does, he allows his vision of that future to spill out of him now, so that they will go to their beds inspired and ready for the Call, whenever it should come.

"I want it now," he says to them. "I want to feel a scrawny Sídhe neck under my hands." They grin back at him, although some shift nervously, not as prepared as they need to be. "And when I return I'll start building a place for the rest of you. We will be the best trained, the strongest in the country. And we ought to rule, not the feeble old farts who have never even dreamed of the Grey Land. Not the bureaucrats. Us. Us! Only we can save the Nation."

"How?" Sherry prompts. She's still fairly new and wants to hear it all.

It's Cahal who answers, his voice a rumble from that thick farmer's neck of his. "The Nation is wasting resources," he says. "On kids who don't have a chance."

"It should be us," Liz Sweeney agrees, her voice high with excitement. She is as tall and muscular as most boys in the year. "People like us. If the best food and medicine and training came to us, the odds would go up from one in ten to . . . to . . . three in ten at least! Five in ten maybe! Instead they waste all the good stuff on walking dead like Aoife and Clip-Clop." Clip-Clop is their name for Nessa.

Conor nods his approval. Nessa, he thinks, Nessa . . . And it's a shame, it really is. Because, from the waist up, she's the most beautiful girl he's ever seen. He dreams of her all the time, a weakness he obviously never shares with the Round Table. Only Sherry knows, because he's called her Nessa by mistake more than once. He's had to strike her then—it couldn't be helped, and he doesn't feel good about it! But he's had to strike her and tell her that he had used that name as an insult because Sherry had sinned in some unspecified way.

Still. She must suspect. •

And it angers him more than anything. The waste of it. How this beautiful girl through her foolishness, or the foolishness of her parents, exposed herself to a supposedly extinct disease and destroyed her future.

He can't bear to look at her and can't help it either. It's as though the Sídhe had designed her specifically to taunt their greatest enemy. What flawless skin they gave her! Pale and smooth beneath the pure black line of her eyebrows, sweeping over well-defined cheekbones and around a mouth designed to smile, although it so rarely does.

"People who are like her," he says now, "won't even be fed after the age of five. Or whenever it becomes clear that they are useless. Our ancestors would have exposed them as babies on a hillside, but we can do better than that because we are not cruel. We can use injections."

"Medicine is expensive," Cahal rumbles. "Pillow will do the job quickly. Won't hurt either."

The door opens and they all jump, as though they should feel guilty for wanting to save the country.

Anto pokes his head in. "Oh," he says, deliberately using English, "is this where we're all meeting?"

Bloody Liz Sweeney actually grins at him!

Anto must have wondered where they were all going and followed along to annoy them. He really should know better after Conor was forced to discipline him. But the little fool never misses an opportunity to mock his betters. He thinks he's a joker, and there's got to be jealousy in there too, knowing that they will survive when he has doomed himself with pacifism and the diet of a sheep.

Conor stands and puffs out his heroic chest. He doesn't need to risk any Cage time by starting a fight when an instructor might pass by—the memory of Anto's bleeding face is enough to remind everybody of his authority.

"It wasn't funny last time you made that joke," Conor says, "and it certainly isn't—"

He stops talking. Anto too falls back a step and clutches that crucifix he wears. Because Cahal's seat is now empty.

"Somebody . . . somebody watch the clock," says Conor. His throat is dry and Anto comes into the room, almost on his tippy-toes. "You don't belong," says Bruggers, a lanky kid from Cork City. But he too turns to watch the clock. A minute has passed soon enough and Conor is struggling to maintain his breathing. He needs to be their anchor now. Their pillar. They must see him unperturbed.

But he's jealous. He always expected to be the first of the group to be Called. As if the Sídhe would want to remove the greatest threat first. Not that they could.

Two minutes, says the clock.

Cahal is a strange one. He has a thick body in an era that builds teenagers to look like greyhounds. But poke him with a finger and you soon encounter rock. Or metal maybe. Cahal is a robot, pure and simple. A machine.

Two and a half minutes.

Conor removes his jacket. "He'll be cold when he returns," he says, confidently. "Everybody step back from his chair."

And then the second hand of the clock on the wall passes the three-minute mark and the last four seconds seem to hang in the air.

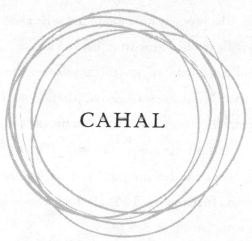

CAHAL

Cahal was sitting, but now he falls to the ground, naked and cold and surprised. He sees the famous silver spirals in the sky above him. He feels his eyes running with the bleach stink in the air. But in spite of the evidence, as has happened to hundreds of thousands before him, he needs a few moments to accept the reality of where he is.

It's a ledge on the side of a cliff.

To his right, a curtain of what might be slime or mucus drips slowly over the cold black rock and down into the dark crevice a long way below him.

To his left, a series of vines offers a way to the top.

Cahal puts his head between his knees and takes a few panicked breaths of the acrid air. He stifles a sob, a sound that nobody back at school thinks him capable of making. But he is the youngest and the last of a family of seven. Turlough was bigger and stronger than he was; Niamh was quick and athletic and ever so kind. She brought him food, and when she returned for brief holidays he ran laughing from her tickles.

The Sídhe Called her one of those times, and Cahal saw what came back before his softhearted parents could prevent it.

The temptation now is to cower on his little ledge and hope the Sídhe never find him. But they will. It's one of the many, many lessons from the Testimonies: You can hide, but not in the place where you first appear. They always know to look there.

So, he wonders, up or down?

The Aes Sídhe must be at the top of the cliff, surely. And indeed, far off a hunting horn blares its excitement.

The climb up will kill me, he thinks. *They'll be waiting by the time I pull myself over the ledge.*

No, it's got to be down, dark and forbidding as it looks. An inky-black hole full of horror. But better some monster should have him than the Sídhe! Why give them the satisfaction?

So over the side he goes. The vines are no help, being full of thorns. And the rock crumbles where the rolling stream of mucus attacks it. But Cahal wedges his toes in the cracks and ignores the resulting pain exactly as he has been taught: accepting the discomfort, but aware of the damage.

It's a long, slow, dangerous way down and his imagination populates the valley floor with the worst visions of the Testimonies.

However, horrors enough inhabit the cliff face. He sees what he takes at first to be a huge spider. But it reveals itself to be a living human head. Its ears have been re-formed into a pair of long skinny arms and it uses them to swing like an ape from one tiny handhold to the next.

When it reaches him, Cahal is hanging between two ledges and helpless to defend himself. He shudders with horror as it brushes against his back. Yet it does him no harm. Instead it swings right over to the dripping mucus and laps at it greedily with a huge, meaty tongue.

From above him, at the top of the cliff, are sounds of joy. "He's here! Oh, he's here! I've found him!"

Tiny stones fall hard enough to shatter Cahal's concentration so that he loses his grip and slides a painful foot and a half to the ledge below. He's not the only one: A male Sídhe tumbles past, laughing all the way down to a crunching impact. The sound informs the boy that he has less than sixty feet to go. He tries to hurry as more falling stones communicate a story of pursuit.

And then he reaches a ledge so wide he thinks he must be at the valley floor. He sees the Sídhe that fell in the light of a torch it must have been holding as it lost its grip on the wall. It has broken its back, but it grins at him through a sheen of sweat.

"I . . . cannot . . . wait . . . ," it manages to say.

But Cahal has no interest in that, because somebody else is there too. A girl. An ordinary human girl. Pretty, sort of, under a layer of filth.

It is not unheard of for children who have been Called to run into others. Sometimes they help each other out. Sometimes a desperate sacrifice will allow one to escape their pursuers, and everybody's favorite Testimony is the true tale of how Jenny Dundon and Mary O'Gara spent their last hour in the Grey Land, back to back with improvised spears.

This girl's eyes are large and they jump with fright when she sees him. Then, however, she realizes that Cahal too is human. "Help me!" she whispers.

The wounded Sidhe widens his smile. "I . . . will be the one . . . to help you!"

The girl is caught in a crevice. She must have tried to squeeze in there to hide, but only half of her—one leg, one shoulder, and part of her chest—fits in, and now she can move neither forward nor backward. She's no Jenny Dundon, that's for sure! Conor would call her one of the "weak." One of the "doomed." But although Cahal is a Knight of the Round Table, although it is his voice that speaks the harshest truths at their meetings, inside . . . inside, his parents still rule, and they are not like that at all.

Ever since what happened to Niamh, he has fantasized about how he might have saved her. And here now is a chance, a real chance, but only if he's quick, because the pursuers are almost here.

"When I pull you, it's going to hurt like hell," he says. "You understand? You'll have to ignore the pain and run for it straight away."

"Of . . . of course. Please. Just hurry. Please!" She holds out the hand that is not in the crevice.

Carefully Cahal steps around the dying, delighted Sídhe and grabs on tight. "Are you ready?"

She grins happily. She opens her mouth and cries, "I have him! I have him! I have him!"

In horror he yanks back, but she is holding on for dear life. Cahal is almost as strong as Conor and more desperate than he has ever been in his life. He yanks her free of the crevice and realizes that she was never stuck there at all: The girl's body ends at the halfway point. She only has one leg, her chest stops at the sternum. She falls against him, and when he tries to right himself another hand grips him by the ankle. It is the fallen Sídhe.

"Dearest thief," it whispers. *Don't let them touch you! Never let the Sídhe touch you!* But it's too late. The creature squeezes, gently, and Cahal's flesh gives way like putty under its grip. Never has he known such pain! As though every part of him under that supernatural touch were made of acid and sawing blades! The glitter-skinned Sídhe twists, and when it releases its hold Cahal's left foot is pointing the wrong way. He falls right over and now a dozen of them are standing around him, palms open, all desperate to get their hands on him.

"Halt!" cries one. A staggeringly beautiful fairy princess pushes her way to the front to crouch down before him. Her glorious hair spills over her shoulder like a waterfall of silver. Her eyes are full of fun and mischief.

"Please . . . ," Cahal says, "please . . ."

She frowns. "As though you thieves listened to us! As though you listened when we wept here in this land without color! But our worlds are getting closer together all the time! And soon you will have a king again to revoke the terrible treaty that sent us here." The frown is replaced by a smile almost lovely enough to dull his pain. "Just this once, I am inclined to mercy. You, we will send back alive."

THE DOG

In the classroom, the last four seconds tick away. Everybody is standing well back from Cahal's discarded clothing. Liz Sweeney has run to fetch the instructors. Nobody else breathes.

And suddenly, something is there: not a corpse and far too large for a human being. Almost seven feet high, it stands on four legs that end in a parody of a man's toes. Its skin is the pale white of most Irish, but it has stretched so thinly over such a large frame that parts of it lie torn and bleeding.

The head is the worst of all: a tiny brainpan with Cahal's brown hair. The mad little eyes too are the same watery blue as those of the vanished boy. They blink, and blink again on either side of jaws wide enough to swallow a basketball. The creature howls. Pain echoes from its throat, along with sorrow, with hatred. And while everybody stands frozen, it grabs the head of Rodney McNair in those mighty jaws and bites down hard. His friends recoil in horror.

"Out of the room!" Anto says, and Conor thinks how bizarre it is that a wilted pacifist is the only one to keep his cool, but then running away is what he does best, isn't it?

"No!" Conor shouts. "We're staying!" The creature drops Rodney and turns toward the sound of his voice. Conor feels the blood turn to ice in his veins. "We can kill this thing," he manages.

"It's . . . it's Cahal," says Bruggers, identifying himself as a weakling right away. But Sherry earns her place at the table. "Not anymore," she says.

The creature launches itself at her, but the girl dives off to one side to crash into the desks and shelves at the edge of the room. It swings after her, but now Fiver and Keith Blake hit it from the left, punching and kicking, barely avoiding the jaws that turn to snap at them. This buys Conor the time he needs to smash it across its tiny cranium with a chair.

The beast that was Cahal collapses, mewling piteously. But Conor will not be fooled. He lets loose an animal roar of his own and brings his chair down two more times until Cahal is silent for good. So is everybody else, their shocked panting filling the classroom. Conor grips the chair hard enough to turn his knuckles white, for if he releases it they will all see his hands shaking.

Liz Sweeney returns with the Turkey in tow. Ms. Breen takes in the scene in a single glance. "Ah," she says, her voice barely shaking at all. "A shame we couldn't keep it alive a bit longer. For study."

"My apologies, miss," Conor says.

"Listen now," she says, "it's rare, very rare, they send them back alive like this. And we never let the parents know, you understand me? So Cahal and . . . who . . . who was that?" She points at the room's other corpse.

"By the Cauldron!" says Liz Sweeney. "That's Rodney! Oh . . . Oh, by Lugh."

"Get control of yourself, Liz Sweeney!" says Conor. "It's Rodney McNair, miss. Cahal . . . the creature killed him."

"I see that, Mr. Geary. Now, boys and girls, when you leave this room, the story is going to be that the two of them were Called, all right? Rodney McNair and Cahal both. If word of this ever makes its way to the parents, the lot of you will spend a week in the Cage." She waits for a nod of agreement from each of them. "Good. Wash off the blood. I'll have some bathrobes dropped up to you until you get your spare tracksuits from the dorm. Dismissed."

They start to shuffle off, but she has one more thing to say. "Wait! I should also add that I'm proud of the way you handled yourselves. More of you would have been killed if you had panicked. The Nation must survive."

"The Nation must survive," they repeat, and Conor feels a surge of energy when Ms. Breen inclines her head toward him in particular. She knows he can kill. Everybody knows it now, and most importantly he, Conor Geary, knows it. One of the silent fears that lived so long in the back of his mind is as dead now as Cahal Dillon and Rodney McNair.

JAVELIN DAY

Twenty-five years ago, empty jetliners tumbled from the sky. Ferries ran aground, their decks crowded with abandoned clothing and whining pets. Foreign radio stations cut off mid-sentence and neither Wales nor Scotland could be seen from the Irish coast, no matter how clear the day.

The world's disappearance trapped tourists and travelers by the thousand. There were soldiers too: Taaft on vacation, aged twenty-two and twice divorced; Nabil, trying desperately to find somewhere, anywhere, quiet and green; a few members of the British SAS, also on vacation, or so they claimed.

But no matter how or why they ended up at the various survival colleges, all of the instructors insist that the students will never be able to kill a Sídhe unless the targets they practice on are as human as possible.

Thus began the traditions of "Pig Day" and "Javelin Day."

A fortnight has passed since Cahal's Call. The Year 1s are all in tracksuits. They arrived less than a month ago, so for the moment, until the soles of their feet have toughened up, the ten-year-olds are still allowed to wear shoes outside.

They won't be penalized for speaking English yet either, but by January they'll get nothing but punishments if they don't ask for things in the unbelievably complex language of the enemy.

"Listen up, babies," says Taaft—she can't speak any Sídhe either, and never will. "This is going to hurt. From now on, everything is going to hurt, but you're going to keep going through the pain, understand me?"

They understand. They look so tiny in their padded tracksuits. Skinny little arms and big, innocent eyes beneath the clunky helmets. They knew nothing but love until they came here, until they woke up naked in the forest. That was just a reminder, to let them know that this is really happening and that one day something worse than they can possibly imagine will occur.

And now it's Javelin Day. The first of many that will pit Year 5s against Year 1s.

Nessa watches them and swallows her pity. This lot are guaranteed two years without the Call, and will probably get four before they lose a friend to it.

Year 5 have lost six of their number already. The bells have rung for Tomasz, Peggy, Maura, Antoinette, Cahal, and Rodney. And going by past performances, those bells will ring thirty more times for Year 5 before any of them celebrates another birthday.

She weighs her javelin carefully. It's blunted but it's going to leave a bruise the size of the Cauldron on whomever it hits. As in unarmed combat, the legs are important for a good throwing technique and especially for gaining distance. But Nessa cheats by making a string to wrap around the shaft. There'll be no strings in the Grey Land. Mind you, it's not as if javelins will be easy to make either. They'll have to grab any the Sídhe throw at them.

When the children scatter on Taaft's command, Nessa picks out a target—a foolish boy running in a straight line. Then, when she releases the shaft, the tether unspools, giving her far more thrust and putting the javelin into a spin for more distance than even Conor will manage. She has researched it and practiced it too. *Thank you, Carthaginians,* she thinks. It flies high and true. It hits the wrong boy, but nobody can tell.

Sorry, kid, she thinks.

In Nessa's day, seeing her waddle away across the field, none of the Year 5s even targeted her. As if the Sídhe would show such pity!

"How?" Taaft cries, seeing what appears to be a perfect throw. "How did *you* do *that*?"

"I'm strong," Nessa tells her in English.

"Well, I'm not that strong, girl." (I.e., nobody is, or so Taaft believes.)

"It's all in the technique, Sergeant."

That's not good enough for Taaft, who searches her for an atlatl or any similar device for the lengthening of spear throws, but she doesn't notice the piece of string under the leathery sole of Nessa's foot.

Still, the instructor reserves her real fury for Anto, who alone of the Year 5s hasn't thrown his javelin at all.

"You know I don't do that," he says to Taaft.

She kicks his legs from under him and he rolls immediately to his feet like the natural athlete he is.

"You could be the best of us," she tells him, "but look at you! The Sídhe don't recognize pacifism, you understand, son? The Sídhe will eat you for breakfast and—"

"I've seen what they can do," he says quietly.

She punches him hard in the stomach for the interruption. Again he is quick enough to move with the force of it, taking as little hurt as possible, although his mother's silver cross now hangs askew. Taaft has to visibly struggle not to break him in two, like Conor nearly did a few weeks before. Instructors are allowed to hurt, but not damage. The whole point of them, some say, is to hurt.

Anto sees Nessa looking and winks.

"What was that, son?" screams Taaft, and Nessa turns away before he gets himself in any more trouble, or before somebody realizes that she cares in any way about the outcome of the confrontation.

After Javelin Day will come Pig Day, which nobody likes. The creatures are as intelligent as dogs, people say. But once a year every student in the school is expected to chase one down and kill it. Even the Year 1s. *Especially* the Year 1s.

Anto wasn't the only one to refuse first time around. But the other little ten-year-olds were bullied into it eventually and no amount of tears or nightmares would get them off the hook.

Anto, apparently, showed no fear of old Sergeant Miller's beatings. He took a lonely, freezing night in the Cage without caving in. Then another. And then a whole week, until they had to carry him out looking like something from out of the Great Famine.

"All right," they told him. "All right. We'll let it go for this year."

But it only got worse, because after a week of regular meals he looked at his plate one night in the refectory and realized it was pork. That was the last meat he ever ate. Again, there was the Cage and other assorted tactics, and lots of "The Nation must survive!"

In the end they started making him his own food: a nutritionally balanced and tasteless slop of beans and whatever else was in season at the time. It looked appalling, but Anto thrived on it anyway, to the disbelief and in some cases outright anger of the instructors.

"The fair folk are going to eat you alive," Taaft is saying now. Not for the first time Nessa finds herself agreeing, finds herself wasting precious time worrying about him. She can't afford to spend nights dreaming of his death. She can't afford the terrible buildup of pressure that will only end in another futile visit to the boys' dorm. *It's not my business. I've got to look after myself . . .*

Even so, even so. She wants to shake him sometimes. She wants to beg him not to throw his life away for pigs and flighty sheep and even fish!

In the distance one of the teachers—Mr. Hickey from hunt theory—is waving at them all to come in, his face bright red like an alarm. Then the bell starts ringing, but the rhythm is different from the sad, ponderous clangs of mourning. This is faster, more insistent, and it can only mean an emergency assembly in the refectory.

"All right!" Taaft calls. "Jogging back. Forget the javelins. Year Twos can collect them in the afternoon."

Everyone has their own tables to go to, their usual seats. The tradition is not to fill the gaps of those who have been Called, and Nessa hates it, the horrible souvenir of Antoinette's passing, of Tomasz. And the two new spaces on the boys' tables remind her of how she humiliated Rodney McNair. Did it contribute to his death somehow? That's such a stupid thought, she knows it is, and can't understand why it keeps buzzing and buzzing around her head no matter how she waves it away.

"There's more people missing," says Megan. "Look! Two from Year One even!"

"Year Ones?" Nessa feels a chill. "That's impossible, isn't it?"

"It's okay," says Squeaky Emma. "I saw some kids heading for one of the classrooms. A few from each year, I think."

Everyone relaxes, which is a mistake, because they are about to hear something far worse than they expect. The signs are already there in the bewilderment of the teachers at the top tables. In the nervous way the Turkey keeps straightening the tattered tweed jacket she always wears. Yes, this is going to be bad.

But Ms. Breen struggles heroically to control herself. For the sake of the children, and, yes, the Nation. She believes in that kind of thing. She clears her throat, and for once there isn't a whisper in the place, not the creak of a chair, and three hundred pairs of eyes are staring at her uneasily.

"I have some news . . ." She is only realizing now that she is in shock and that she is about to spread that shock to those in her care. To boys and girls who need to stay focused on survival. This isn't like her at all. But she hovers on the edge of saying nothing, of making matters worse, until Nabil covers the microphone with one hand and whispers into her ear, "They will hear of this anyway."

She nods and he fades away into the background.

Ms. Breen takes another breath. "Something . . . something . . . unfortunate has occurred." Another breath. She has never spoken so badly in her life. When she started out in her scholarship, when she published her first papers on Sídhe history, there were still a hundred and fifty survival colleges in the country and pupils were assigned to one or the other depending on the day of their birth. Nobody will say how many schools remain open, but these days the children who come to Boyle can have their birthday any time in the month of September. And it's even worse than that, because this year, for the first time, the number of new entrants has fallen below the fifty mark.

She grabs the lectern, aware of her cracked nails, of the wrinkled skin on her hands. *What use am I?* And then, in anger, she smacks the wood hard enough that the pain brings tears to her eyes and everybody jumps.

"It's like this," she says, and she's speaking in English so that even the Year 1s will get it. "Mallow Survival College is gone."

Everybody stares. Her statement has no meaning. "What I'm saying, children, is that everybody there, everybody in the whole college was murdered in their sleep. Those children who had relatives in Mallow have already been . . . been taken aside by the counselors. That's why they're not here with us. As . . . as always, we must be supportive—"

Everybody starts speaking at once. Children shouting questions or hugging each other or crying. Ms. Breen is normally more careful than this. She prepares all her big statements, preempting questions and concerns, heading off destabilizing rumors, consulting with the counselors in advance. She's been at this a long time after all. Too long.

Now she just goes back to her seat at the top table, staring straight ahead. It is up to the portly Mr. Hickey to put a stop to the riot.

"Enough!" he cries into the microphone. "We don't know any more than that, all right? There were survivors—a few of the veterans who were drinking in the town and gave the alarm when they came back. The night watch were killed too. So something put them to sleep first. And that's that. Enough! Shut your traps! Enough!"

And it is enough. The questions cease.

"Now," says Mr. Hickey, "we've spoken to Ms. Fortune"—he is referring to the chief cook—"we're going to be having lunch early today, so stay in your places. And from now on, starting with this meal, all food will be tasted by the dogs first, under the supervision of Mr. Downes and Mr. Connolly." Behind him, the other teachers are looking surprised. When was any of this agreed? Hickey is on another of his solo runs. But nobody objects because these precautions are obvious and sensible and somebody has to take charge.

Ms. Breen continues to stare into space, but the hunt master hasn't finished quite yet. "And finally," he says, "I can't speak for the government, or for any of my colleagues here behind me, but I don't think this outrage could have been committed without the help of somebody inside the school. I think that's obvious. We don't want any witch hunts here in Boyle, but if you see anything strange from now on, anything at all, please report it at once—at once! To one of the instructors. Nabil? Will you take charge?"

Everybody trusts Nabil. Except Taaft maybe. It's a good choice, so good that it takes a little of the tension out of the room.

But here and there children of all ages are still crying. Sure, they got all the siblings to the counselors before the announcement

74

was made, but the world of the Irish teenager is so small now that many of them know somebody who attended Mallow. At Nessa's table, Aoife has her face in her hands while Squeaky Emma tries to comfort her. And Megan says, "Crom twist the Turkey inside out! Has she no sense?"

But Nessa has no idea how it might have been done differently.

A school. A whole school full of trained killers destroyed in their sleep. And she remembers the drugged dogs in the corridor. She remembers them and she shivers.

She leaves the rest of them behind and finds the big Frenchman. "Nabil?" Unlike Taaft, he does not like to be called "sir" or "sergeant" or "master." He hates salutes, and once, when a pot smashed behind him, Nessa saw him launch himself into the bushes. But other than that, he seems sane enough.

"I have something to report," she says, "about the dogs." Because what she could not admit to Ms. Breen, she will tell him. She must tell him, if she and her friends are to live.

BY CROM

It's nighttime again and Nessa is in the loo, trying to persuade herself to flush the poetry down the toilet and go back to bed. The news today has shaken everyone, but that's not why she's here. It's because she's an addict of her own dream. She imagines a farm in Donegal and somebody to share it with.

> *If I had wealth*
> *Silver in my pocket*
> *I'd take the shortest path*
> *To the house of my beloved*

After she made her report to Nabil and sat down again, everybody was hugging everybody else. And she needed a hug too, she really did. But not their pity. Not that. Alone of everybody at her table, she sat straight and impassive until Anto walked right up to her.

"What are you doing here?" she asked sharply.

He looked so handsome, his eyes all but black in the low autumn light. She glanced away, and his disappointment was so very obvious.

"Don't worry," he said, nodding back to one of the boys' tables. "I told them I would ask you what you were saying to Nabil, that's all."

"All right," she said. "But . . . but I can't tell anyone."

"Fine." And he was gone. And she is here again, in spite of the fact that Nabil has forbidden it and that he will know who is responsible if she is seen.

She bangs her head against the wooden walls. "By Crom," she says. "By Lugh and Dagda, go back to bed."

She pauses to wonder how it became a fashion among the children of Ireland to swear by the gods of their murderers. Even as a six-year-old, with no knowledge of what was to come, she and her little friends had a long list of sacred names to take in vain. Why not swear by sex as their parents do? Or by plague and the devil like their ancestors?

But people like to shock with their words, don't they? And what could be more ugly than the fair folk?

"Doesn't matter," she mutters now.

She opens the window and finds a waxing moon that's far too bright for comfort. Her bad idea is looking worse by the minute. But she's smiling anyway, every muscle thrilling with excitement. And then she hears somebody shouting. Shamey, one of the "veterans," has wandered into the unused parking lot at the back of the school.

Three years ago he returned from the Call completely unmarked. Well, physically unmarked anyway. Nessa sees that he has been into the town of Boyle—shrunk now to a single inhabited street and an empty church. It retains just the one pub, and that's enough for Shamey. He's seventeen years old, just about. His hair is long and he sports a scraggly beard that has failed so far to submerge the spots on his cheeks. He shouts, "I'm not having kids, you hear me? You all hear me, you Sídhe-twisted scum? Just to send them to . . . to *that* place? Are you mad?"

Veterans serve no real purpose. In theory they give talks or lead classes when teachers are ill. Mostly the post is a chance for them to recover from the Call before finding a place in the real world. Meanwhile, they get to do pretty much anything they want.

But not this.

Shamey's words are an attack on morale that cannot be tolerated, and indeed the two night guards, Tompkins and Horner, ex-SAS, as it happens, bring him down as gently as their training allows. Which isn't gentle at all. Nessa watches as Horner gets him in an armlock and Tompkins stuffs his mouth with a rag of Lugh knows what.

At that moment, as if he knows she's there, Horner looks right up at the bathroom window. He has such a youthful face—like that of a boy's corpse, lying drowned in a river with large, large empty eyes.

"Get a move on!" Tompkins says. But it's still a full count of three slow heartbeats before Horner turns away. They spirit Shamey off and Nessa finally finds the courage to shred the poetry and go back to bed.

———————

Like Antoinette's parents, Mr. Hickey was one of the first survivors. That puts him in his late thirties, or would do if he hadn't spent every one of the last twenty years eating and reading, drinking and reading. Going AWOL in Dublin to steal books . . . And all the other usual behaviors inspired by a short visit to the Grey Land. But the kids like that he's close to them in age, and especially the fact that a good chat can sidetrack him for entire lessons at a time.

"No!" he protests. "Burke, you know this is hunt theory and not history. You know it."

Everyone is grinning at Solomon Burke—Bruggers, as the boys call him. Everybody except Heather, who came from the same town as Rodney McNair and whose red eyes show she liked him more than she's been letting on.

"But really, sir," says Bruggers, using the English honorific instead of the Sídhe term "High One," "the legends say they used to steal our babies from the cradle. And that they'd substitute their own young ones instead—"

"If they ever did such a thing, Burke—*if!*—they stopped it a long time ago. And anyway, there are plenty of stories of them stealing away older children too."

"How would we know though?" Bruggers grins at Conor, hoping his triumphant derailing of the class is properly noted. "About the babies, I mean? Maybe the Sídhe never stopped swapping them out. Maybe that's where we get our Hitlers and our Cromwells and all."

Mr. Hickey throws his eyes to heaven. He was born into a world where even the dustiest academics knew no more than a few hundred words of Sídhe, or Primitive Irish as they called it. There were no survival colleges back then.

"Listen," he says, "we don't need the Sídhe to teach us evil. We were the ones who put them in the Grey Land, remember? And not for just a day or however long it is the Call lasts. We Irish . . . we trapped an entire race of people in *hell* for all eternity just so we could take their homes for ourselves. You can read it in *The Book of Conquests*. I mean, look at it from their point of view. The Tuatha Dé Danann, the People of the Goddess Danú . . . There they were, a few thousand years ago, living in a place they loved so much that they called it the Many-Colored Land. Then this other group arrives, pretty much the same as them, speaking the same language even, except this new lot—our ancestors— were the first in the world to have iron weapons. They thought it gave them the right to take everything! Everything!"

The truth of it is undeniable, but it's not a popular opinion, and the cheerful mood of the class instantly chills.

"Look," he says, "I'm not saying that anybody here deserves what's happening to them, all right? By the Cauldron and the Spear, I was training for the Olympics when it happened to me!" And his voice cracks. "I was thirteen." He takes deep, deep breaths for a while, and it's clear he must have one of the better counselors because he steadies himself soon enough. "The point is, we'll never beat them if we don't understand them. And it might even be that we can't beat them, but that we can find some kind of compromise and make peace with them. Forgive them even."

This is too much for Megan. "Crom twist you!" she cries. It's enough to earn her a night in the Cage, but not in Mr. Hickey's class. "You actually expect us to forgive them? *Sir?*"

He shrugs. "Let me ask you this, Ms. Donnelly. Do you want them to stop what they're doing? Do you? Because, if so, then *they* will have to forgive us."

"I'll forgive them with my fist," Conor says, and even Megan nods, her jaw tight. "They agreed to the treaty, to leave Ireland to us. That's in *The Book of Conquests* too, isn't it? Now they need to stick to it."

The only person in the room who has survived a Call shrugs sadly. "All right then, class. Back to work. Here's what I want you to concentrate on when you're out in the woods next week . . ."

HUNTING

O nce a fortnight, Year 5 stages a hunt. On this particular evening, Nessa will join the prey. She always needs more practice in learning to hide, although she's not so fond of the non-damaging but painful beating doled out to those who are caught, or the freezing misery of the losers' showers.

But as Mr. Hickey often reminds them, it's just as important to be one of the hunters: to put yourself in the minds of the Sídhe as they seek out the only remaining thing that can bring them joy.

Halloween creeps ever closer. Trees shiver with the previous night's rain, and the first ice of the year is only a week away.

Nessa has done her usual trick of making crutches for herself, and so good is she with them that she can go several steps at a time without her feet touching the ground, using them more as stilts than anything else. If only she could keep up such gymnastics for more than a few minutes! If only she could outpace even one of her classmates . . .

Tonight she needs to stay free a mere six hours as teams of four comb the woods, hoping to win the privilege of a hot bath and a hot meal; hoping to deprive her of the same.

They'll have plenty of light to find her. A splendid full moon sprinkles silver through the trees, and this, apparently, is the closest that beautiful planet Earth can ever get to the Grey Land's sickly pallor.

Nessa pauses at the base of a large pine, breathing heavily, her nostrils filled with the scent of resin, her keen ears picking out the sounds of smaller creatures fleeing her presence. And then she jumps, as less than three hundred feet away she hears a shout. It's Bruggers calling, "All clear, east! Advancing!"

Conor's loud tenor replies from somewhere to her right. "I see a few holes in the ground. It's Clip-Clop and her crutches! She can't be far!"

All the advantages are theirs. Those are the rules. There'd be no point otherwise. Mr. Hickey gave his hunters time to look over the terrain and to set traps. They get to choose their own teams too, and so, not surprisingly, Conor has a bunch of his cronies around him. They even carry flashlights because, unlike the Sídhe, their eyes are not so well adapted to the environment. The beams pass through the branches around her, but create more shadows than they kill.

Nessa has to force herself not to plunge away off into the trees. Conor's no fool; he just isn't. He knows how to stay quiet, so if they're calling to each other, it's because they want her to hear and to panic. They're hoping she'll flounder into whatever trap the remaining two members of the hunting party have prepared for her. *Of all the teams, why must it be Conor's?!* He glares at her sometimes like he means to eat her, and she has never figured out why, when Megan's the one who always stands up to him.

The flashlight beams swing left and then right. Nessa eases herself to the ground and feels around for a stone. By the time she's upright again, a dozen steps and the trunk of a pine tree are all the protection she has left. Bruggers whispers in his singsong Cork accent. "She's come over the stones, see? Smart bitch, our Clip-Clop. But she can't be more than three hundred feet from here. Probably half that or her arms will have fallen off by now."

Nessa's arms *are* tired. Bruggers is to her left and Conor must be nearby too, but he doesn't reply and has turned off his flashlight. It's nerve-racking not to know where he is, to think he could be looking right at her. But if she freezes they're going to find her anyway, so Nessa takes a gamble. She eases herself around the side of the tree. Bruggers is ten steps away, his back turned.

But where is the other one? The glorious leader?

And then she spots him, like a giant predator in the branches of a nearby tree, his head swiveling from side to side to catch her scent on the air.

She stills her panicky heart. But then she thinks, *I could split him open with this stone. Claim it was an accident. After all, sooner or later he'll try to get Megan back for the fool she made of him . . .*

But the urge passes. Instead she waits for his attention to swing away from her before launching her missile down into the forest behind her pursuers. It's not a big stone. Its impact is tiny, but suddenly Bruggers is charging down through the undergrowth and Conor, who barely has to flex his knees when he drops from the branch, calls out, like an absolute lúdramán, "To me, knights! We've got one!"

Two more figures come pelting down the slight slope behind Nessa to join their master, and off she flies herself, in the opposite direction. Four more hours to go, she thinks. Four more hours to stay free. She's getting better at this: twice now, in the last six months, Nessa has avoided capture.

She plows through some bushes, careless of the noise she's making, desperate to put some distance between herself and the knights. She stumbles, half falls over the edge of an ancient man-made ditch, breathing hard, and comes to a stop.

She needs to move more quietly again. There are six other hunt parties out there after all, any of whom could condemn her to a beating and a cold shower if they find her. But what, she thinks, if it's Anto who comes instead? "Tell nobody you caught me," she'll whisper . . .

That stupid thought is delicious enough to quicken her heart. Magical here in the moonlight. And why shouldn't she kiss him anyway? it whispers. Others are doing it all the time. And more. Soon enough Nessa will be dead. *Everybody* knows it. Her poor parents. Her friends. Surely here, all alone in the dark, she can finally admit the truth.

"No!" She says the word aloud and it's like a thunderclap in the otherwise silent forest.

It's a mistake. Out of nowhere, a hand reaches into the ditch and covers her mouth. She jumps, ready to struggle, to fight to the death. But only for an instant. She's been caught fair and square and that's that. Final proof, if any were needed, that daydreams of love will get you killed.

A voice whispers, "Promise not to say anything?"

And Nessa nods, feeling relief roll into her. No hunt party would require her silence.

"Megan?"

"You're a Crom-twisted wee whore for making so much noise. That's not like you! Now shut it. I've got Squeaky Emma on my tail with Aoife and Nicole and Lugh only knows who else. Maybe I should send you out there for them to catch instead, eh?" But of course Megan would never do that.

"Listen," Nessa says, "we'll have to move away from the ditch. I've left quite a trail for the last few hundred yards."

"All right. No more talk then. Come on."

Megan's not the fittest girl in Year 5, or the most studious. But she actually enjoys the hunts, and Mr. Hickey's is one of the few classes where she keeps up with the rest. Yet Nessa finds herself criticizing internally as her friend breaks bracken or scatters twigs behind her.

And who am I to talk, with my big bloody crutches?

Throughout the woods they catch glimpses of flashlights combing the ground for prints, and sometimes sudden, excited calls ring out in the distance.

After ten minutes of exhausting creeping around, the two girls are sweating enough to fill the Shannon river. They have reached one of the known forest trails. They could make a lot of distance here and leave very few tracks. And yet at least one of the hunter teams will be lying in wait somewhere along the path's mile and a quarter.

Megan puts a hand over Nessa's lips and Nessa nods. Her friend will go on a little by herself to scout. Nessa points back the way they came, to indicate that she will check on the progress of their pursuers. They each nod once and off they go.

Nessa doesn't get very far before she spies dark figures creeping through the bracken behind them. Heart in throat, she ducks out of sight and returns to the tree where she left her friend.

But there's no sign of the other girl. No sign at all, except for a vague shape on the ground. Nessa creeps forward, feeling a rushing in her ears. Her heart is beating faster than it ever has in her life; her limbs are on the verge of just giving up and dumping her on the ground. She crouches to touch the shadow. It's her worst fear: a jacket. Megan's jacket. And Megan herself is gone. Nessa falls to her knees in the chill, damp leaf litter, her head spinning. The calm part of her mind has already started counting down from three minutes and four seconds, but there is bile creeping up her throat, trying to force its way past a suddenly dry and swollen tongue.

And then Megan steps out from the forest and leans down toward her.

Nessa's response is completely automatic. She slaps her friend across the face. Once. Hard. And Megan, being Megan, responds in kind, holding nothing back so that Nessa's head is ringing. Then they embrace and Nessa clings on to her like a life preserver.

"By Lugh," says Megan, "you thought I'd been Called? And then you belt me hard enough to flay the skin from my face?"

"Your . . . your jacket."

"Sorry. I'm sorry. I thought I heard hunters. My hood got caught on a branch and I just abandoned it, ran up the hill." They're still hugging and smiling, but Nessa feels nauseous. Finding Megan's jacket was more than just a fright. It was a sign of the unavoidable future. She knows that going by the odds, one of them will be Called by Christmas.

"Listen, Ness," Megan whispers. Her voice is suddenly tense. "I found something . . . something *incredible*. You have to see it!"

"What is it?"

Instead of an answer, Nessa gets a flashlight beam in the face.

"Two?" says Aoife. "Whoever caught two before?"

And Squeaky Emma, with real hurt in her voice at the sight of them hugging so tightly, says, "That's not fair, Megan. I came out to *you*. Before I even told my mother!"

And the two friends burst out laughing.

But on the way back to the college Megan still isn't herself.

"What is it? What did you see when you ran up the hill?"

"I need to find Nabil," Megan says. "I need to find him right away."

GIRL IN A ROCK

Their friends have hardly beaten them at all. Even so, they've been caught and must suffer now through a cold shower and a meal as chilly and bland as the cook can make it. But even that dubious pleasure must wait.

"Nabil first," Megan insists. "It has to be. And you're coming with me."

Nessa pushes aside the hunger and allows herself to be dragged along. She's never seen her friend so agitated before.

They meet the Frenchman in the "barracks"—a corridor of small but comfortable rooms belonging to the staff and the veterans. He is old-fashioned enough to worry about being alone in his quarters with two young girls, so, to Nessa's dismay, and maybe his own, he invites Sergeant Taaft to join them.

"I hear they were caught together" is the first thing Taaft says. "Helping her out, were you, Megan?"

"No, Sergeant. She was helping me."

"Because there'll be nobody to protect her over there. You need to train as if you're working alone. That's the whole point!"

Nabil intervenes, a hard edge to his voice. "Sergeant Taaft, please."

He has cleaned his room to the point of sterility: a bed, a prayer mat, a desk. Not so much as a photograph of his family mars the walls. Even the bookshelves hold little more than the contents of the college curriculum: the Turkey's *History of the Sídhe*; the hunting manuals; and year after year of survivor Testimonies, the later volumes in the language of the enemy, which he speaks fluently. But Nabil has to revert to English now for Taaft's sake, and there he struggles, a national stereotype straight out of the old movies they show in the gym on Saturday nights.

"So, girls. I do not worry that you 'ave . . . that you work together. But what you need to report?"

"A corpse, Nabil," says Megan. "We saw a corpse. Human maybe."

Nessa opens her mouth to object, to say that she herself didn't notice anything, but a good hard stare from Megan shuts her up. *You want to see it or not?* seems to be the message. So Nessa goes along with the story for now. And who wouldn't be intrigued by the use of the word "maybe" in relation to a human body?

"But it's more than just a corpse," Megan says. "I think . . . I think you might want some of the teachers to come along with us. Mr. Hickey maybe. Ms. Breen and Ms. Sheng."

"I'll get the flood lights," says Taaft, all business now.

Nabil nods. He scratches the scars cutting through his beard. He always looks tired, but never shirks on courtesy, "Megan, go please to fetch Ms. Breen and anybody you need. Nessa, tell Mr. Hickey to call in the hunt before he reports to us here. And get some sandwiches from the kitchen on my authority. We will all have need for energy."

He's right. It's an hour before they're back in the woods, shivering and wet, with Mr. Hickey's labored breathing loud enough to kill any conversation dead. But it takes Megan surprisingly little time to find the place where she left the path, and as they climb the slope, Nessa too feels a strong sense of familiarity.

Have I been here before maybe? During the day?

Clouds have covered the moon, but soon enough the flood lights are placed around a great moss-covered boulder, and everybody gasps at once.

There is a girl in the rock. Or rather, a rotting corpse, the sight of whose glistening flesh threatens to squirt Nessa's sandwiches right out of her stomach. But it's only half a corpse really, because from the hips down the girl merges into the surface of the stone, and her hands are positioned in such a way that it looks as though she were trying to climb out of it when she died.

"It's one of the Aes Sídhe," says Ms. Breen, and Mr. Hickey agrees. Still panting, he points out the large empty eye sockets.

"Less than a fortnight old." He spits. "Haven't seen one of the monsters in twenty years. Must have got trapped on the way in."

"She's been here more than two weeks," says Ms. Sheng, the skeletal teacher of field medicine. "Trust me." And then her voice rises an octave. "But this is a mound!" she cries. "We're standing right on top of one!" And all of the teachers gape at the dirt between their feet as though it's poison.

"This is a Fairy Fort?" asks Megan. "An actual Fairy Fort?"

But she is ignored.

"Nabil," says Ms. Breen. "Sergeant Taaft. No more exercises here for a few days. Please keep all students to the fields until we can get a team up from Dublin."

And that's that. The two girls and the instructors too are hurried away back to the college without any answers to their questions. In fact, when Megan tries to insist on the basis that "We found the thing!" she's told by Ms. Breen, "Your job, girl, is to survive. For the Nation. You do that, and you decide you want to work on something a bit deeper, come back to me. Until then, you need your rest."

"And I'm supposed to sleep after seeing this? An actual Sídhe corpse? *Melted* into the rock?"

"You'd better, child," and the principal is struggling to suppress the quaver in her voice, "because it's the *living* ones you need to worry about. Now go. And tell nobody what you've seen here, or you'll spend the rest of the week in the Cage."

"What was it?" Squeaky Emma wants to know the following morning. "What did you see?"

The two Donegal girls have come in early for breakfast and have grabbed an empty table for themselves, but Emma won't take the hint.

Megan, enjoying the attention, smiles enigmatically. "Bet you wish you hadn't caught us, eh, Ems? I might have told you then."

"What about you, ice queen? Will you tell?" This is directed at Nessa, who only shrugs and keeps her attention on the porridge-like slop in her bowl.

But Megan and Squeaky Emma are good friends, and when Nessa looks up she catches the exchange of a wink that brings a grin to the smaller girl's face and stops all her questions in their tracks. Squeaky Emma returns to the usual table, where everybody else is finishing up.

"I hope you're not planning on telling her, Megan Donnelly."

"Why ever not?" Megan's innocent rosy cheeks are like something straight off a Victorian biscuit tin. "People are dying for something to talk about."

"It's the Cage though, if word gets out. And it *always* gets out."

"Well, I'm no stranger to the Cage, Ness, as you know. I'm even growing to like it." But she grins and squeezes her friend's hand. And then she changes the subject so transparently that

Nessa can't help rolling her eyes. "But what about that triple-F, Nessa, eh? Right on the grounds!"

"Triple-F?"

"Feckin' Fairy Fort." Megan smiles around a face full of dribbly porridge. Bad as the food is, they won't leave so much as a smear of it behind them. "I thought they'd found all of the triple-Fs in the country."

Everybody knows about the line in *The Book of Conquests*, the one where the Aes Sídhe traveled into exile by passing "under the mounds." And the island has no shortage of artificial hillocks to match the description: Iron Age forts, Stone Age grave sites, medieval cattle corrals. For centuries they have attracted stories of malicious and beautiful creatures that steal away the young. Fairy Forts, people have always called them, a mere double-F at best.

"I thought we'd surveyed every last one of them," says Megan. "That's what Harvey big boobs said in archaeology class, didn't he? All of the triple-Fs dug up and destroyed and nothing in them but trinkets and moldy bones."

Nessa shrugs. "They had to be sure. The legends hold a lot of truth."

"And bullshit too! Holy Danú's milky tits! All that stuff about the Sídhe world being a paradise! The Blessed Isles! The land of eternal youth!"

That's what the refectory looks like now, the land of youth, as more and more students come in to queue up the sides for bowls of congealing mush.

"The Sídhe *are* all young though, Megan. Eternally young, for all we know."

"True, Ness. That's true." Megan's eyes take on a faraway, greedy look. "And our girl is young too, isn't she? By Crom, I'd love to see her again in the daylight. An actual Sídhe!"

"We can't, Megan."

"We're entitled though!" She bangs the table. "The whole point of a survival college is to teach us about those scum. Everyone in the class should be walked past her body and given a chance to spit on it. To take a bite out of it even!"

"Megan!"

Megan grins. "Nah, you're right, Ness. She's gone all moldy by now. Probably doesn't taste much better than this stinking porridge!"

And her words wake something in Nessa. "Wait!" She reaches for her friend's hand. "There was no smell though, was there? I mean, I saw a dead sheep once. There should have been a smell of rot, shouldn't there?"

"Good!" says Megan. "Curiosity. That's very good. So you'll come back with me then?"

"You know I won't—"

"Because if *you* won't come with me, Squeaky Emma certainly will."

Nessa, still holding her hand, squeezes hard enough to get her attention. "Listen. Just listen, will you? We're in Year Five now."

"Bah!"

"We can't risk the Cage. Neither of us. More than half the class will be Called, you know that, and—"

Conor's team burst through the door and make their way over to the boys' tables, their faces still flushed and healthy from their morning stretches. Normally they would be loud and boastful, but today they all stop talking the moment the doors swing shut behind them, and their eyes swivel toward the two girls. Word has spread, obviously, and the boys' tables want to know the secret as badly as anybody else. But Conor suddenly laughs and points at Nessa.

"We nearly had you last night, Clip-Clop," he says, "but we wanted a challenge! Right, lads?"

Nessa doesn't look up from her bowl. She is shaking, but with temptation rather than anger. She heard Conor and his boys calling each other "knights." Ridiculous! Like seven-year-olds and their wooden swords.

She has the power now, right here, to humiliate him with this knowledge. Her breathing increases and she opens her mouth to speak. However, he is a real danger to her and she will *not* give in to the urge for the sake of a meaningless victory. She clamps her mouth shut. Her control is excellent.

Megan's is not. "Woof, woof," she says, to remind Conor of her previous insults. He smiles, pretending confusion, but his eyes narrow and Nessa knows Megan will pay sooner than she expects.

CURIOSITY

A week goes by with experts from Dublin out in the forest, tight-lipped and middle-aged. Alexandra from Year 6 is Called and has a miraculous escape. She's the college's first survivor since Ponzy and, unlike him, she seems unaffected, at least physically. Everybody celebrates! And even though the mourning bells ring twice more in the week, hope suffuses them all.

But Nessa feels divorced from the joy. Her only real friend is spending rather too much time in the company of Squeaky Emma, the two of them thick as thieves and surely planning on a visit to the girl in the rock. Of course they are! When the woods are swarming with instructors and researchers and the Cage awaits anyone who is caught. By the Cauldron, are they mad?! But Nessa knows better than to oppose Megan on this, so she concentrates on her studies. She practices new techniques in the gym. She scours the hunt manuals for clues, while nearby laughter tells her Anto is entertaining his friends with tales of the "overly curious gerbil" or the "drunken aunt."

Nessa strains against the muscles in her neck that want her to turn and look in his direction, that want him to be looking back. But mostly, when her self-restraint fails, it's not his eyes she finds, but those of Conor.

Friday comes and it's Nabil's day off. It's also a morning when Year 5s have the whole library to themselves. It's a sprawling room of narrow aisles and musty shelves. Hidden nooks lie everywhere, with old computers quietly rusting, their ethernet cables still plugged into sockets that go nowhere.

But Nessa prefers books anyway. Especially the endless volumes of survivor Testimonies, which, by definition, are all success stories. Since coming to college she has filled a dozen notepads with an illegible scrawl. Clues to the Grey Land. Strategies for dealing with the various hazards should she encounter them when her time comes. Hopes.

Today she is sitting in her favorite cul-de-sac with a battered edition of *The Book of Conquests* in front of her on the table, along with the most recent Testimonies. The only other chair is empty right now, but Megan's pen is there, a notebook open and the page, as is typical for Megan, still mostly blank and mostly written in English. Nor does any of it make much sense: "Grab ankle." And "keep to the right of it."

Not for the first time Nessa wastes precious minutes fretting about her friend. Foolishly she allows the worry to grow. It's normal for the young to imagine their companions dead whenever they fail to turn up for something. Whenever they spend too long, as Megan is now doing, in the bathroom. This is pointless, and for a while Nessa focuses back on the book in front of her, her attention like a spotlight on the story of Rose Smyth, who stabbed a Sídhe prince in the face with a sharpened bone. But what really interests Nessa is the fact that Rose is one of the few survivors to have witnessed the "windows" phenomenon in the Grey Land. Yet her concentration fades again, because every line Nessa reads is another in which Megan has not yet returned.

She stands with a sigh. It's going to be just like that time last year when she knocked on the cubicle door only for Megan to respond, "What? You want to stick your hand up there and drag the turd out with your fingers? I swear, after that lasagna, it's like giving birth . . ."

But Nessa gets up anyway, walks down a towering aisle of books and then along the narrow gap between the archaeology section and the windows that leads toward the girls' bathroom. And that's where she sees her friend—or at least the back of her, because the library looks out over the lake and the path into the forest, and Megan is hurrying along it with Squeaky Emma and another girl with a blonde fuzz on her head who must surely be Aoife.

Nessa watches them disappear, a slight pang of jealousy settling in her throat. *You could have gone with them,* she thinks, leaning her forehead against the chill glass, allowing her breath to fog it up. Best to study now though. She needs to get through a few more Testimonies. Five a day is her target, but on a library day she can easily double that and still find time for a poem or two.

The girls disappear into the trees, and she's about to turn away when she sees another group taking the exact same path. It's the knights. Or some of them: Conor and Liz Sweeney and Chuckwu. If anything, they are moving even more carefully than the girls had before them, and Nessa realizes at once they are tracking them. And it won't be for any good reason either! Conor is finally going to have his revenge on Megan for the jibes about the dogs.

Don't get involved. She made her bed and she can lie in it . . .

But that's just the jealousy talking, and Nessa is already moving toward the back exit that will lead down a rarely used stairway to the outside.

"You'll need help."

She jumps at the whisper. It's just Anto, however. He's only a hand taller than she is, but he's as lean and well built as any of the lads, despite his strange diet.

"How do *you* know what I'm doing?"

"Oh"—he smiles, totally unafraid to show the gap where he lost a tooth last year—"*nobody* ever knows what you're doing, Nessa. That's the point, isn't it? But Megan . . . now there's a different story. She's gone to find again whatever you two discovered the night of the hunt. And the great galloping Knights of the glorious Round Table—they want to find it too."

She fights and fights against his magical grin. So he knows about the "knights" too?

Maybe she really does need Anto's help. Not that she knows exactly what she plans to do yet, or if there's even anything to worry about. Conor, after all, might simply want to know the secret for himself. But she doubts that. He owes Megan one, and knows she won't dare report him even if she were to return with a broken arm or worse. Snitches never prosper in the school.

"Come on," Nessa says, turning to hide the coloring of her cheeks.

They have other classmates in the library, but the full shelves hide their departure.

The third week of October has brought a chilly eastern wind that has them longing for coats and especially shoes. Frost lies on the grass this morning, and everywhere are drifts of damp and slippery leaves.

Anto ignores the discomfort to get down on his knees, his face close to the ground.

"We don't need to track them," Nessa says. "I know where they're going, remember?"

"You know where they'll end up," he corrects her. "But they'll be avoiding the instructors and whoever else is supposed to be keeping us out of the trees."

"A point to you," she says, feeling foolish. She leaves him to his work and selects branches to make crutches out of, breaking them off with the strength of her arms that she has worked so hard on, keeping the sound to a minimum.

"I always wondered," Anto said, "why you don't just make a permanent pair for yourself?"

"It's the rules," she says, removing twigs and excess bits of wood. "Like the way the college forbids us from wearing shoes, because we won't have any when we're Called."

Anto nods. He has seen the way she has learned to move with those crutches of hers. And the practice of making them has served her well too, because she has created a new set in less than two minutes: springy but strong staves of ash, that she knows instinctively are just barely the right thickness to hold her weight.

"They went this way," he says.

"The knights or the girls?"

"Both, far as I can tell."

And that's the last they'll speak for some time. They know what it is to play the hunter as well as the hunted. They can communicate by numerous signals and signs, but so practiced is everyone in Year 5 by now that even such communication is hardly necessary.

By day at this time of year, with little cover and such careless prey, they barely need to slow. Neither group ahead knows they're being followed, but Nessa too can't shake off the feeling that somebody is after her. She spends as much time looking backward as forward. What if Taaft is out there, ready to catch them all out? But no. That wouldn't be her style. Why sneak up on them when their presence here is already enough to condemn them to the Cage?

But Nessa's skin crawls the farther they move into the trees. Anto's too, by the look of him. He clutches the little crucifix his mother gave him so hard that his knuckles gleam white.

By Crom, she thinks, he's lovely. Even the way he moves is magical, every part of him in balance, his footsteps too light on the forest floor to disturb the fallen leaves.

The two of them make good time and work together well as a team. Although Nessa—she can't help it—shows off rather more of her skills than are strictly necessary for the task at hand. At one point, risking both the snapping of her crutches and the twisting of an ankle, she springs right over a fallen tree that Anto himself has to clamber past. She plays it cool as she waits for him to join her, pretending to examine a mark in the mud on the far side.

He grins when he reaches her. He uses his hands to mime her flight through the air, his eyebrows raised in appreciation at her feat. He's so close she can almost feel the heat of his skin. She'd pull him to her right now, she would, if it wasn't for the weird sensation that they're not alone. Every hair on her body is standing on end.

Focus, she tells herself. Focus. She needs to work out what a girl on crutches and a pacifist can do to stop the likes of Conor. And she'd better come up with it quickly, because up ahead a voice, *Megan's* voice, shrieks, "Oh, Crom! Watch out!"

FAIRY FORT

This is gonna be amazing," says Megan. She might as well be speaking to herself and she feels her temper begin to rise. Look at them holding hands like that! Aoife couldn't care less about the wonder she's about to witness. She's always got that lottery-winning grin on her wide peasant face when Emma's with her.

"She'll break into a bloody song next," Megan mutters.

"What was that?" Emma asks.

"I said we need to get a move on. It's too quiet."

Let them moon over each other if they like, she thinks. But it's Crom-twisted rude when they're all supposed to be out here together and her the one doing *them* the favor! And what will Nessa say? Playing the Goody Two-shoes back at the library? Scowling? An unworthy thought, Megan realizes, because Nessa's loyal unto death and will provide the world's best alibi without the tiniest flicker of a lie showing on her face.

"What do you mean, quiet?" asks Emma. The girl looks strangely uncomfortable. Megan's not sure she's ever seen her sweat so heavily after so little exertion.

"They're supposed to be excavating the thing. To be keeping us away with instructors and the like."

"They're on a tea break," says Aoife. "Every day at this time. We've been watching."

I have, you mean!

Mind you, it was Emma who had spotted the pattern. Aoife on the other hand has weighed them down. Oh, she's a generous soul. She smiles the biggest smiles in the dorm. She gives away glorious cakes, each crafted to genius levels of perfection by an obsessive old Pole. But she would sleep twenty-four hours a day if she could, and has no more initiative than one of these dead branches. Only Emma keeps her in this world at all.

They are crouching under the skirts of a few evergreens. The ground is dry here and the branches provide cover from the wind and any instructors that might be about. No more than sixty feet ahead of them, the ground slopes dramatically upward into what they all recognize now as a Fairy Fort.

"Lucky for us they're not leaving any guard dogs around," says Emma. Her voice is hoarse. She clutches Aoife's hand hard enough to hurt.

"That's cos the poor things went crazy," says Aoife. "You remember the first night? The noise of them! Can't have the dogs out here now. Strange that even the corpse of a Sídhe will upset them."

Megan checks her grandfather's mechanical watch. "Only ten minutes left of the break," she says. "It's now or never." But she's reluctant to leave the cover of the trees, and that's not like her at all. Someone is *there*, she thinks. But she's not even sure where "there" is. It's just a feeling she has.

She crawls from under the evergreen on hands and knees and hears Aoife following, but not Emma. Nobody ever hears Emma unless she wants you to. And yet she must be there, or Aoife wouldn't have moved at all.

Megan runs in a crouch from tree to tree, regretting the swishing sounds she makes in the leaves and the panting of her breathing, as loud to her as a fire alarm on a still night. But she feels a grin rising on her face. *I love to be bad!* she thinks. *Danú's hairy tits, I love it!*

She scrambles up the slope, and moments later the girl in the rock is revealed. But it's all she can do to smother a cry of delight, because the sight is so, so much better than she thought it would be.

The researchers are not like the archaeologists of old, whose passion for their subject caused them to spend weeks carefully brushing dust away from moldy bits of pottery. This lot have come down from Dublin as part of a war effort. Lives—the entire future of their nation—might depend as much on their speed as their diligence. And so they have not hesitated to chisel away the boulder from which the young Sídhe woman sought to free herself. The girl is exposed now from the hips down, and it is extraordinary for two reasons. The first is that the rock has prevented the rest of the woman's flesh from rotting at all. Her gold-flecked skin is bared for all to see. What a fine specimen she is, except . . . except . . .

"She shrank!" said Aoife, a little out of breath, either from the run, or from the bizarre sight of the dead Sídhe.

The lower body is much smaller, way out of proportion. The farther down you look, the more she seems to shrink: her buttocks belong to a child of ten; her knees to an infant; her calves to a newborn; and her feet, her feet are no longer than the first joint of Megan's thumb with the toes too tiny to see at all.

"I don't like it," Emma whispers. She has a slight Galway accent that gets stronger when she's afraid. It's been very strong the last few minutes, all the O's changing to "ah," the S's to "sh" when they crash into the consonants. Her narrow shoulders shiver in the wind. "There's someone here," she says. "I . . . I feel it. There's definitely somebody here."

THE GLORIOUS CHARGE
OF THE KNIGHTS

Conor is grinning. He has his two best knights with him, and they are hiding under the very same tree their quarry was using just moments ago. What better proof of their weakness could there be than that they didn't even look behind themselves to see that they had been followed?

The girls have scrambled up the hill together. Megan, Squeaky Emma, and the useless Aoife. All of them are a waste of resources, he thinks, except perhaps for Emma, who is as lucky as a devil.

Chuckwu lies on his belly, chewing away, as always, on who knows what. Liz Sweeney waits to his right, and she breaks discipline now to whisper, "Forget the stupid secret. Let's just kick the shit out of them while we have the chance."

Conor mulls it over. He takes no special pleasure from cruelty, and only Megan, after all, is guilty. But it might be a good thing to blood his troops.

"We should just go back," says Chuckwu.

Conor almost chokes. "What are you talking about?"

The boy is one of very few in the school to have truly dark skin, but the queasiness shows in the set of his mouth and the rapid blinking of the eyes, as though he is one swallow away from throwing up.

"Are you *scared*, Chuckers?"

The answer is yes. It's written all over the boy's strong young body. "Not . . . not of those three . . . Lugh no! But can't you feel it?"

And as it happens, Conor can. Not as strongly as Chuckwu, or Squeaky Emma before them, or Anto, still two hundred paces away behind them. But he can feel it. Whatever *it* is. An unpleasant tingle. A pressure.

It's a dare, he thinks. A challenge to his authority, to his great future. He decides to meet it head-on.

"I like Liz Sweeney's idea," he says now. "We're running up there and we'll take one each. A good kicking, but no permanent damage, you understand me? I'm looking at you, Liz Sweeney! I know Emma made a fool of you a few hunts ago. But nothing permanent that will affect them if they're Called. They'll die anyway, but it shouldn't come back on us."

They nod, but Liz Sweeney, red-faced at his reprimand, asks, "What about the secret though? We need to find what they're hiding out here."

"We'll see it when we climb the hill, I'm sure. But no matter what it is, we investigate *after* we've taught the lesson that needs teaching. Understand? Distraction has killed thousands in the Grey Land. Focus on the task in hand." His words are as firm as those of any commander and he makes sure they both nod at him, although Chuckwu looks unhappier than ever.

They crawl out from under the tree, and like the magnificent athletes they are they run silently through the leaves and up the steep slope. The girls have their backs to them, but Megan looks up in time to cry out the alarm, rather louder than she should in the circumstances. "Oh, Crom! Watch out!"

Already spooked, the quarry scatters, darting behind the boulder and all the equipment.

Liz Sweeney dives for Emma, but her feet catch on the cord that stretches between a power drill and a small diesel generator. Down she goes. Neither Chuckwu nor Aoife are anywhere to be seen and Megan has no time to worry about them, because Conor himself is coming for her, his fists pumping like a locomotive.

Megan stumbles over something—she has no idea what— but she is already on the far slope of the mound and is tumbling downhill, crashing through bracken and stopping just long enough at each rock along the way to draw blood.

She fetches up against a lightning-shattered stump, dazed as a turnip. She has been taught well, however, and wastes little time in getting up again. And here comes Conor, charging down toward her, foiled only when she stumbles in behind a nearby ash tree so that his own momentum on the slope carries him a dozen steps too far. Then she shakes off the shock and flees back around the base of the mound, heading for home. Her two friends will have to fend for themselves. Nobody can deny that Conor is the greatest threat that Year 5 has to offer, and he's been waiting, waiting for just this opportunity . . .

Conor would punch himself if he could. He allowed his emotions to get the better of him, hurtling down the slope like a bull so that his victim can elegantly sidestep away from his flailing fists. But he catches himself on a branch and swings around after her.

Facts are facts. He's one of the fastest runners in the year, and Megan is not. He's the best fighter in the whole school; a natural leader; a fine hunter. She will never be any of these things.

Megan has no more than a hundred-fifty-foot head start on him, and even though he has already had to run up the hill toward that weird statue in the rock, or whatever the hell it was, there is simply no way she can escape the future king.

Megan's only talent is a smart mouth, and already the idea of seeing it sputter in fear and drip with blood is filling him with glee.

Soon he has narrowed the distance to sixty feet. They are passing the tree under which both groups were hiding earlier. She is running well, he notes. Not wasting all her energy in panic; not throwing any pointless glances behind her. Anything can happen. If he stumbles, if he twists an ankle, she might reach the path in time and come out the gap there into the playing fields, where even now the high voices of the Year 1s can be heard.

But he too has been taught too well to fail now. Part of his attention is always on the ground ahead. He avoids slippy piles of leaves and pointed rocks and broken branches. Sixty feet become fifty, become fifteen . . .

And then, from his left, Nessa arrives. Nessa! She has never moved so fast on those crutches of hers. Each is like a long, long leg, giving her—with enormous effort!—a giant's stride. Nobody could keep up such a pace for long using only their arms, but she doesn't need to.

He sees her land on the top of a hummock just to his left, balancing there on her weak legs, swinging the crutches down ahead of her. Then she seems to shoot toward Conor, feetfirst, a human arrow. The crutches shatter, but it makes no difference. Pain explodes in his belly and his hip. Then his head bounces off a tree trunk and he's on the ground.

An eternity passes.

"Is he . . . ? Did you kill him, Ness?"

Two girls swim into focus above him.

"He'll be all right," says Clip-Clop. "We need to get out of here. We'll find Anto first. He's around somewhere . . ."

"Are you sure Conor will be all right?"

Nessa must have nodded, because Megan sighs, then spits— she actually spits at him! It runs down his face and he sits up, in agony, in fury. But everything hurts.

"Stay down, big boy," says Megan, "or you'll be getting this here rock in the face."

Somewhere Aoife is screaming, and Conor thinks, *At least Chuckwu succeeded in his mission.*

But that's not it at all.

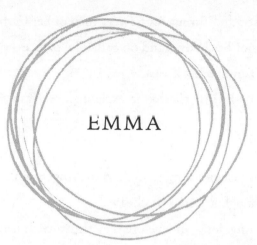

EMMA

Emma never gets caught on the weekly hunts. Her ability to hide is her pride and joy. So much so that it's always her first boast, when, late at night, she sneaks into Aoife's bed. "They'll never catch me," she whispers. To which Aoife inevitably replies, "Well, you're in my web now!"

That's only if Aoife's awake of course. Otherwise her greeting is a lot less seductive and is made up of nothing but swearwords.

They will never kiss again.

Not everybody arriving in the Grey Land is fortunate enough to find themselves alone. Squeaky Emma has appeared naked in front of a group of Sídhe, who sit before her, for all the world like an interview panel in a movie. She gasps, backing slowly away. And now, now she learns that there are others of their kind right behind her, that she is in a circle of them.

Then a princess, the most beautiful girl Emma has ever seen, her skin glittering in the silver light, her eyes unnaturally huge, rises to her feet and closes the gap between them with a single stride.

"Please . . . ," Emma says. Every inch of her flesh is prickling as the hairs of her body stand on end. The princess places a hand just above Emma's left breast.

"Oh, its heart!" the Sídhe exclaims. "So fast! A marvelous heart!"

"Please . . ."

"I *must* taste it for myself." And the fingers sink into Emma's chest, as though it were soft cheese.

It's a long, long time before they finish with her.

ANTO AND CHUCKWU

Anto watches Nessa take off the second she sees Megan running for her life through the trees. With her crutch-fueled superpower, she might just make it in time to distract Conor from his quarry. But she'll arrive there exhausted, and then it'll be trouble all round.

Everyone in the college thinks Anto is a pacifist, and they're sort of right: He won't eat any animal that's not trying to eat him. And he'll take a beating rather than lower himself to the level of the bullies.

But if Conor harms so much as a hair on Nessa's head, all bets are off. So he chases after her, the forest a blur to either side of him. He sees her swinging up to the top of a hillock . . .

And then, just like that, Nessa disappears! Anto cries out, certain she's been Called.

But it's not her, not Nessa. The whole world around him has melted and reformed itself in grey and silver and black. The air has turned sharp enough to scald his throat. It forces its way down to his stomach, and there it lingers like a diseased hand, lazily stirring the remains of his breakfast.

Eyes streaming, naked, he falls to his knees. How can this be?

In front of him, where Nessa had been just a moment before, lies the crest of a hill, jagged with slicegrass and immature spider bushes, scrabbling for life in thin soil and loose stones.

He's got to run. The Sídhe always know when they have guests, and the exact point of arrival. A welcome party will turn up any minute, and if he ever wants to see Nessa again he'd better be gone. But where?

And then he hears the shouting—a human, he does not doubt—from beyond the lip of the hill in front of him. It may be a trick, but Anto has to look anyway and he crawls right up to the edge, to where an astonishing sight awaits him. The slope on the far side is scattered with shattered tree trunks—Crom only knows how they got there—and farther down, Chuckwu is swinging a branch, fighting for his life, hopelessly, pointlessly, against a dozen laughing Sídhe.

They dance around him, leaping over his attacks, rolling under them to bounce joyfully to their feet, the grey spider silks of their clothing fluttering behind them.

Anto doesn't hesitate, doesn't even feel afraid. This is all still a dream to him. So he grabs a long rotted trunk and, holding it lengthwise across his belly, charges down the hill. Bones crunch and Sídhe go tumbling in all directions. The violence should sicken him, but instead, as Anto drops his weapon and continues his run down through the scattered enemy, he is screaming in exhilaration.

As he hoped, Chuckwu has come pelting along after him, but not the Sidhe. A glance over the shoulder shows them taking a moment to pick themselves up, milling about excitedly.

The boys keep going. Downhill, always downhill. They can't yet know what a terrible decision this is, for who has time to think amid all the wonders and horrors of the Grey Land?

They pass a swamp where head-sized bubbles rise into the air and pop, each one releasing a cry for help in any one of a dozen languages. They see twisted creatures, former men and women, hunt each other through ankle-high forests; they drink from streams whose waters taste like tears, and indeed each swallow fills them with a few heartbeats of deep sadness.

They seem to have left the pursuit far behind them when Chuckwu takes Anto by the shoulder and says, "Thank you."

It's been hours since they've paused to rest. Maybe a whole lot longer, but who can ever tell in this place?

Anto nods. "You'd have done the same for me."

"I wouldn't." The admission makes both of them uncomfortable, but the truth has always been important to Chuckwu. He is half a head taller than Anto, and nearly as well built as Conor. He has more endurance than anybody else in Year 5, and looking at him now, Anto thinks, *He's not even breathing hard.*

"What about now though? After what we've been through?"

"I'm sorry," Chuckwu says with a shrug. "I'm just not brave like that. I'll save myself first, and it's only fair you should know."

An awkward silence follows.

Anto cracks first. "You're braver than you think. You were fighting a dozen of them by yourself! And you were kicking the crap out of them."

"No, I wasn't." But Chuckwu grins shyly. "They weren't even trying to fight. Just dancing around, you know, like that game where you take a Year One's book from him and play keep-away?"

They're walking now, away from the stream, through woods of startling, frightening noises, battling slimy fronds that wrap around their ankles.

"I was amazed to see you coming down that hill for me, Anto. Isn't fighting—I don't know—isn't it against your principles or whatever? I mean, you spar pretty good in the gym. But I heard bones breaking back there!"

Anto heard that too, and is starting to feel a little sickened by it. Still he says, "I'll always fight for my friends. Always."

"But we're not friends, are we, Anto?"

"Of course we are, Chuckwu! We must be, or I wouldn't have helped you out."

Chuckwu laughs, he can't help himself, and in that unguarded moment, it's easy for Anto to see the tiny child who arrived at the college five years before, clutching a teddy bear that was not abandoned until after two full years of the worst bullying.

"The Sídhe haven't given up," says Chuckwu, "and they know this place better than we ever will. So where are they?"

"Ahead of us," Anto guesses.

"Right, they're ahead of us. Behind too maybe. How long have we been here? I don't even know."

Anto feels cold, and it's not just the normal chill of the Grey Land. Their ordeal has barely begun. A whole day of struggle awaits them. Above their heads, a dozen spirals of silver light slowly turn through the sky. There is no day or night here, but some of the books posit that the speed of the spirals or their relative positions can be used to tell the time. Maybe.

"So here's the deal," says Chuckwu now. "I know I said I wouldn't fight for you, but there's no reason we can't still work together. When they spring the trap, you run left and I'll run right. Regardless of where we are. Left and right. As fast as we can."

"Unless they're coming from the left. Or the right."

"True. True. Maybe we should just split up now then, eh, Anto?"

Maybe they should, but it turns out to be too late. A dozen Sídhe come jogging from the direction of the marsh and drive the boys before them, downhill, always, always downhill. They run for what feels like hours. Perhaps it is. They are ragged, bleeding from clashes with slicegrass and dive-bombing pigeon-sized men. They encounter a dozen sights more horrifying than anything they could have imagined, even after years of reading Testimonies. The air tears at their lungs and the linings of their eyes. But the Sídhe never close with them.

"They'll have to make their move soon," says Chuckwu.

Anto doesn't need to ask why. The enemy will want time to "play" with the boys before they kill them. He's half thinking they should turn and try to barge their way through the crowd of hunters behind them, but arrows keep them moving until they are pushed onto what looks for all intents and purposes like a paved path.

It leads into the narrowest of valleys with slopes angling steeply to either side of them. They can run comfortably here side by side, faster than the leisurely pace of the hunters, so that they seem to be getting away again.

But it is not until they are in the middle, the very middle of the valley, that they realize they are quite alone. They slow to a complete stop. Anto is bent over and breathing hard while sweat chills on his body, but Chuckwu is looking up at the steep climb to either side.

"You hear that?" Chuckwu asks.

Anto pauses, straining his ears, and yes, he can hear it. Giggling. He regards the mud-covered sides of the valley. It's only a climb of maybe a hundred paces to get up to the boulders and trees at the top. The slope is too smooth though, without so much as a weed to grab on to. But it doesn't matter anyway, because both boys now recognize that this is the place where the Sídhe wanted them all along. This is where they're going to die.

The path continues down the valley in front of them and seems to open out down there.

"We should sprint for it," says Anto, although he hasn't got the strength.

Chuckwu shakes his head firmly. "Up the sides," he says. "They'll be waiting for us down there. The whole welcoming committee is—"

"Look out!"

A boulder comes flying down the hill and each dives out of the way just as it smashes onto the path. It bounces ten steps up the far wall and tumbles down again. Neither boy wastes time catching his breath, because more rocks are coming both in front of and behind them. Giant pool balls crash together and splinters fly to sting and shred their skin.

A rock comes for Chuckwu—it's barely the size of his head, but he saves himself only by diving in behind the rubble from previous attacks. He finds Anto already waiting for him, the shorter boy's face a mask of blood-spattered dust.

The avalanche pauses. Applause and laughter break out at the top of the far slope. When Anto looks out from the protection of the rubble, he can see Sídhe rolling more rocks into position above him.

"I'm making a run for it," he says, pointing down toward the far end of the valley.

"You can't!" says Chuckwu. "You'll be crushed. We have cover here now. We just need to wait for them to use up their rocks. Then we can fight them off. If we can hold them until—"

"No! No!" Anto grips his arm tight enough to bruise. "We can't afford to wait. I know we can make it! We—"

He doesn't get to say anything else before more rocks begin to fall. Anto pulls at Chuckwu, but the bigger boy wrenches himself free. "Please, Chuckwu!" But then he has to dive out of the way.

True to his word, he starts sprinting and Chuckwu curses him for a fool. All along Anto's path, the enemy releases boulders to roll down on top of him. Except . . . except, none of them strike the boy. He always has plenty of time to avoid them, and now, at last, Chuckwu realizes what Anto has been trying to tell him: The Sídhe want them alive. Of course they do!

He begins to follow Anto, but it's too late. The enemy, beautiful men and women, are sliding down the walls of the valley, laughing all the way. Their intention is clearly to hunt down Anto, but it also puts them between Chuckwu and the only way out of the valley. Others of their kind are coming in from behind him and that means he's dead. One way or the other, he's dead, and the right thing to do is to find a way to finish himself before they can lay their terrible hands on him.

Chuckwu has always been a scaredy-cat. When they took his teddy away, he wrapped his arms around a pillow instead.

And later it was Conor's sermons he relied on, to keep the nightmares at bay and imagine that he might live.

But that is not to be. Chuckwu's only hope now is to avoid pain. To bash in his own skull. To cut his throat with one of the sharp fragments lying around.

Instead he flies forward, as fast as his powerful legs can carry him. He screams, "For the future!" and crashes into the Sídhe that are pursuing Anto, lashing out with a rock, so that two of them fall dead straight away. He throttles a third, and punches another in the side of the head.

And when they finally grab him and begin to twist his body into terrible, agonizing shapes, Chuckwu the coward does not freeze in horror as so many have before him. No, Chuckwu bites and kicks and delays. "Run, my friend!" he screams, the sound already more animal than human. "Rnnnnnnnnnnnnnnnn frrrrrrrrrrrrrrrnnnnnnnnnnnnnnnnnnnnnnnnnnnd Rnnnnnnnnnn nnnn."

The Sídhe are both astonished and delighted.

———

Anto has yet to escape the valley. Rocks shatter all around him, loud enough to hurt his ears. He ignores them, relying on the Sídhe's desire for live capture to keep him safe. A shard of stone rips into his shoulder and lodges there. Powdered rock stings his left cheek. And still he runs.

Once they realize what he's up to, the enemy start throwing themselves down the slopes, heedless of injury. They're behind him because he should never have made it this far. But they have plenty of time to catch up on their fading prey.

I'm done for, Anto thinks. *Done for!*

But then he hears Chuckwu screaming, "For the future!" Like a ridiculous war cry from one of those movies that's so old they made it in black and white. Anto should go back and die with him, but instead he weeps and finds the strength to accelerate.

Only twenty paces away lies the mouth of the strangely artificial valley. Here the sides of the hills become actual walls too steep for the Sídhe to slide down. Yet a laughing gang of them waits at the top with a final boulder, larger than five of the others put together. A great heave, and it drops like a sledgehammer. No matter how fast Anto runs, it will reach the bottom before he makes it to the exit and there's no way he'll climb over it before the hands of his enemies take hold of him and melt his flesh.

"Rnnnnnnnnnnnnnnn!" he hears behind him, the heart-freezing cry of a beast in agony. "Rnnnnnnnnnnnnnnnn frrrrrrrr rrrrrrrnnnnnnnnnnnnnnnnnnnnnnnnnnnd."

He throws every ounce of energy, of courage, into his charge.

The boulder strikes the path like God's fist, close enough that Anto might have reached out and touched it. Instead he is already diving forward, brushing underneath it as it hops once, before finally settling to block the valley.

He crawls on all fours for a few minutes, his breath hoarse, the only sound the war drums of his own pulse. But he knows he can't let up. It's hard to gauge how much time has passed, but there may yet remain hours of pursuit. Certainly more than he has the energy for. His muscles barely have the strength to tremble and he is leaving a steady trail of blood behind him. Surely they'll bring their terrible dogs to bear now?

Even so, when he has staggered one or two hundred yards farther, the hills and trees open up and fall away completely to reveal the most astonishing panorama.

The sea of the Grey Land lies before him: an expanse of black molasses-like liquid, barely stirred by a lazy, putrid breeze. He has read about it of course, but not this part of it. He's looking out over a sheltered bay, maybe two and a half miles wide, and from one end of it to the other are piles of wreckage: shattered airplanes; fishing boats; military landing craft; and far, far out toward the horizon he spots the outline of an overturned cruise liner like a massive carcass, lying where it died.

Farther down the beach is something that should be equally strange here in the Grey Land: spots of color—real color. He knows they must be "windows." A phenomenon that fascinates Nessa.

It's amazing he can think of her here, in this place. The curve of her cheeks. The set of her jaw as she fights and fights to hide that she cares. He knows, deep down, that she will be dead within the year, for she would never survive what he has been through so far this day. Fast as she moves on those crutches—if she even has time to make any—she just won't last long enough.

"Oh, God," he prays, "that's how I know you don't exist. Because how could you do this to *her*?"

So tired is he, so confused, that it takes Anto a few minutes to recognize this as an opportunity to save his life. There must be a thousand great hiding places in that graveyard of ships. A million! And no "dogs" will find his scent in all that water. But he'd better be out of sight before they follow him out of the valley. They can't be more than a few minutes behind him.

Anto staggers forward. First comes a sterile beach of hard pebbles that dig into his torn feet. After there's a wet, itchy sand, that sends out clouds of the most appalling vomit-like smell every time he breaks its surface. And then there's the water itself. Sludgy as old porridge, and it leaves an oil-like sheen on his skin when he washes off the blood. Otherwise though, if the Testimonies are correct, it should be harmless.

The sea has risen to his waist by the time he reaches the first piece of wreckage—a jetliner—and still there's no sign of any pursuit.

Water passes inside through a rip in the fuselage. It might be a good place to hide, but he'd feel more comfortable if there were another way out of it. So he moves on, deeper, allowing the chill slime of the sea to creep up to his sternum. A likely looking fishing boat is waiting only a little farther along. And now that the bulk of the plane is hiding him from the beach, he can take his time getting there.

But then, just as he's pondering trying to swim the last hundred feet, what appears to be a floating sheet of metal *moves*.

The water around him shivers like a lump of jelly, sliding away in great lumps as the rusting metal reveals itself to be the shell of a tank-sized monster. He freezes—the natural response of tiny prey since the beginning of time. *Maybe it won't see me here, worthless crumb that I am, hardly worth the trouble of eating . . .*

But he draws attention to himself by crying out. For he has seen that it has not one face, but dozens and dozens of them. They are crammed in together beneath the lip of the crablike dome of its shell. All of them are human, melting into each other, mouths twisted in pain or fury or hunger. A thousand blinking, tearful eyes; the features of every ethnicity in the world.

Nearest Anto, at the surface of the water, is a woman's head, half covered by the rags of a pilot's uniform, squashed up against, and growing into, the moaning weathered skin of a middle-aged man in a rotted fisherman's cap.

And then all the mouths open at once and call out in a chorus of rage and hunger. Massive fists slough off the water, and these are rough things, made of multiple human torsos, each great knuckle protected by a sheet of metal torn from the hull of a ship.

But Anto won't die just yet. The creature is not the only one of its kind. Another has heaved itself to the surface and is already shoving old wrecks from its path as it powers toward the first. Such is the force of its passage that the waves lift Anto and fling him gasping against the fuselage of the plane behind him. In no time at all the "crabs" are battering at each other. Their metal shells dent and tear with a sound that can be heard for miles in all directions. Their many voices cry out in pain as blood seeps into the black water, and a terrified Anto, gasping in horror, can see that several of the faces at the front of each titan are already dead.

But eventually one great fist breaks through the enemy's shell. It tears out whole handfuls of body parts, and these it pushes gently but urgently into its own flesh, growing in the process. The loser, meanwhile, staggers back toward Anto, already diminished, no larger now than a minibus, bleeding, disoriented.

Anto has seen enough. He knows that if he doesn't leave right now, he will finish his days under one of those shells. Or parts of him will.

He swims, or rather he claws his way through the water under the body of the plane to come up on the far side. He's got to get out of here. Got to.

Screams from behind tell him that the two giants are not quite finished with each other yet. They're making more waves now, and one of these is so large it lifts Anto from his feet entirely and flings him head over heels toward the beach.

This is not the place where he entered the sea: nowhere near it. He has fetched up, in fact, beside the "windows."

Anto's strength has left him and has taken with it all will and imagination. He is incapable now of wonder. But still his eyes are drawn to the color.

"Windows" are a well-known but poorly understood phenomenon. They are like holes in the air. Each is double the height of an adult, and three times as wide, and through them you can see views of Ireland as it was a few decades ago. The Testimonies have recorded eighty separate scenes so far. Without exception they are displays of happiness.

The one farthest from where Anto lies shows a herd of colts, prancing in a spring meadow. The green of the field burns into his retinas, so intense does it seem amid the misery of the Grey Land. Another window displays a cocktail party, with dancing and the like, in old-fashioned clothes. Anto wonders what music can make the people move so vigorously that they look like they're about to crash into each other in a joyful mess.

But the people in the scene nearest to Anto are all, like him, spending a day by the seaside. They stretch out in the glory of the sun, heedless of the intense beauty of their plastic buckets, their bathing suits, their towels. A sob escapes his throat, and even though it won't work—it can't work!—he climbs to his feet and tries to reach into the scene . . .

And that's when the Sídhe arrive. A group of twelve.

Anto can't run. He's got nothing left in the tank. Even standing is too much for him. For the second time in less than twenty minutes, his fear freezes him.

They approach, and he sees now that their beauty is all illusion. And they know it too. Because although they are supposed to be searching for him, their eyes are drawn first to the horses and the green and then to the dancers.

He sees the longing in their perfect faces and he wonders who designed this hell. Who, in their cruelty, left these windows behind to remind them of all that had been stolen from them? To remind them of the thieves themselves, enjoying every shade of green and gold and red? Feeling the sun and the clean, pure rain on their skins?

For once the Sídhe are not smiling. They beat at their chests like maddened gorillas. But they keep moving, and now they turn their eyes to Anto, until every one of them, the full dozen, is looking right at him.

But then they begin to walk past, and he realizes, he realizes, they think he is *part* of the scene in the window. Laughter bubbles up inside him, but it's death to make a noise and he manages to squash it. Three Sídhe women come by in cloaks of spiky leaves. Four men follow along, bows half cocked in their hands.

"We have no time," says one. "The thief has escaped us."

"Every one that gets away," says a second, "is another to fight us when the worlds align again. It will not be long . . . But this one, I think, is still here. I felt it arrive, and a hundred heartbeats remain before it can leave."

Two more men and two women go by. In the scene, through the window, a girl is standing next to Anto. Blonde hair has blown into her eyes and she brushes it away. He moves his mouth silently, pretending to talk to her.

Then a hand closes around his wrist, and for a moment Anto thinks it's the girl, that she has come to him through the window. But it's the last of the Sídhe. A tall woman with huge, sparkling eyes and a wide, wide grin of triumph.

"Oh, cleverest of thieves," she says. She is *so* happy to see him. A child at Christmas. "Yet I saw that your hair does not blow in the same direction as hers."

And she begins to squeeze. And the pain is incredible.

"You, we will make a giant!"

MOURNING BELLS

Nessa and Megan walk right past Anto's empty tracksuit without ever seeing it. They don't even know he was Called. Beyond the mound where the girl in the rock forever struggles to free herself, Aoife is still screaming.

The noise has attracted some instructors too: Tompkins and Horner, materializing between the trees like a pair of ghosts. Tompkins, the one who talks, turns his head toward Nessa. "Go back. This is forbidden." But he doesn't stop to ensure obedience, and the two girls skirt around the face of the hill to where Aoife, her voice now hoarse, weeps over the appalling remains of Squeaky Emma. Liz Sweeney crouches nearby, trying not to look but unable to help herself.

"I . . . I'm not sure I want to get any closer to *that*," says Megan, and Nessa can only agree. Squeaky Emma has always been a strange fish: secretive, but cheery and irreverent. She could talk for hours about foods and dishes she had never tasted, but showed little interest in actually eating. And she could be fun, sometimes, when the mood took her. Nessa doesn't want to see what has become of her now. The parts of her that appear from behind Aoife and Liz are scaled and oozing. That's more than enough.

They turn, to find Sergeant Taaft clumping along toward them through the fallen leaves. "Oh, you're for it now," she says.

But just then another voice calls out. "Chuckwu! We've found Chuckwu! I *think* it's him anyway." And Taaft curses. "Two together so soon? Back! Get back to the college. Now!"

They return the way they've come, and if they didn't see Anto's empty tracksuit on the way here, they certainly won't notice that it is now missing. Only the crucifix remains, dull in the forest gloom.

The mourning bells ring twice that day, both times for Year 5. In the refectory Megan is trying to comfort the weeping Aoife, but gentleness was not one of nature's gifts to her, and besides, she has wet cheeks of her own.

Nessa's not much help to anybody either. It's because of Marya, who's running around telling everybody that Anto was Called too, but that he's come back alive.

Nessa's thoughts are spinning and spinning with it. What will happen now? What *can* happen? She's in a daze, and yet she's not, because every time the door swings open her head jerks up, expecting to see him come in, to see him stride over to her for her congratulations.

Such things have happened before: survivors paraded in front of their peers; injuries tended, faces washed, and awkward in civilian clothes and even—by the Cauldron!—shoes. More often, however, they need "help" processing their experiences. Sometimes they don't return to society for months. Sometimes they are kept on a suicide watch. Forever.

And yet, in spite of that, their untested peers envy them and celebrate these rare victories more than they mourn the losses.

In the refectory, songs are sung and cakes are served along with precious coffee. It makes everybody giddy and loud. Under the cover of this racket, Megan leans in close to Nessa; her eyes are red from crying over Emma. "You happy?" she asks. "I always know when you are. He's your boy."

"He's not my boy."

"He's yours if you want him."

Nessa doesn't respond. Megan's right though, isn't she? Half of the impossible fantasy has come true. And Nessa wonders if Anto will return to the college as a veteran. Many do. Like poor Shamey. Like Diane Mallon, who, with seconds to go in the Grey Land, jumped off a cliff and got home just before hitting the bottom. Both of them seem reluctant to begin new lives and she wonders why that is. And then there's the third veteran, poor Melanie, whose heart will literally burst if she ever comes under real stress again. What if Anto is like that? The Grey Land kills in many ways and not always quickly.

Please, God—she never prays! *Holy Mary, let him be all right.*

For the second time that day, Taaft appears behind the Donegal girls. Her hands grip their shoulders. "Ms. Breen wants you," she says. "Did you think we'd forgotten you were in the forest today?"

Nessa looks up to see Conor glaring across at her from the boys' table. His special hatred for her is never far away. So much so that she rarely notices it anymore. And after what she did to him in the forest, surely she has earned a bit of it now.

They have to drag Aoife out of the warmth along with them. It's no easy task. The poor girl walks as though in a dream, and Nessa imagines she would have the same look on her face if it had been Anto who was lost, rather than Squeaky Emma. Except Anto is only a fantasy boyfriend rather than a real one. She wouldn't have a right to feel that way.

Taaft leaves them with Liz Sweeney, who's already waiting outside the principal's office. "What about the puppy-lover?" Megan asks her. "He too busy today?"

"Who?"

"Ass face. Your boss. Conor turdbreath."

"Crom will snap you in two, you hateful little redheaded bitch."

"Seriously. Where is he?"

"The instructors never saw him in the forest. Nobody knows he was there, and there's no reason for you to tell, is there, Megan Donnelly?"

Megan shrugs. "I'm no snitch, Liz Sweeney. Unless he saw something useful for the Testimonies?"

Liz Sweeney says he didn't, so that's the end of the matter. Megan knocks on Ms. Breen's door. "It's the Cage for all of us," Liz Sweeney says.

And in they go, the four girls squashing in between piles of books and stacks of yellowing notes that must never have been consulted in the quarter century since a religious order ceded this building to the State. The place stinks of the menthol tobacco that Ms. Breen uses in her pipe, and she takes another pull of it now as she looks up at them from the keyboard of the patched-together computer she uses.

"You will be punished," she tells them conversationally, "but not until we've figured a few things out, because it's strange, isn't it? For three people to be Called so close together, so soon. Within a radius of, what? Fifty, a hundred feet?"

"It's the girl in the rock," says Nessa. Because of course she has been thinking about the coincidence too.

The Turkey nods. "But why weren't *you* Called? You and Megan discovered it only a week ago. You walked right up to . . . to *her*, didn't you?"

They nod.

"Did you touch her? Did Emma touch her? Or Chuckwu, or Anto?"

"We didn't get a chance," said Megan. "We were followed by—"

"*We* followed them!" says Liz Sweeney hurriedly. "Me and Chuckwu. The *two* of us. That's what she's saying. We were . . .

we were curious, but the girls ran from us. They must have thought we were teachers or instructors. So they ran."

Ms. Breen's voice turns hard. "Did any of you touch her or didn't you?"

"I don't think so," said Megan. "Like Liz Sweeney says, we scattered before we got the chance."

"And Anto definitely didn't get the chance," said Nessa. "He couldn't have."

"You were together?"

Nessa feels her face redden, but manages to keep her voice steady. "We were in the library, miss. We saw . . . Liz Sweeney and Chuckwu and wondered what they were at."

The principal sighs. "And so," she intones, "all of the lemmings run over the cliff. Brilliant."

She puffs at the pipe for a moment, ignoring them, deep in her own world. But Nessa feels compelled to speak.

"I think this happened because they cut open the rock, miss," she says. "There was a strange feeling among the trees that wasn't so strong the first time we saw the . . . the Sídhe girl. And . . . and it affected Anto more than me. He was grabbing at that cross of his and sweating."

"By the Cauldron!" shouts Liz Sweeney. "It was the same with Chuckwu!"

"And Emma . . ." These last words are a whisper from Aoife. "She . . . she never was afraid of anything, but she . . . she seemed more nervous than Megan did. Or . . . or me even."

"Good," says the Turkey, the folds of skin at her neck gently swaying. "This is good." Keys clack-clack on the filthy computer as she takes notes, the pipe dangling precariously from her cracked lips. Only her command of the Sídhe language is beautiful. "Is there anything else?" she asks. "Anything at all?"

Nessa does have a question. She has a ton of them actually. For example, where is Anto? Is he coming back to the school? Is he all right?

But it is Megan who speaks.

"Why was the Sídhe girl getting smaller, miss? The farther her body went into the rock?"

Ms. Breen shrugs, as if the question is unimportant. "You're getting three days in the Cage" is her answer.

"That's too long, miss!" Megan protests. "And since we were at the rock today with Squeaky Emma and Chuckwu, how'd you know we aren't about to be Called too?"

"We don't, child. We never know. But we have to maintain the system for everyone's sake and—"

"And things are getting worse," Megan interrupts, "aren't they, miss? Coming to a head. Everybody says so, what with that whole school in Mallow that got done! But none of you teachers are admitting it. I think—"

"Enough!" The Turkey's voice is sufficiently cold to stop even Megan in her tracks. But Nessa fancies she can see doubt in her eyes. "You, my dear lass from Donegal, you are getting an extra day for insolence."

Even Megan knows better than to push it and snaps her mouth shut in time.

"Nessa," Ms. Breen continues, "I won't be sending you to the Cage."

"You . . . you won't?"

"You were the most foolish of all. Following the others for no reason. So I have something much worse in mind for you. You will stay behind. The rest of you"—she waves the stinky pipe toward the door—"I hope you ate all your cake. Find Tompkins and ask him to escort you upstairs."

Out they go, leaving Nessa to her fate.

"We'll give them a few minutes," says Ms. Breen, her voice more kindly now.

"A few minutes for what, miss?"

"You've never been to the Cage, have you, Nessa?" She waits for confirmation. "Well, I'm not sending you now."

"So what is my punishment?"

"Oh, there isn't one. I just didn't want to embarrass you. The thing is . . . we can't have you weak now, can we?" And she winks. She actually *winks*. As in, I'm doing you this massive favor because you're a useless cripple type wink.

It takes every scintilla of Nessa's willpower to keep her face straight, to prevent herself from lifting up the table and battering

Ms. Breen to death with it. She takes a few deep breaths, and this too, she realizes, will be read by her tormentor as "relief." As weakness.

But what it actually is, is strength. She will use Ms. Breen's idiot pity to get what she wants. And so she comes straight out and asks about Anto.

"Is Anthony Lawlor coming back here?" Her voice is perfectly disinterested. Perhaps too much so, for who wouldn't be curious about the first member of her class to survive the Call? It is a massive event for Year 5. Massive.

"He's on his way up to Dublin."

"Is he all right?"

Ms. Breen's face twists around the stem of the pipe, as though she is carefully working through a dozen different wordings in her mind, before she finally settles on, "The doctors are . . . they are *confident*."

"C-confident? Confident of what?"

"Oh, child. You've had a long day, haven't you? Go on back to the refectory and tell the rest of them you've been punished terribly. Make something up. You're smart enough. Go on."

Nessa finds herself back in the corridor. She stops halfway down, in front of a window blurred with rain. She's thinking about all the Testimonies she's read, about the bizarre and terrible conditions inflicted on some of the unluckier survivors. The mermaid girl, Angela Heffernan. That lad from Tuam, what was his name? The one who was given bats' ears and a voice too high for anybody else to hear.

And there are far worse things than that! Look at the veteran Melanie, right here in this college! A beautiful, beautiful girl. But that's not why people whisper about her. Her Testimony is one of the most popular in the library because everybody wants to see the sketches of her incredible "injury."

"Confident," Ms. Breen had said when she'd asked about Anto. "The doctors are . . ." And she hesitated, didn't she? She hesitated right there! As if to say they're not bloody confident at all!

Nessa turns to go back to the refectory, her mind still wrestling with her fears. And then she stops.

Conor is there. Lounging in an alcove that held the statue of a saint back when this part of the college was a monastery. He's watching her and must have been the whole time she stood at the window.

"I think you broke my rib," he says. He's like an apparition. He doesn't belong here when her mind is so focused on other things. "A foolish risk you took there for Megan. It was my duty to teach her a lesson, but I wouldn't have damaged her. She can take a bit of a beating, can't she?"

Nessa never stands next to Conor unless they're paired off at sparring, and that hasn't happened in several months. She has forgotten just how large he is, in all ways, and she has a sudden realization that no matter how many weights she pumps or how much of the terrible refectory food she eats, she will never be as strong as he is.

"What do you want?" she asks him.

He's not unintelligent, and yet this simple, obvious question throws Conor into confusion. As though it has come to him as a surprise. He looks once around the empty corridor and then back at her, and his breathing changes.

"Listen," he says. His voice becomes a whisper. "Listen. This is your chance. Nobody has to know."

"What . . . what are you talking about?"

And then his lips are crushing hers. Just like that, and it takes all of her considerable strength to push him away. "What the . . . ?! Conor!"

"Don't be a fool," he says. "You might as well take it when it's offered. Obviously I must forbid you to tell anyone. But you're not like that twit Sherry. I've sent her away, and it's for you."

Then he's kissing her again. Rough and inexpert. Callused hands are pushing under her tracksuit, straight up toward her small breasts, his whole, massive body pressing against her. "You might as well," he breathes. "All of us who were out there today are going to be Called now. So enjoy it! Enjoy!"

And then he screams.

Never once in their sparring has she successfully landed a blow on him, but for some bizarre reason he's not expecting one now. Certainly not a vicious punch between the legs. Or a second one before his nerves have had time to tell him something terrible is wrong. Or a third. He's not ready to have his ear yanked, or to have it used as the handle of a battering ram, as she slams him into the wall. And that rib? The one she damaged earlier in the day? Why, yes, yes, it still hurts, especially when she strikes at it with stiffened fingers.

When she has him down and helpless, she staggers away from him. But Conor has had the same training as herself. He knows that to stay down is to die, regardless of the damage suffered. He leaps to his feet and charges along the corridor after her, half blind with dripping blood. He grabs her before she can get through the door into the back of the refectory and flings her away from it, as though she is no heavier than a paperback. She hits the polished floor and slides along it to end up against the very same alcove where their encounter began.

She's not going to catch him by surprise again, she thinks. The Cage, the Cage would have been far better than this! She tries to stand, but suddenly Sergeant Taaft is there and keeps her down with a polished black boot.

"A lover's tiff?" she asks.

Nessa can't see the sergeant's face, but genuine eagerness fills Taaft's voice as she says to Conor, "You want to fight me, child?"

Conor's battered face shows no fear at all. But eventually, and with regret, he answers, "You have more training than me."

"No kidding."

"But I'll keep getting stronger."

And now Taaft sounds like she is spitting. "Not in the Cage you won't. Picking on the handicapped! You make me sick."

But it's Nessa who feels sick, battling to keep the tears of shame at bay.

THE SNOW

It hasn't been the best week in Liz Sweeney's life, and now, now the snow!

Everybody says the winters are colder than they used to be, that nobody should have to put up with temperatures like these the week before Halloween. But nowadays thermometers always take a dive after September, and the instructors think nothing of dragging the class for a pre-breakfast, barefoot run through the slush.

"No offense," says Aoife to Horner. "No offense, sir, but me and Liz Sweeney, we're just out of the Cage. That biscuit was our first food in days, sir. Sir?"

Horner rarely speaks, English or Sídhe or anything else. He doesn't even like to shrug, but he manages one now, dragging it out of the black hole of war that ate his personality thirty years before. He has a tiny smooth face, with greying curly hair and great big eyes that any Sídhe would be proud of. Liz Sweeney has to drag her gaze away from his before it sucks her into nothingness. Just looking at him is enough to make her shiver, regardless of the weather.

That Aoife's a lazy shit, Liz Sweeney thinks, but for once she'll keep that opinion to herself. The girl cried every day in the Cage and it wasn't about food, although all of them were bent double over cramped bellies. And looking at her tears, Liz Sweeney didn't think of weakness, as Conor did. No, she wanted to weep too. For herself. For Chuckwu. For the sister she lost. For her brother Kieron, in Year 6 up in another college and not yet Called.

She'll hear news of him very soon. Yes, because farther north, near Bangor, Kieron Sweeney has also been ordered to go for a run in the snow. It's heavier there, practically a storm, and half an hour from now his abandoned tracksuit will spend three minutes and four seconds getting wet.

Liz Sweeney can't know any of that. As part of the Round Table, she constantly tells herself how strong she is. How little she feels—other than scorn—for the Aoifes of this world, and admiration for the Conors.

Her life is about to be turned upside down.

KIERON'S STORY

Kieron has survived the Call. Now he is back and everything is different. He stands naked on top of his soaking tracksuit with snow falling around him. He shivers violently and then falls to his knees, his mouth open, braying like an animal. He has seen things no human should ever witness.

Parallel welts run down his chest where a "dog" of the Sídhe raked his skin, but the wounds don't bleed: They have an ancient, gnarled look about them, and he cries out, "I wish you'd killed me! Why didn't you kill me?"

But this is just shock. Disbelief. And while the dreams will haunt him the rest of his life, he will fight them, fight to live, fight to be happy.

He has been trained for this, and in spite of what he has just experienced, he is one of the lucky ones.

His teeth chatter. *Don't freeze to death.* The idea makes him laugh like a madman. He spent all his energy in the Grey Land, but he grabs up his soaking clothing and staggers, tripping through the ankle-deep snow. *Nearly there, nearly there.* There's nobody around of course. Everyone else gets to enjoy a lazy breakfast, but he was foolish enough to mock one of the instructors, Sicari, where she could hear him.

"Out, Sweeney! Out!" she cried. "A whole circuit of the park."

"How will you know I've done it?" he couldn't help asking, and her eyes narrowed so that the combat scar across her forehead turned white under his gaze.

"You think I couldn't track you in that?" She jerked her head toward the freezing blanket that had settled onto Bangor overnight. "You're lucky it's not the Cage, you little shit. Year Sixes act out sometimes. Everybody knows it. You're like little children. Now go, puppy, go. A full circuit or, by God, you'll not eat for a week."

That conversation seems like so, so long ago. Another life, which, of course, it is. An innocent one, in which he hadn't seen the . . . the *fruit* trees of the Grey Land. Oh, Danú! Oh, Lugh! The thought of them drives him to his knees to retch from an empty stomach.

It was just bad luck that he was called halfway round his circuit of the park. He knows this place like the back of his hand, but now the snow is falling thicker than ever, disguising familiar landmarks—the statue, the yew trees, and so on. He can't feel his fingers. He can't think straight. But right beside him there are footprints, as bare as his own. Perhaps a boy in another year has been punished in the same way as he was. Most likely a boy, because the prints are too large, certainly, to belong to any of the girls. And where could this other lad be headed but to the college?

"Thank you, Lugh," he says, a meaningless prayer to the enemy's god.

He manages to stand. If the footprints are to save him, he will need to follow them before the snow hides them completely.

Off he goes. They lead him away from the track and through the silent trees. Now, he thinks, here's somebody who doesn't fear Sicari will be checking up on him!

This is a direct route, and soon the back of the kitchens emerges from the white curtain.

Entry through that entrance is forbidden to pupils, but nobody will refuse a survivor anything! With a hundred yards to go, he wastes precious seconds deciding whether to put his wet clothes on to hide his nakedness from the cooks, but he realizes that he must be in an even worse condition than he imagined, because his useless fingers have dropped the tracksuit somewhere along the way.

It doesn't matter. Nothing matters except getting inside to those warm lights. Kieron finds he is crying. He doesn't need the footprints anymore. But when he looks at them again, he sees that they might belong to one of the girls after all, for they are smaller than he thought. *No, you idiot. It's the snow that's filling them, that's all.* And on he goes.

At the entrance he fears he will have to scream to be let in, or to beat on the steamed-up windows with nerveless hands. But no, the door lies ajar. It's still bloody warm though! He cries out in joy. Pushing it shut behind him and sliding to his bare bottom, babbling half-remembered prayers from his childhood.

It is some time before he realizes he has heard no voices. His whole body aches as the numbness wears off, and it is now that Kieron notices something strange: There are footprints on the linoleum floor, an obvious continuation of those seen in the snow. He has to squint to make them out properly, because they have dried in the heat, leaving behind an outline in dirt.

And whoever owns these feet can't be any larger, surely, than an eight-year-old.

Did he really see man-sized footprints out in the snow? He was exhausted. He was shaking with horror and slowly freezing to death. He *must* have imagined their larger size.

"Who cares?" he says aloud. There are coats belonging to the cooks hanging just above his head. He pulls himself up, heedless of any damage he might cause in the process, and borrows the largest of them to cover his nakedness. The effort is almost too much, and he wants to fall down again and sleep under a blanket of old jackets. But he's come this far.

"Kieron," he mutters. "Kieron the Survivor." He's going to be a hero. He's going to get married. He can do anything, anything he wants. "Kieron the Survivor. Kieron Sweeney."

And then he steps into the kitchen, where everybody, everybody is asleep. With their eyes open.

It is such a strange sight he walks right past it, as though in a dream, and on into the refectory. Unlike his sister's school, Bangor SC has been set up in what used to be called a "Great House." Eighteenth-century stable buildings have been knocked together with a series of mismatched extensions to make a long, confused series of rooms, stuffed with tables of all shapes and sizes.

The students are all here to greet him, Kieron the hero. They lie about the place, mouths open, eyes staring, their limbs like a rag doll's. His mind refuses to switch on and tell him what's happening.

He remembers something about another college, but what? What was it?

And then, from behind him, he hears the faintest of noises. He follows it back into the kitchen.

A little man, no larger than his hand, sits beside a great vat of porridge. Kieron approaches to within a few paces and notices that the creature is laughing and laughing. "I didn't do this," it squeaks. "But a promise allowed me to come and I wanted to see!" It is as naked as he, but has the features of a Sídhe, the glittering skin, the big eyes.

Kieron lets out a bellow and grabs for the man, but an intense pain causes him to let go at once—an indent has appeared in his palm that he will carry the rest of his life. The tiny man springs away. Furious, Kieron chases him across the counters while the man seems to shrink and shrink.

The tiny Sídhe skips across the top of the gas cooker, but now it is no larger than Kieron's thumb, and this proves the creature's undoing, for it falls into one of the rings on the top of the cooker and the boy can trap it by simply placing a pot over it.

And then, with animal pleasure—for his palm still aches— Kieron, lights the stove and removes the pot.

An ever tinier human torch stumbles around for a moment. Then, as though choreographed, both killer and victim fall. One as ash, and one asleep.

MEGAN RETURNS

Apart from Conor, Megan is last out of the Cage. Already condemned to lie there a day longer than the others, she couldn't help herself and found a way to extend her sentence even further by antagonizing Tompkins when he arrived to release Aoife.

She shuffles from her cell, half bent over like an old man.

"What if they Called you now?" Nessa asks. "Why do you do this to me?"

"To you?" Megan grins. Her red hair is already too long, and now there's a good handful of it, clumping all to one side. And of course she still speaks in mostly English. "Anyway, Ness, why're you here? I thought you'd be over in the library writing a wee poem—oh! Scrape that face off yourself, there's nobody listening. You think I'd say anything if there was?"

Nessa knows she would not. Megan is a terror, but she's Nessa's terror.

"Come on," she tells Megan. "They said I could take you to the refectory. You can have broth for now. And you need a haircut."

Megan rolls her eyes, but follows along, her pace even slower than that of her lame friend as they make their way down the stairs. But she's not so far gone she doesn't detect that something is wrong. "Spill it," she says. And Nessa does, in a whisper.

"Another college is dead."

"What? Like . . . like the one in Mallow?"

"Yeah, just like that. And listen . . ." She takes a deep breath, shocked even now by the magnitude of it. "Liz Sweeney's brother was up there and he was the only survivor. He was . . . he was Called at the same time it happened. *Exactly* the same time. Or so the rumors say. And he's supposed to have seen one of *them*, a Sídhe. In *our* world."

"No way!" Megan pauses, swaying at the bottom of the stairs. "All those stupid stories of spies are real?"

"Well, sort of. The stories say the Sídhe wander around disguised as people, or even wearing a person's flesh over their own. But this one . . . it . . . it kept shrinking, the longer it was here."

Both of them think of the girl in the rock, although only the bottom half of her shrank, as far as they can tell.

"Wow," says Megan. "I can't believe it. Wow."

The Cage—really a series of locked little rooms—sits directly above the staff quarters, aka the barracks, to the north of the refectory. They have to go outside to reach the main complex of buildings, with Megan shivering every step of the way. But already they can catch the fading smells of breakfast and hear Ms. Fortune's husky voice calling out orders over the sound of chopping.

"Shouldn't you be at class, Nessa? Or is it sparring today?"

"The teachers are all having a meeting. And . . . and wait till you see this." With a flourish, Nessa opens the door into the refectory, and Tompkins is right there, standing guard. Three or four other instructors, all of them armed, lounge around to keep an eye on the food supply. And for the first time ever dogs are in here, sniffing at the corners and wagging in delight.

"Taaft is in town to . . . to make sure nothing gets poisoned before it reaches us. Everything is to be tasted first by the pigs."

"Well"—Megan manages a wink—"that explains why they let me out. I'm to try the broth for them. Not that I'm even hungry, if you can believe that."

They talk as Megan slurps down her food. Nessa tricks a grumpy but handsome Doberman into allowing his ears to be scratched. "What about Anto?" Megan asks. "No word yet?"

"No."

"That's it? All you have to say on the subject?"

Or any subject. Nessa really wants to explain what happened between herself and Conor, but isn't sure of where or how to start.

She damaged him, she really did, but it was only through surprise. The one time he'd caught hold of her, his strength had been terrifying. Nessa used to sleep so easily, but now she relives that moment again and again: dangling from his arm like a weed pulled from the garden, then flung onto the compost. And during it all, that terrible, terrible feeling that she was helpless. That she was nothing. Doomed. All her training and determination, all her clever workarounds and tricks, counted for nothing and would count for nothing the next time he got hold of her.

"You all right, Ness?"

She nods. She smiles. "It's good to see you, Megan."

"Damn right."

"You're my bodyguard."

"The very best."

The high five is spontaneous and perfectly coordinated, so that the smack of their palms makes the Doberman jump and start growling again. But they only laugh.

Lunch occurs at the usual time, but now the refectory is more crowded than it has ever been, for all of the teachers and veterans are present. Extra chairs are brought in and some of the Year 6s and the last two 7s, a boy and a girl, are moved out of their usual places so that the top table can be lengthened.

Even Frankenstein has been dragged out of whatever hole he lives in, his eyes as large as an owl's in his underfed face. He picks at his food as if not convinced the pigs have done their job properly. To his right, Mr. Hickey shovels his meal down with military efficiency.

"By Danú's tits," says Megan. "Somebody get that man a funnel before he starves!"

Diane Mallon has finally left the college, so of the veterans only Shamey and Melanie remain. They both sip from something they keep under the table, even though the rumor now is that she's pregnant and he's the father. Ridiculous of course. Everybody knows pregnancy would kill her with that heart of hers.

Farther along, Ms. Breen, the Turkey, raises her tiny chin so that her gaze sweeps the room and every student feels her suspicious glance pass over them. And not a word is spoken at the top table, not a single word until the last hideous lump of "bread pudding" has slithered its way into the Turkey's stomach.

Then she stands and waves off the kitchen workers, who are already dumping hot pots of nettle tea onto the Year 1 tables.

"Listen," she says, and they do. Even Megan's gob stays glued shut. "We know you have heard by now what took place at Bangor Survival College. And Mallow, of course, before that. And many of you are asking why these things are happening. Why the Sídhe, the enemies of all our people, can't just continue to murder us bit by bit. Why, after thousands of years, they are now so . . . so *impatient*. Well, let me tell you, there are minds all over the country working on this. But if you ask me, their impatience is a sign of our success. Of *your* success. We learn more about them with every survivor, and we're getting more and more of those." She grins horribly, working hard at believing her own words. As though losing nine in ten of a nation's people, on and on into the future, can only end well.

"But things must change around here. So, on to good news. Another of our wonderful veterans, Shamey here, will be moving home." He looks up, startled, woozy. This is news to him. But he makes no protest.

"Probably going to a hospital to get him off the drink," whispers Marya, and Nessa can only agree, but her heart is beating, thumping with excitement, because she knows what's coming next.

"And our own Anthony Lawlor—Anto, to most of you—will be returning to us. To share his . . . um, his fresher recollections and his survival strategies."

Nessa feels her face burning. This is what she has wanted, but as her guts turn to water, as her mind darts from joy to fear to confusion, she realizes how hard it will be to keep her concentration with him back in the college. His return will be a danger to her if she can't learn to control her emotions. And of course she can't. She knows that now. Her only skill is to hide them. The first test of this comes mere seconds later when Marya says, "He's a handsome lad, that Anto. Swimmer's body, as my mam would say. I wouldn't mind, I'll tell you that."

"You never even looked at him before, Marya!" This from Megan, who has no time for boys, or girls for that matter.

"Well"—Marya has thin wrists and tiny little hands that dramatize everything she says—"he had that whole crazy vegetarian thing. The not-fighting thing." In other words, she expected him to die. "Maybe we should all give it a go! Seems to have worked for him."

Conor won't be giving pacifism a go. He's been let out to hear the speech and sits in his usual place between Fiver and Keith. Liz Sweeney is sitting with them at the boys' table, and after what happened to her brother, none of the teachers even think to tell her to move. As though she is some kind of miracle, or maybe a disease. Some from the top table whisper and look at her. Some of them don't see her at all.

Conor turns around and locks his gaze with Nessa's. She used to think he hated her, and she couldn't have been more wrong about that. It's only now that she sees what his spite actually looks like, and it's an electrical current that moves from his eyes to pass through the rest of his body, stiffening him like a board, lowering his chin so that his forehead points toward her, the horns of a bull. It is not the look of a boy. Or a wild animal. Or a serpent. This is the spirit of the Call itself. Deadly and inevitable and imminent.

Nessa actually jumps as Megan speaks right at her ear. "That poor Conor looks like he's constipated."

Is that all she sees? Nessa wonders, as her friend goes right back to picking at her dessert without a care in the world. Is that all that anybody sees in him?

HIDING

It's hard to avoid somebody in your own year, and most especially Conor. His so-called knights are everywhere and all of them pay Nessa special attention. Tony with his old man's eyebrows and pocked skin; Bruggers, the scrawniest of them all, but with the reflexes of a reptile taking a fly; Keith and Liz Sweeney and even members of other years, like the now mournful and abandoned Sherry, desperate to be queen again.

Nessa's ability to hide her emotions has left her with no defenders other than Megan, who can never be in more than three places at once.

Thus, when sparring a few days later, Bruggers takes Nessa down and wallops her head into the floor. While she's still trying to clear the ringing sound from her skull, she hears him apologizing. "By Crom, I'm sorry, Nabil. I thought she was still over the matting."

At lunch, Liz Sweeney drops a cup of scalding tea, and only luck keeps it out of Nessa's lap. "Oops," says the big girl. And Nessa grabs her by the wrist.

"What are you doing, Liz Sweeney?"

"I said, 'Oops.' Doesn't anyone speak English in Donegal anymore?"

"This is serious, Liz Sweeney." Nessa is proud of how calm she sounds. "We don't . . . we don't actually *injure* each other."

"Well, you should have thought of that before you snitched on Conor to get him Cage time. And the lies you told about him! As if! As if he'd want to sleep with Crom-twisted *Clip-Clop!*" Nessa has never seen her so angry, and this in a week when her brother survived the Call! "You're like something out of *The Elephant Man.* So, yes, Nessa. Yes, it's serious. You've brought this on yourself and the gloves are off."

And then Liz Sweeney gasps and her eyes bug out, and Nessa realizes she is still gripping her classmate's wrist, hard enough to feel the bones rub together.

"I could break it," Nessa says. Broken bones are a serious matter in Year 5. A potential death sentence. "You're like a twig."

"Go on then, bitch. I won't scream."

"But I don't *have* to break it. Just say you'll keep the peace between the two of us."

"*Go on*, I said. Deliberate damage means expulsion. Conor will be delighted."

"You would risk this just to get back at me?"

"If you're not going to do it, I need to fetch more tea."

And Nessa, with a fake shrug, releases her, but she feels chilled.

Two more days pass without further attacks from the Round Table. The mourning bells ring several times, but not for Year 5. Nor are there any new survivors for the college to celebrate. At least the snow has gone again, melting away in the face of a driving frigid rain.

Shamey stays off the drink long enough to make his good-byes, mainly to Melanie, his fellow veteran, and to Anne-Marie, the last of the Year 7s, who still awaits the Call. He is a sad little boy, walking away toward Boyle in donated clothing, awkward in his shoes. Nobody has come to replace him. Not yet.

The next morning is Halloween. To celebrate, the Sídhe have left a gift in the boys' dorm. It is Keith, one of the Round Table. They have sculpted his face into a delicate flower of blood and skin.

Outrage and doubt consume the remaining knights. "We are the elite," Conor has told them. "Our odds are better than anybody else's."

But Keith and Cahal and Chuckwu have all been caught, and caught early enough for the Sídhe to have had their fun. And Rodney's gone too, when he was too slow to get out of Cahal's way. Thus far, Year 5's only survivor has been that grass-eating rabbit of a boy, Anto.

When they meet that morning before breakfast, Conor knows he's in danger of losing them.

"It's just the odds," he keeps saying. "At least three of us are going to make it. I can guarantee it." But they need more than this, and so, strangely enough, does he. He feels a grin twisting his face.

"At least we'll get Clip-Clop," he tells them. "They've cleared out the Sídhe girl in the forest and fenced off the mound. And that means the weekly hunts are back on. So"—his great height is imposing, his gestures those of a wise old man—"we need to put her in her place."

"Her place is in the ground," says Bruggers, still basking in his triumph from sparring with Nessa in the gym.

And Conor nods, meeting their eyes one by one to show he's serious, challenging them to join him at this new level.

"We should do Megan too!" says Bruggers, yet Conor, the exasperated but proud parent, shakes his head.

"The little red whore deserves it for sure. But we only get to have one . . . one *accident*. You understand me? Any more than that would attract all kinds of suspicion. So . . . so here's the plan."

Nessa avoids Conor's friends where she can: feigning illness if she finds one of the knights opposite her at sparring, keeping herself in the sight of instructors as much as possible. But in a small school it can only work for so long.

She makes it a full week into November before she figures out that *they* are avoiding *her*. Why? What are they planning? It has to be something more than a beating. Something far worse.

A realization begins to dawn on her that she needs to transfer away from Boyle. She saw the way Conor was looking at her the other day and there was nothing in his face to suggest even the possibility of rational restraint.

Ms. Breen will arrange a move for her if she asks for it, but the one time Nessa finds herself outside the office, she raises her fist, yet fails to knock. That's right. The girl who above all else yearns for survival, leaves herself surrounded by enemies in the hope that one more time, just once, she will get to see Anto.

She imagines talking to him, really talking to him, and the feeling is the same one she had when she climbed out the bathroom window for the first time, vertiginous, giddy, joyful.

Nessa will apologize for doubting him, the way everybody doubts her. Both are stronger by far than they appear, and they belong together. Or will do, when she proves that she too is worthy.

And that very evening—the day she fails to ask for a transfer—Anto returns. Marya, who never can resist a bit of scandal (she refers to it as "ska"), witnesses his arrival and she flies up to the dorm to tell everybody.

It's already dark outside and, apart from Aoife, the remaining Year 5 girls hug one of the two radiators that stick up from the floor, equidistant from all of the beds.

"What's happening, Marya?" asks Nicole, who fancies herself quite the smart aleck. Her chunky head is always cocked at an angle, her generous lips twitching upward. "You win the lottery?"

Marya beams in reply, her arms twitching with excitement. "Oh, I'm a bit closer to it than I was, girls! I surely am! I saw Anto!" She tells them of the minibus that pulled up behind the school.

"And what were you doing back there?" Nicole wants to know, but other voices tell her to "shut it or prepare to swallow teeth." There's not a girl in the room that doesn't have the training to make good on such a threat, although Nicole is as wiry and wily as anyone there.

"It screeches to a stop," Marya says, her brown eyes wide, her hands palm out, as though she herself had halted the vehicle, "and this guy hops out. But listen! He was wearing a cloak, like something out of *Dracula*. And the moment, the very moment his feet touch the gravel, he's sprinting, and I mean *sprinting* for the door at the back of the instructors' building. I've never seen anything like it. He runs funny too, like he has a limp. And then, when he gets there, it's locked or something and he's banging and banging at it, all panicky."

"Sounds like Anto all right," says Liz Sweeney, rolling her eyes.

And Marya wags a finger at her. "You don't talk about a survivor like that!" Heads nod all around and even Liz Sweeney ducks in embarrassment. "Anyway," Marya continues, "I didn't know it was him yet, did I? It was dark out there. And Ji—I mean, I was alone. I was by myself out there and had to squint. And then he turns around and I see it's him. And I wave and call out to him. 'Hey, Anto!' And I start walking toward him. And—" She gulps, and now Nessa, who has been hanging on every word, sees that the girl is actually a bit upset.

"Go on!" says Megan. "By the Cauldron, squeeze it out of you!"

Marya takes a deep breath. "I was slow getting to him. You know the gravel out there. Sore on our bare feet."

"That's why they put it there—" Nicole starts to explain, but the others shut her up.

"And he sees me and . . . and he's terrified. He's . . . he's banging at the door and screaming to be let in. Hammering it with his fist until somebody opens up and he falls inside. And me just stopped there with the stones digging into me."

"He thought you were a Sídhe," Megan says.

"Crom take you, you useless red-haired slut!"

But Megan holds up the palms of her hands in a sign of peace. "No, Marya, I didn't mean it that way."

"That's a first!" Nicole says.

"I *meant*," Megan continues, "that it's just the post-traumatic stress, right?"

And Marya relaxes at once. "Oh, right. What was I thinking? Oh, right. In the excitement I forgot." Relief fills her voice and everybody nods wisely, as if they know the first thing about it. "Anyway," she says, "Anto's back."

AOIFE MOURNS

It's not that people don't talk to Aoife these days; it's that she's invisible to them. She brings the Plague of Doom with her everywhere and nobody wants to catch it.

Oh, she's not stupid, in spite of her legendary laziness, her overindulgence in just about any vice she can gain access to. She is aware of her own peril, sliding through one empty experience after another: through listless sparring in the gym; through runs in the hills; through spear-making classes. She lifts no weights in circuit training, and when the time comes for push-ups she is face-down on the mat, and only Taaft out of all the instructors has the heart, or the lack of it, to scream her into a shadow of obedience.

"The problem," somebody says—Nicole, in fact—"the problem is the lack of funerals. I liked Squeaky Emma." She scratches at the brown bristles on her scalp. "And I miss her too. We need a proper chance to mourn and we never, ever get it, do we?"

Liz Sweeney has only sneers in reply to that. "And what else would we have time to do, if there were two or three funerals a week? And anyway, what the Sídhe sent back of Squeaky Emma wouldn't fit into any coffin I've ever seen."

At this point Aoife pulls the pillow over her head. She has to. She preferred it in the Cage. A cell as cold as death all to herself, whose black walls she painted with her imagination—always a talent of hers. She is a girl who can dream about anything she wants. But it's hard work and it crumbles at the slightest mention of what happened out in the forest.

She does not know how many days have passed since then. Enough for everyone to stop asking her opinions, for Marya to stop drawing her into the latest "ska" or for Nicole to openly rifle through Aoife's locker right in front of her. Has Nicole always done this? Does she steal from her dorm mates? It's the first interest that Aoife has felt in the world for some time. However, it's still not enough.

Her awakening does not happen until two days after Anto's return, when Sherry comes into the dorm to find Liz Sweeney alone there. Well, except for Aoife of course, who no longer counts.

She has a pillow pulled over her head, and it muffles their conversation.

"You're not allowed in this dorm. You're a Four, in case you forgot."

"I'm not staying." The younger girl's voice is resentful and a little bit shaky. "I need to talk to you."

"So talk."

Sherry must have made a gesture of some kind, because Liz Sweeney snorts and says, "Oh, she's not here, you understand?

That one will sleep right through the Call when it happens. She's one of the dead now."

"I'd prefer—"

"Crom eat your preferences, little girl. You need to get over it. The king doesn't want you anymore."

"But . . . but he *has* to. I need you to make him."

"Make him? Make him talk to you? Why on earth—*Oh.*"

Oh, indeed! No pregnant girl has ever survived the Call. A few deliberately got themselves with child way back in the early days in the hopes it would mean they were no longer "adolescents," but adults. That was the theory anyway, but it didn't save a single one. In fact, when the State first set up the college system, strong arguments were made to separate out the sexes altogether. Aoife can't remember why that never happened. It doesn't matter to her. Gay students are ignored. They do whatever they want until they survive the Call. At which point all of society leans and leans on them to have children, regardless of their own wishes . . .

"I'll get it fixed," says Sherry. "They'll let me fix it. But he deserves to know. And I won't turn him in."

"You'd better not! Or I'll break that slutty little face of yours!"

"Oh!" and Sherry's voice hardens. "Oh! Of all the people, you call me a slut, Liz Sweeney?"

"What's that supposed to mean?"

"You want him for yourself, is what. As if he'd touch you, Liz Sweeney, with your man features and your man's body. Maybe Bruggers the bugger would be more your type!"

The springs of a bed sound and Liz Sweeney must be leaping to her feet right now to give the younger girl a beating, although some of the Year 4s can give back as good as they get.

And then Liz Sweeney comes to a stop. "You . . . you brought a *knife*? Are you crazy?"

"I'll do whatever I have to," says Sherry. "Isn't that what Conor taught us? Rulers have to act, and here I am, acting. Now listen, he doesn't want you and he doesn't want me either, for the moment. He wants her. Clip-Clop."

"He . . . he what?"

"You believe me. I can see you do. I'll cut her throat. I swear by the Cauldron I will."

"No." Perhaps Liz Sweeney is shaking her head. "He doesn't want Nessa, and you'll see the proof of it tomorrow. The hunts are starting up again."

"You have a plan? A plan to get her?"

"It's Conor's plan. In the forest she . . ." Perhaps Liz Sweeney thinks better of what she was going to say with Aoife in the room. Perhaps she makes some kind of a gesture. "All I'll say is that she's finished here."

Deep inside Aoife, her spirit stirs. It's not that she dislikes Nessa, in spite of the fact that Emma always fancied her. "Shame you're not her type, Emma," Aoife told her once, pretending not to be hurt. And she has to admit to the charms of the girl from Donegal: those dreamer's eyes, that regal bearing. The air of tragedy that hangs over her, like the cancer-suffering heroines of the books Aoife liked so much in her first years here. Aoife has had more than a few fantasies about Nessa herself, but they always shatter against that haughty exterior.

But still. But still. Are they really planning to *murder* her?

"I . . . I can help," says the younger girl.

"What? You can show off for him, can you, little Sherry? *Pregnant* Sherry the idiot?" and Liz Sweeney, from the sound of her voice, is grinning like a mad thing. "You're a Year Four and you won't be hunting tomorrow, will you? You'll all be in your beds clutching teddies and scared of the dogs in the corridors."

"What if I get to her first?"

"Don't be an idiot!" And her voice turns to a whisper. Too low for Aoife to follow. Not that she's trying.

Sherry leaves and the doors swing shut behind her.

For a moment Aoife is thinking she should warn Nessa that something awful is being planned for her. But then the image of Emma's corpse pushes to the front of her mind and it's all she can do to keep her gorge down.

The Testimonies are crammed with nightmare images. And over the years students have hidden forbidden photographs of some of the Sídhe's worst victims in between the volumes of an encyclopedia in the library. But never has Aoife seen anything worse than what they did to her Emma! Nessa will be caught early enough to suffer such a fate. There can't be any doubt in the matter. Terrible hands will turn her skull inside out while she yet lives.

Conor's gang would be doing her a favor. They'll avenge whatever slight they think they've suffered and she will be free.

Besides, Aoife can't interfere. She has too much of a fight on her own hands as it is: She needs to reinforce the walls of her imagination against the horrors that wait beyond. If she works at it, Aoife will be able to imagine the field trip to an Iron Age site where Emma, out of the blue, first kissed her. Nobody ever heard Emma coming! Quiet as the mouse that gave her that stupid nickname. And the kiss! With Ms. Buckley just behind a lump of scattered stones! She feels those little hands on hers, and remembers how her body bent of its own accord so that their lips could meet . . .

And then the pillow is jerked away from her face and sunlight gouges at her eyes.

"If you say a word," says Liz Sweeney, "even a word about this, to anybody, you'll wish that Crom himself had come for you!"

"Leave me alone," Aoife replies, outraged to have Liz Sweeney's big feet trampling over her most precious memories.

Perhaps it is the red, red eyes. Or the lost weight. Or the quivering lips. But Liz Sweeney simply sneers and drops the pillow before leaving the dorm.

Hours later, Aoife jumps at the clang of a bell. It's just the sound of dinner, however, and she realizes she's been asleep. She used to be a great eater, and now habit carries her downstairs and across two corridors to get to the refectory. So slow is her pace that she's among the last to arrive. The rest of Year 5 are in their seats. Many of them are laughing, faces flushed, hair glistening after the run they must have returned from. It's raining outside and the windows are fogged and the whole huge room reverberates with clinks and voices and shouts.

Aoife can't help looking at the empty places around the tables. There aren't so many yet: The Sídhe have killed less than ten out of sixty Year 5s. If the pattern holds, it'll average one death a week until summer.

She walks in to take her seat beside Marya and Megan. And here she sees an empty chair she wasn't expecting. For a moment she wonders if she missed the sound of the mourning bells, but then she remembers that Nessa always finishes a run ten or twenty minutes behind her classmates, depending on the length of the course.

Megan shrugs. "You're looking more awake."

"I am?" Across the way, at one of the boys' tables, Liz Sweeney is braying like an ass and Aoife surprises herself. "I'm hungry!" she says. Her waking is as slow as spring, but deep inside, a new purpose is germinating and looking for the light.

But then she pushes the hunger away and stands.

"Where're you off to?" asks Megan.

"I . . . there's somebody I need to see. Right away! But I'll need to talk to you too, Megan. Later."

She leaves the red-haired girl gaping after her.

THE VISIT

Rain makes the going hard for most of the students, but Nessa, with superb coordination, with excellent reflexes, can always move faster with a bit of mud on the ground. She likes to slide. She takes advantage of every feature of the landscape: skidding on the slopes while swinging around on trees, and springing from rocky areas on her crutches. If they don't snap of course. It's exhausting though, and as always she soon falls behind.

But this one time, instead of soldiering on, she simply stops and waits. By now Nabil and Horner have loped off with the main pack. When they get to the end, instructors and students alike will pile into the showers before racing down for dinner. Nessa won't even be a blip on their radar—she's always last anyway.

She walks quite sedately for a while, shivering a little, listening to a thousand and one rustlings from the undergrowth around her as she goes over her plan.

Now that Shamey is gone, his room in the staff accommodation block is freed up for Anto, and she will tell any lie to get in there to see him. In this way she can say her good-byes before winning a transfer from Ms. Breen.

As she walks, she's already battling the sadness she'll feel in parting from Megan. Anto, at least, is a survivor now, but the odds are that she'll never see her only friend again.

Stop! she orders herself, when tears threaten. *Just stop.*

It's only five o'clock by the time she creeps out of the trees and onto the painful gravel near the staff entrance. This late in the year, and with the rain, lights are on everywhere in the school and they guide her up to the door, illuminating the signs that threaten Cage time for anybody going in unescorted. In spite of everything, Nessa, whose avoidance of the run is already begging for punishment, hesitates.

But it's not the Cage that holds her back.

She knows Anto won't be the same after his ordeal. She knows it. She pauses on the step, shivering at the rain running under the collar of her tracksuit. And what if he doesn't want to see her? He ran from Marya, didn't he? Like she had the plague.

The door opens easily and she pushes through to that familiar corridor lined with instructors' rooms, each with a name on the door. And she follows it down, toward the darker end, where the communal laundry basket overflows with filthy tracksuits still damp from the run. And there, sure enough, is a handwritten sign: ANTHONY LAWLOR.

And now the nerves come! The oh-so-sweaty palms; the continual swallowing. She makes a fist and holds it over the door.

Thinks better of it, and leans her ear against the wood instead. She hears nothing, nothing at all.

Who or what lies inside? And yes, the "what" is important, because some of those who return are as damaged in body as they are in mind. Like Eithne Fitzgerald with her knotted legs. Like Ryan McMurty, who bore the impressions of a Sídhe's fingers in his forehead. For the rest of his short life, he suffered headaches as well as bizarre visions he claimed were prophetic. All were faithfully recorded, but nobody has yet made sense of them.

I should have brought a poem. She might have slipped it under the door for him. A reminder that somebody cares. No matter what he has become. And she realizes that she has to tell him this in person. Before the Call spirits her off to the Grey Land.

And then the main door is opening—the one she came in, at the end of the corridor. Nessa throws herself under the stinking tracksuits, not even taking the time to leave a peephole for herself and praying that the movement remains undetected.

Footsteps come all the way down to her position and she expects at any second to have her cover pulled away. Instead she hears the faintest of tapping against wood and a stage whisper.

"Anto? Anto, are you there?"

"Go away." Nessa jerks in spite of herself at the muffled sound of his voice. The parched emptiness of it.

"It's Aoife. Can I come in?"

Aoife? Of all the people, she is the last Nessa would expect to find here. Not that she and Anto are enemies—quite the opposite actually. Aoife rarely keeps any of her grandmother's cakes for the boys' tables, but Anto's gentleness has won him a nibble or two over the years.

"Anto? It's about Nessa." Nessa stiffens in her burrow. Never has she strained so hard to hear, but all the dirty clothing, the distance, the wood of the door frustrate her. For all she knows, there's no response at all.

"Listen," says Aoife, "there's a hunt tomorrow afternoon and Conor's gang . . . Conor's gang are going to . . . I *think* they're planning to kill her."

What? Nessa thinks. *They're planning what?* Yet she feels no surprise and realizes she'd been thinking the same thing herself, ever since Liz Sweeney spilled the tea on her.

Anto's response is only heartbeats in coming, but Nessa crouches there, like the cat in the box, waiting, waiting, to find out if she's alive or dead.

And then all the possibilities collapse into one outcome, and it's a sentence of death.

"I don't care! Go away, Aoife. I want all of you to go away."

"Then why did you even come back here? You didn't have to work as a veteran!"

But Anto, it appears, has nothing more to say.

Aoife departs and Nessa must have left shortly after her, because she finds herself wandering out in the rain, not sure where she is going or why. She was the one who was supposed to reject him. For her own safety. She was the one who'd fought forever against a poisonous fantasy, who'd regretted romantic gestures, who'd pitied him and feared for him.

Every time she met him, when he focused those liquid eyes on her, she would say, "Oh, no, thanks! I couldn't possibly!" And for what? For what?

In her mind's eye the farm in Donegal dissolves, becomes a dirty flat in some town where Nessa lives alone.

Eventually it is the cold that drives her indoors, and for the second time that day she enters through a forbidden door and plonks herself down next to one of the ancient radiators, shivering and too empty even for tears.

The dogs find her shortly afterward.

There's always a pack of them wandering together, a bizarre mix of breeds and mongrels of varying levels of aggression and friendliness, so that when a Jack Russell growls at her, it is up to the big Doberman to shove it off. Then he settles his warm stinking body up next to her and snuggles down. A few of the others follow until she has a pile of them crushing in around her, panting, yawning, farting. And there she falls asleep.

———

The following morning, she's in Ms. Breen's office.

"Your behavior, Nessa . . . your behavior is getting stranger all the time. You realize that, don't you?"

Nessa is standing before her in the cramped office with its menthol stink. She responds no more than a corpse would.

"The Lord knows I've tried to keep you out of the Cage, but you've made it impossible for me. After we found you with the dogs last night! In the Year Seven corridor of all places!"

Ms. Breen looks expectantly at her, waiting for the excuse, the apology that never comes. And finally she sighs. "Very well then. You can report to Nabil tomorrow after breakfast."

And finally a feeling finds its way through the girl's hope-lessness: It is puzzlement.

"*Tomorrow*, miss?"

"Ah, you think we're going to let you out of this afternoon's hunt? When your year hasn't had one for three weeks now because of . . . because of that Sídhe you found in the rock? No, no. I'm sentencing you to two nights, but starting tomorrow."

This is the perfect opportunity for Nessa to ask for her transfer, to explain the threats to her life, or at the very least the integrity of her limbs. And yet moments later she finds herself back in the corridor, with grey daylight pouring through the upper windows and leaching her will.

She needs to turn back. It's not too late. Instead, as happened with the dogs the night before, a pack of girls finds her, Megan at their head. Again she is surrounded by warmth and, yes, by love.

"Aoife told me everything," said Megan. She hugs a shattered Nessa to her muscled shoulders. "I'm not letting those vomit-lickers have you. Understand?"

"Mmmm."

And Megan slaps her hard enough that Aoife, Marya, and Nicole all jump back.

"That's right, Nessa! It's wakey-wakey time! Come on. Frankenstein's class is up next, followed by a riveting hour with the Turkey. After that we're going to plan a humiliation for King Conor and his merry men. You hear me? One more screwup and even Liz Sweeney will have to drop him like the stickiest sock in the basket."

And now Nessa feels a smile come to her face, and for once she makes no effort to hide it. Instead she hugs each of the girls. She knows Megan would do anything for her, and Aoife is kind enough to help even an enemy. But the presence of Marya and Nicole comes as a great surprise.

And she lets them lead her off to class.

———

To avoid suspicion, they don't sit together.

Aoife, looking thinner than Nessa has ever seen her, lies facedown on her desk and goes to sleep right at the front. If Frankenstein notices, he says nothing. His hollow owl eyes blink moistly and his failing voice drones on and on. He always sweats these days, as though melting under the intermittent heat of the radiators.

"Of course, the Sídhe have other art forms. Music and dance are obvious ones. They carve marvelous tools of bone . . ." He chews his own flaking lips, and if rumors are to be believed, he'd like nothing better than to wet them with cheap vodka. Even three rows back, students shy from the foulness of his breath. "But they save their greatest inspiration for the works they do in human flesh. It is the only form of magic for whose existence we have actual scientific proof."

"How is it proved?" asks Bruggers, shocking Frankenstein with a pertinent question.

After a few more pitiful attempts to moisten his lips, the teacher mumbles something about the cellular structures of the bodies, both living and dead, that have returned from the Grey Land, but Nessa is no longer listening. All of a sudden she finds herself staring at Frankenstein's face. There is something about it that she can't quite put her finger on.

He has been a teacher here since long before her arrival, and when she first knew him his lectures on the strange biology of the Grey Land were among the most interesting for her. But then that thing with his wife happened. A bad death by the standards of this world, and he mustn't have had any friends to pull him out of it again, because he went so far downhill that Ms. Breen was overheard saying he was on his last warning.

Nessa has always thought it a sad story, but a romantic one too, and she paid it no more interest than that until now.

She puts up her hand. "Uh . . . Frank?"

He stops his mumbled explanation for a moment and she continues. "Are you, uh . . . are you ill, sir?"

"Ill, child?"

"Your face, sir. It's . . . yellow." Not completely, but little streaks have appeared there under the sweat that trickles down his face.

"Oh, lord, not again," and his voice is the saddest sound Nessa has ever heard. "It's . . . Not that it's anybody's business here. It's just jaundice. I've been . . . I've had to cover it with . . ."

"Makeup, sir?" This from Bruggers, who can't be bothered to hold in a snicker. And Frank O'Leary pushes back from his desk and all but runs from the class.

AN APOLOGY

Mourning bells ring twice more at lunchtime. Anne-Marie, the last of the Year 7s, has met her fate, along with a boy from Year 6. So it is a somber crew that sits down to eat.

"Imagine," says Marya, "Year Seven is gone now!"

Aoife, who has started eating again, doesn't even glance up. But Nessa can see the two tiny dorms in her mind's eye, the beds empty and quiet until September.

"They didn't even make their one in ten," Marya continues. She comes from one of those homes where nobody saw anything wrong with speaking from a full mouth, so that food could be consumed and generously shared all at the same time.

"We'll make up for it!" says Nicole, but nobody likes to say such things, or even to hear them, and she shuts up when their eyes slip away from her.

"I would hate to be the last," says Marya now, waving little fists about. "Can you imagine?" And they can. Among all the terrible outcomes, it's one that crops up again and again. Watching your friends live or die, while all the time the odds of finding yourself in the Grey Land keep climbing. Far better to be taken soon. But not now. *Never* right now!

"Look, how're we going to do this?" asks Megan at last. "I was thinking, we wait for the lists of hunters and hunted to go up. The chances of all of us being in one of those groups have got to be tinier than Conor's wee piggy eyes. Am I right?" They all nod. "And then, if Nessa is a hunted, she arranges to meet up with one of *our* hunters so she can be 'caught' and get out of the forest right away. Or vice versa."

It's such an obvious plan that there are specific rules and penalties against it. But Megan thinks that even if they get in trouble, they'll have saved their friend's life for another fortnight. And that might be enough, for who knows what will happen in two weeks? Conor could be Called. Or Nessa.

"I'm always nervous of the Cage," says Nicole, but Megan rolls her eyes.

"It's the best and only time off I ever get in this place. Away from your snoring, Nicole."

"I do not snore!"

"It must be a drill you keep under your pillow then!"

And Marya claps her hands and Nicole groans, because there's nothing she can do now: Megan's poor witticism will reach every dorm by nightfall.

Nessa grins too, until she realizes she hasn't thought of Anto all morning. But already he's creeping back into her head. *"What do I care?" he said.*

But here is Megan again, dragging her back to reality with a squeeze of her arm. "I need you focused," she says. "Danú's tits, but you're a dozy slut." This is Megan's version of gentle.

"I thought that's how you liked your sluts?" says Nicole, finally scoring a point. She's off her game today. Maybe afraid of what will happen tonight if she takes part in balking Conor of his prey.

And so she should be! thinks Nessa.

Then everybody jumps, because Liz Sweeney is right there at the table with them.

"Well, well," she says, looking from one face to another, before finally settling on Aoife. "So you weren't able to keep your mouth shut, I see." She grins as if she doesn't mind at all—which means Conor doesn't. He's no fool, whatever else Nessa may think of him, and that means he has already guessed their oh-so-obvious plan, and that he has taken it into account.

"Mind if I join you?" she says.

"Yes," Megan replies, but Liz Sweeney simply grins and slides into Squeaky Emma's empty chair.

Ms. Breen is not yet at the top table. She's stuck in her office with the human wreckage that calls itself Frank O'Leary squashed into the hard chair in front of her. His face is thinner than ever now, his legs too long for the space between him and her desk, his eyes glistening hollows.

"Oh, Frank," she says, "you're not leaving me with much choice, are you?"

"You promised . . . ," he says. It's the voice of an Egyptian mummy—far away and all the words crumbling to dust the instant they reach her ears. His breath too stinks of the tomb. It is all she can do not to gag. "You said . . . after she . . . when I lost my wife. You said I'd retire with dignity at the end of the year . . . Over Christmas, you said."

She sighs, rubbing her eyes and thinking they can't look much better than his. She sleeps badly, always waiting for the sound of mourning bells, despite the fact that they never ring without her say-so, and never at night. But there's only so much a mind can take before it snaps: year after year of watching the murder of her beloved children here in the school. Of pretending wisdom and calm when all she wants is to be locked up somewhere quiet where the decisions are taken away from her.

But unlike Frank O'Leary, every morning she finds anew the strength she needs. She has been at this horrible game so long now that in the worst of times habit alone is just enough to keep her back straight.

"Listen, Frank," she says, "you walked out of a class. I'm pretty sure you've had a nervous breakdown. Aren't you? That means you're delicate now. Too delicate for this kind of work." She knows her words are cruel, that her job has made a monster of her, yet she does not stop. "The students need the best if they are to live."

"Nobody knows more about the Grey Land than I do."

"I know that. Your writings are brilliant. Why don't you concentrate there?"

He manages to raise his chin. "Alanna," he says, using her first name, as he has not done in over a year, "listen, I . . ." And then he shocks her by slipping out of the chair and going onto his knees in front of her, his long fingers damp on the edge of her desk. "There's only . . . a month to go. Six weeks anyway. Let me . . . let me leave with dignity. In my own time. I couldn't take it. I just . . ." He hangs there, and Alanna Breen thinks to herself that he is the most pathetic thing she has ever seen.

But she remembers his laughter from his better times, a great, braying roar that filled the staffroom from end to end. And it might not be the worst thing to wait for Christmas. The students will spend two weeks with their families, allowing time for the induction of a new member of staff. Less disruptive all round.

She sighs. "Get up, Frank. It's all right. Until Christmas will be all right, but not—I repeat—not if you can't handle the children, do you hear me? Walk out again like that and I'll have to get somebody else. Now, if you'll excuse me, I need to address the students." She flies out the door before he can babble his gratitude. And straight away, in the hallway, she runs into Horner, yet another broken man. He stops to allow her past and, as always in his presence, it is a struggle not to break into a run to get away.

Only Tompkins can get through to that man, and only Tompkins, it seems, can tolerate his fishlike stare and his eternal silences. Not for the first time, she wonders what they must have gone through together, that the steadfast, overwhelmingly . . . *normal* Tompkins can subject himself to all of that.

And then she's through the door and into the steamy warmth. The students are already on their tea, so she wastes no time in calling for silence.

"All right!" she says, and pauses as her eye comes to rest on the empty Year 7 table. She remembers a year when one poor girl had to linger there alone all the way to March.

"Listen now," she says. "I speak so that the Nation will survive." These words always sober even the rowdiest of Year 4s. "We, the staff of the college, would like to apologize to you, our students." She sees their puzzled looks. "A few weeks ago, during a hunt, some of our Year Fives found . . . well, you all know by now what they found, don't you? And our attempts to cover it up proved to be not only pointless, but dangerous. Yes. Your curiosity is natural. Especially when it pertains to your survival. When we hid the girl in the rock from you, it resulted in three Year Fives being Called at once." And she makes no mention of Anto, the boy who returned alive and who refuses to come out of his room to sit at the top table with the remaining veteran, Melanie.

The doctors have sent a report down from Dublin about his "condition," and she is itching to read it. For the moment, however, Ms. Breen's business is here.

"I'm sorry we were secretive. So let me give you my word on this: The girl has been removed from the forest along with all traces of the boulder she died in. We think the . . . the power of the place has gone with her. But we can't be sure, so we have fenced off the entire mound. Let me emphasize, the fence is not there to stop you seeing anything, because I'm giving you my word now that there is nothing more to see. And I further promise that should the scientists make new discoveries about the girl in the rock, we will be open about it from now on."

This is a lie.

She doesn't tell the children that some of the scientists were against fencing off the mound in the first place. The strange feeling reported by the students once the rock had been cut open fascinates the investigators. "We could learn so much more," one grey-beard suggested, "if we could map that feeling of theirs. If we could deliberately provoke the Call somehow."

She growled the scientists into silence, protecting her young from the monsters from Dublin. She worries that certain parts of the government might yet try to force her hand.

But for the moment she is confident that the problem has been resolved.

THE FINAL HUNT

And it's back to the forest again with a head start that's barely enough time to allow Nessa to make crutches for herself. This is not to be a nighttime hunt. The shade of the trees in mid-November is thought to be dark enough to give the feeling of being in the Grey Land, or so the staff like to think.

As soon as she's ready, Nessa heads straight for the Fairy Fort.

She had the idea to go there when she heard Ms. Breen's speech. "Listen," she said to her allies, once they'd read the lists of hunters and hunted on the Year 5 board, "everyone will be afraid of the mound now. Of being Called."

"They're right!" Nicole said.

"Possibly," Nessa said. "Look, I know it's terrifying, but there are only two possibilities: The power is still there, or it isn't, right? And if it is, if we're going to be Called, what better time than at the start of a hunt, when we're fit and well fed and ready? You couldn't plan it any better than that."

Nicole didn't look like she agreed, but Megan interrupted her. "Oh, for Crom's sake! The girl in the rock is gone now, and we won't even be able to reach the bloody mound. It's just a place to meet that they won't be too keen on checking. Nessa—we'll see you at the south end of it and 'catch' you there. Then it's an early shower for all of us."

"A cold one for me," Nessa replied. She grinned, and not just at her best friend, but at Aoife and Marya and Nicole. In spite of her coldness to so many people over the years, here they are, four girls—young women really—ready to risk the Cage, to risk Conor, just to keep another person safe.

The only problem is that Conor has certainly guessed what they're up to by now. He'll be looking for Nessa, checking for a weak footprint that points slightly inward, for the indentations of improvised crutches. And he'll know to follow her comrades too if they're not careful.

Nessa has a plan to keep the Round Table from tracking her, but it's not going to be fun. The sky is spitting hailstones and an east wind slips between the trees to suck all the warmth from her bones. "By Crom," she mutters. "By Crom . . ."

She throws her crutches over a pile of boulders before crossing them on hands and knees, keeping away from moss and lichen to hide her passage. On the far side lies a freezing-cold stream.

Lots of Testimonies recall survivors who walked through water to hide their scent. But with no "dogs" to fear, and the summer long gone, it's not something any sane girl would want to do now.

"Oh, by Crom!" she says again as the water starts to work on her, as the ache spreads up to her ankles and her teeth chatter enough to catch her tongue.

And then she hears the horn that releases the hunters to the chase. The Round Table will have seen where she entered the trees and will follow her there. She has five minutes, maybe ten, before they get here and she'd better be long gone. Her allies, on the other hand, will run straight for the mound . . .

"Hello, there."

Nessa jumps in shock. The hunted should all be well ahead of her by now and the hunters well behind. But then Liz Sweeney steps out onto the rocks she has just crossed.

"W-what are *you* doing here?"

Liz Sweeney's lips twitch into a smile colder than the stream that's numbing Nessa's legs.

"I'm a hunted, just like you. I'm entitled to be here." The big girl is an excellent athlete and crosses to the far bank of the stream with a single jump. Then she turns to face Nessa. "We're allowed to work together, you know? And I've brought something for you."

But all Liz Sweeney has brought is a trick. She grabs away one of Nessa's crutches and snaps it in half. It's all very sudden, and she's grinning wide enough to swallow Ireland. "I bet you weren't expecting—"

Nessa hits her across the face with the other crutch, water spraying from the tip. Then it becomes a spear, taking Liz Sweeney hard in the solar plexus while she's still clutching at her mouth. And down she goes, winded and gasping.

Nessa flees, as fast as she can with only one crutch, and it isn't more than a brisk walk, with a trail left behind her that her granny could follow. Her only hope now is that Liz Sweeney won't get up for a while and that Megan will spirit her away before the Round Table in all their Monty Python glory run her to ground.

Ten agonizing minutes pass, as she pushes her useless legs harder than ever. She is panting and sweating enough in the cold that her tracksuit is glued to her. The Round Table will have found Liz Sweeney by now. They could just "capture" her and go back to the college for a warm meal and a shower. Somehow Nessa doubts they'll be doing that today.

She thinks she has somehow gotten lost when she comes across a two-man-high chain-link fence. There is a strange feeling in the air, as though somebody is standing right beside her. She felt the same way once before, and she knows now that this is the fence Ms. Breen promised for the mound. For some reason, in her mind's eye, she had pictured a wall of pine planks with a warning sign on it. Nothing this anonymous, this easy to climb over.

She begins to follow it around, looking for a place to hide until Megan and the rest can get here. The wire gives her something to hang on to over the uneven ground, but that itching sensation, that *presence*, only seems to strengthen the more she walks and she has a horrible, horrible feeling that she shouldn't be here, that she is about to be Called. It's so strong that an involuntary whimper escapes her. She clamps down on that right away.

Nessa is fitter and stronger than she's ever been in her life. Probably more than she ever will be again. Isn't that what she said to Nicole? That this would be a good thing? *Let it come!* She utters the mental challenge several times more. When nothing happens she peels her clawed fingers away from the fence and continues on her way.

She is straining for the sounds of pursuit, for the voices of her friends. But halfway around she finds a break in the barrier. One of the metal poles that holds the iron links in place has been knocked over. As if a boulder, or an elephant, has smashed into it from the *inside*, popping the links to leave them scattered around like petals in the summer.

Never has a generation of Irish children been so aware of its own folklore, especially as it pertains to the enemy.

In olden days farmers lived in terror of blocking "Fairy Roads"—those secret ways by which the Sídhe were said to travel the country at night. No work of man could long survive in such a place! So anyone building a house would ensure the Sídhe had no prior claim to the land by marking the outlines of the site with loose stones. By the following morning, if the stones had been moved the builder would be wise to go elsewhere.

If that isn't a Fairy Road, Nessa thinks, looking at the torn metal, then nothing is. Indeed, the horrible feeling that someone is right here with her grows all the stronger as she passes the broken part of the fence. So powerful is it that twice she spins to look behind her. But nobody is there, and the feeling eases as she moves away.

Finally she reaches the southern end of the mound. She crouches behind a weary rhododendron. She can see right down the overgrown path, where nature walkers and joggers took their leisure in happier times.

There is no sign of her friends yet, but Nessa's patience is infinite. She knows they can't be more than ten minutes late, that they're likely just working to make sure nobody is on their tail.

"They're not coming." Nessa jumps. It's Conor who speaks, his voice and demeanor sorrowful, dignified. He can't see her—he's looking in the wrong direction! But he'll be ready to move should she so much as twitch a muscle. Three boys emerge from the trees to stand with him on the path: Fiver and Bruggers from left and right, with Tony to bring up the rear, although he should have been another "hunted" like her. He looks particularly queasy, and must sense, as she can, the power of the mound behind her. But Conor displays no doubt.

He swivels his head as he did during the last hunt, raking the undergrowth, twitching his nostrils. He takes a sudden stride forward, hoping his very presence will make her dart from cover.

But although she is terrified by what she thinks he will do to her—what he *must* do, to avoid losing the last of his authority— Nessa is a girl who imagines a great destiny for herself: survival. She will fight anyone who threatens to steal it from her. Most especially, she will fight her weaker self. The self that copies other people's poetry and pines for a boy who doesn't care. The self that wants her to run like a startled rabbit for the pleasure of the wolves. She stills her pounding pulse and bares her teeth in a silent snarl.

"We've driven them off," says Conor to the undergrowth. "All your little friends." His Sídhe is excellent and formal, the R's rolling, while every lenition and conjugation falls gratefully into place. "Megan ran like a red-haired rat. Nicole squealed when we threatened to break an arm. Only Aoife put up a fight. Am I right, Bruggers?"

"Crom curse you," says the other boy, and he has blood running from his nose. "You should have let me bend those fingers for her."

But the king is shaking his head. "I told you. We can only afford one accident today. And that's you, Nessa. That's you."

"Clip-Clop's hiding behind that bush." Liz Sweeney has arrived, her face already swelling from where Nessa got her with the crutch.

They all turn at once toward Nessa's rhododendron.

"Are you willing to bet your dessert on that, Liz Sweeney?"

"Are *you*? But listen, Conor, I want to be the one to do it to her. She's loosened a tooth on me."

The king shakes his head regretfully. "I'm not cruel, but the responsibility is mine and I cannot shirk it."

And then, with no warning, he leaps forward, as light on his feet as any goat, landing right on top of a rock beside Nessa's hiding place. She wastes no time on startlement, but sweeps her crutch across his shins so that he has to hop back again, laughing and shouting, "Leave her to me! I owe her this!"

That should have been the end of it. He should have had her in a flash, but now Megan arrives from the left, her head connecting with his stomach, tumbling him over even as his allies cry in outrage. She is already leaping to her feet to flee down the path. "Go! Nessa! Go!"

And she does. She drops her remaining crutch, preferring to pull herself along the chain-link fence with the power of her arms. Years of weight training, of determination, move her over the rough ground almost as fast as the others can run. She hears more voices shouting behind her now: Nicole and Aoife. All her friends have come to buy her a slim chance at escape . . .

But neither Liz Sweeney nor Bruggers has been caught up in whatever chaos Megan has arranged, and five minutes later Nessa meets them coming the other way.

THE TWISTED PATH

Nessa ducks out of sight. The two knights haven't seen her yet. Their pace is reluctant and sweat rolls down their foreheads. Each is spooked whenever the other makes a sudden movement, leaving Nessa in no doubt that the mound is getting to them.

But their imminent approach leaves her with an awful choice: crawl off into the forest, in the hopes that the poor autumnal foliage will cover her tracks, or slip through the break in the chain-link fence.

The latter is not an option. It *can't* be. Every muscle in her body—no!—every cell recoils from it. And that's how she knows it's her best chance. For who will follow her into that?

She ducks under the wire, aware of Bruggers's rough voice only ten steps away.

"I've had enough. She's dead anyway when they Call her. Don't see why it's our business to begin with."

And Liz Sweeney's practiced sneer. "Are you jealous, Bruggers? You want Conor for yourself?"

"So what? I don't hide it. Unlike some."

And Liz Sweeney doesn't like that one bit, but Nessa is struggling to concentrate on her own situation. She needs to get under cover quickly before they figure out which way she's gone. Right by the break in the wire, a little animal track begins, zigzagging its way up the mound between rocks and bushes and tufts of grass. Almost as though it were designed to conceal her from anyone outside the fence.

She crawls forward on her belly, fighting through spells of dizziness. No sooner does she pass the first turn in the path than she hears her pursuers arguing again.

"There's no way she went in there! She didn't! She couldn't have!"

"You're a dirty coward, Bruggers! Of course she went in there. Her tracks stop exactly at this point. Exactly!"

"Then she's been Called. That's what this feeling is! Oh, gods! Oh, Crom. You stay if you want!"

And Liz Sweeney's voice, full of bravado and trembling just a little, cries, "Run then, you coward! *I'm* going in."

Nessa has used the sound of their argument as a distraction while she pulls herself along. She feels sicker than ever, but the feeling comes in waves, and every time the tide goes out just a little she drags herself farther along, farther up the slope.

Liz Sweeney can't be more than five footsteps away, but her voice is faint as she calls, "I'm coming for you, Clip-Clop! Not even the Cauldron will fix you after I'm finished." And then the sounds of throwing up.

Nessa's journey feels like an eternity. The path must be twisting around the whole mound, because no matter how far she crawls, she never reaches the end of it. And the rocks! Why didn't she notice them when she came up here with Megan? They're huge! The only explanation she can think of is that the scientists must have dug them up. But that can't explain the tree-sized ferns growing all around her.

I'm hallucinating, she realizes at last. That sickening feeling, like a diseased finger lodged in her throat, is affecting her mind too.

Liz Sweeney is still following. "I'll get you . . . ," she wheezes, some way back.

Nessa could take her in an ambush, but somehow that never crosses her mind. All she can think of today is flight. And on she goes, around and around the base of the artificial hill, until at last the path comes to an end.

Before her lies what can only be described as the face of a cliff, many times taller than herself—taller indeed than the whole mound should be. And in the rock is a door. Although "door" seems like a poor word for such a thing, so large and weighty, carved into the very stone of which it is a part. Were it to open, an elephant could charge through without scraping its sides, and the riders on its back wouldn't even bow their heads to pass underneath.

Two body-lengths away from the door, Nessa comes to a halt, unable to approach any closer, unable to bear the sight of it. This is when the contents of her stomach come up. Her thighs are damp with her own urine, although she doesn't remember when that happened.

"Come back," says a voice behind her.

It is Liz Sweeney, all aggression gone, her face like parchment, like that of an ancient.

"Come back," she says again. And Nessa can only agree. Her own death is meaningless here. Her mutilation, her life. Liz Sweeney's life.

Together they turn around, and although nobody is hiding from anybody else now, they remain on hands and knees, the lowest of creatures, without even the dignity of a worm.

Both are starving by the time they reach the break in the fence again. They've spent a whole day climbing the hill. Exactly a day—they must have. The sky is the same color it was when they went in; the same hailstones bounce from every surface.

People will be wondering where they've gotten to. Year 1s will be combing the forest for their bodies, expecting that they will have been Called.

So it comes as a huge surprise to both of them to find Conor, Tony, Fiver, and Bruggers waiting for them, with Megan tied to a tree at their backs. She looks as if she is sleeping.

"Well done, Liz!" Conor's smile is broad, genuinely warm. "That was quick indeed!"

Neither of the returning girls speaks. Neither can. They only stare as Conor gently separates them. Then he pulls Nessa close and whispers, "I wish you hadn't made me do this. I ought to kill you. I should kill you. But I'm just going to break your arms today. I don't enjoy hurting people." His breathing is fast, however, like a boy before that first, longed-for kiss. And he takes her unresisting left arm and Bruggers says, "Do it!"

And Keith and Tony both nod, although the latter looks away in shame.

"And Liz Sweeney?" Conor asks. "What's your vote?"

But Liz Sweeney is too far away to cast any preferences. She has fallen to her bottom against the base of a tree, her chin stained with vomit.

"Well then, if we're all in favor . . ."

He turns her around so that the others can see his face, see how mature and measured he is being about this whole thing, and indeed, how little Nessa means to him.

Still, she does not resist. She is facing the mound now. She doesn't care about her arm. She is thinking, *I could walk to the very top of it in two minutes!* No huge rocks dot its surface. No prehistorically large ferns. Just waist-high ones, pushing up through the soil and through clumps of fist-sized stones.

"You will leave her alone."

Nessa is released to fall at Conor's feet. It is not an instructor that has found them, but a stranger: a boy wrapped in a filthy bedsheet, his short hair wild, with a patchy beard struggling to cling to his face.

"Anto?" Conor is surprised.

A man-sized bush is all that stands between them: two boys, one at the peak of physical perfection, an Olympian, the other a ghost.

"Nessa?" Anto whispers. She manages to drag her gaze away from the mound. He flinches from her, lowering his eyes. "Aoife knocked on my door yesterday. Said you were . . . threatened. You . . . you can leave now."

But she hasn't got the willpower to move.

As for Conor, he just laughs. "So, the mighty conqueror returns, does he? You? *You* escaped the Sídhe?" He steps closer. Anto sways back and Nessa idly thinks that there is something not quite right about the way he is moving, about the way the sheet that covers him lies across his body.

"Conor . . . ," he pleads.

"Not such a hero after all?" The king grins. "I took two pints of your blood last time. I will have another if you force me to. Now back off!"

"Nessa?" Anto whispers. "Come. Come on. Just . . . just don't look at me."

"No!" cries Conor. "She's not going anywhere! I don't care that you're a veteran. She will pay the price for her disrespect.

Two arms broken." He leans down to take Nessa's hand again. "Your only job is to watch."

"Don't . . . ," says Anto, a bit louder than before, and when Conor moves his grip to Nessa's elbow Anto cries, "Don't! Don't!" Tears of distress are pouring down his face.

"I will!" shouts Conor, "I—"

And Anto screams.

He grabs the bush between them by its trunk and pulls it right from the soil, roots and all, swinging it about his head like an enormous club. Stones fly from it to strike enemy and friend alike. Megan jerks into consciousness and cries out in fear. Bruggers and Fiver fall back, staring and staring at this impossible feat of strength. And that's not all they see.

Conor and his allies, with the exception of the silent Liz Sweeney, flee for their lives. And slowly Anto's passion cools and the bush falls to earth. Hurriedly he covers himself with the sheet, but not before Nessa has seen his left arm. It is twice as thick as his right and long enough that the tips of the fingers reach down as far as his ankle to form a giant's fist.

"Don't look," he begs her, and never in her life has she seen such despair. And then he too is gone, running lopsidedly, with the bedsheet flying behind him like a superhero's cloak.

It is an hour before Megan frees herself and gathers up the two other girls to lead them back to the college. Darkness has fallen, and slowly Nessa beats back the numbness that afflicts her.

"That was Anto," she manages.

"Yes," says Megan. "That . . . was . . ." She is bleeding from her scalp and bruised about the face and neck. It takes all of Nessa's willpower to get out a "thank you" to her best friend for saving her life.

Somewhere ahead of them, on the way into the shower block, Tony's tracksuit falls to the ground, his body gone from it.

TONY

L ike most teenagers of this time and place, Tony's story is not a long one, and it will come to its end no more than twenty minutes after his arrival in the Grey Land.

Tony can run as fast as anyone in Year 5, save maybe Anto. His sparring is good too and he takes great delight in tracking others in the hunt, or in fooling them by leaving elaborate false trails of his own. It's this intense focus on the ground, on the secrets of soil and twig, that prove his undoing.

He has sprinted away from the area where he appeared, and is now leaning against a tree to catch his breath. He never will catch it. Instead a great, soft weight smacks into him hard enough to smash him to the ground. Bones are broken in the fall, and he is on his face in acidic muck, barely able to turn his head in order to breathe.

And then the strangest thing, a voice, speaking English with an American accent. "Oh, thank you! Thank you, Jesus!"

"Who . . . ?" Tony manages.

"Hush now! Hush! You're the answer to our prayers." Needle-sharp teeth rip a fist of flesh out of Tony's back. He twists like a speared eel; he screams, until a filthy claw piles mud into his mouth and begs him, "Oh, no! Please don't! By God and all his angels, you are so delicious. I'm sorry, I have to—" And then Tony is thrashing again.

"Papa, Papa!"

"I'm here, girls, I'm here! Quick now, before they come for him. Eat what you can, you hear?"

Heavy, furry bodies land hard enough to fracture more of Tony's bones. New teeth tear at his flesh, filling his vision with red . . .

Only his skeleton returns for examination, picked clean of even the marrow. Nor is his the only corpse to turn up that day in the school. Two others, a Year 4 and a Year 6, will add to the silence in the refectory this evening.

THE MAPMAKER

D ozens of the latest Testimonies lie open on the narrow
desk in Mr. Hickey's office. His tongue sticks out in fasci-
nation, and every few minutes an ink-stained hand wanders up
from the books to push his glasses back into place.

"Interesting," he'll mutter, his breath clouding the cold air.

But he's not searching for evidence of plants or new dangers
to document, as he's supposed to. Instead, like thousands all
over the island, the hunt master is indulging in the pointless
hobby of "mapping" the enemy's world.

Teenagers stumble through horror and chaos. They flee
every kind of peril, from Sídhe arrows to sucking mud, from
god-sized storms to murderous "insects." All they can think of is
survival, and those few who return are often so traumatized from
the events that it can take trained psychiatrists months to get
anything useful out of them. And these addled accounts then
form the basis of Seán Hickey's . . . pastime.

Let's say that a decade ago a girl wandered through a swamp full of singing "lizards"? And just last year that boy, the famous one from Cork, nearly sank to his death with some kind of music in the background? It *might* be the same place. And the river he skirted could well match up with the one that appears in a hundred other accounts. And so on. Hopeless, but somehow compelling. Thrilling even, because sometimes Seán thinks he is the first to recognize a geographical feature that will appear in the *Mappers' Newsletter*.

"Come in!" he calls when a knock sounds at the door to his little room.

Ms. Breen does just that.

Her ugliness is extraordinary. Like something the Sídhe made from an unfortunate captive, and when he first came to the college he always referred to her in his own thoughts by the names the students gave her, "the Turkey" or "Gobbler." But nowadays he can't hide from the fact that she is far more intelligent than he is, and so dedicated to the survival of the students that she has put herself in harm's way for them more than once.

When he thinks of her now, it is by her first name only—Alanna—and he speaks it with the deepest respect.

As always when she enters his office, she spends a few minutes perusing the drawings on his walls—little more than single sheets of paper with hills and coastlines and caves and rivers. Each labeled with names of his own or those taken from the *Mappers' Newsletter*.

"You know this is pointless?" she says for the umpteenth time. "There's a whole world over there." She smiles as she speaks because she knows she is just provoking him and that even though he has tasted this bait again and again, still he will rise to it.

"That's not what the treaty said." And by this he means the legendary agreement between the ancestors of the Irish and the Tuatha Dé Danann, whom they replaced in the Many-Colored Land.

"We don't know there really was a treaty," she says.

"Yes, but *if* there was, then there is good reason to believe that the Grey Land is no larger than Ireland. In fact, it may even be exactly the same size and shape as Ireland was back then."

Or it may not. *The Book of Conquests* is 1,500 years younger than the events it describes, and contains a great many elements that are easily, demonstrably false.

Seán sighs and forces his fingers to unclench from around the pencil before they snap it.

"What can I do for you, Alanna?" He doesn't bother asking her if this is a social visit. She has no hobbies and exactly the same number of friends as he has. Her whole life is the college and the Nation.

"Why adolescents?" she asks.

"Why always the same question?" he responds, but then he sighs again, because she won't leave him alone unless they play this out to the finish. "The Sídhe take them because they can.

Because they are our future and because it breaks our hearts and our spirit to see them die."

But that is no answer at all, as well he knows. So he adds, "Alanna, you and I both know that it's not just teenagers they take."

"Go on," she says. They're not supposed to talk about the others, but there's nobody else present and clearly she's come in here today to use him as a sounding board. So he gives her the rest of it.

"They'll take newborns sometimes, as long as they're less than a day old." And he thinks of the panic that would cause if it were generally known! "But it's harder for them to do that, a lot harder, because the window of opportunity for the . . . the Call is so brief."

"And who else?"

"The dying, sometimes. The window is even shorter for them. The Sídhe have got to Call them within hours of death, but that's even rarer than for the babies. It's the old Gateway theory. When we cross certain thresholds in our lives, it puts us closer to their world. And since adolescence is the longest of these, it's easier for them to . . . to find us."

She smiles and pulls up the office's spare chair so that he knows she's finally ready to get to the point. She fiddles with her pipe, but she never lights it outside her own office.

"I'm an idiot," she says, and he sits up, because he rarely hears anger in her voice. "Telling students to stay away from the mound wasn't enough. How could I not know that? I was a teenager once myself, and *I* never left well enough alone. I should have had instructors guarding that stupid fence day and night. Teachers even! And now there's been another Call that may be a result of the students' presence in the forest. But"—and she licks her lips, the scholar in her fascinated—"one of the students came to me after, Vanessa Doherty."

"The polio girl? Nessa?"

"The same. She's spending her first night in the Cage, by the way. But listen, Seán, listen to what she told me."

He gasps as she describes the path up to the top of the mound and the door that waited there.

"You think the path is actually part of the Grey Land? But no, no, you don't! There were ferns and so on. Oh, Crom! The ferns she saw, were they the same as ours?"

Alanna Breen grins. "I knew you'd get it, Seán. And so did Nessa, the smart girl, after she had recovered. That's why she risked extra Cage time to tell me, because this is too important. The ferns, as you say, were the same as ours, except they were enormous. And these are the words she used, the very words: 'It's like I was shrinking,' she said. *Shrinking!*"

He covers his mouth, thinking of the way the girl in the rock had grown the more she emerged from her stony prison. And then there was that story out of Bangor about the footprints Liz Sweeney's brother had seen, getting smaller and smaller all the time. And the thumb-sized man the boy claimed to have incinerated, of which no evidence could now be found.

"People have told stories like this forever," Alanna says. "About little people, even though we know the Sídhe are not little."

And all the hunt master can do is nod, gobsmacked. Thinking about a conclusion that is so obvious neither of them need voice it aloud: the closer we get to the Sídhe world, the smaller we become. Indeed, the toes of the girl in the rock were too tiny to be seen with the naked eye. And Seán Hickey immediately stands and rips the useless maps from his wall. But more from wonder than despair. He is imagining a world small enough to fit into a single drop of water, or a human hair, or an atom. He is wondering if somewhere in all this there also lies an explanation for the way time stretches during a Call.

He laughs, startling his guest. "By Crom," he says, "does this mean if we found their world, we could just step on it and squash it?"

"I doubt it," Alanna says. "I doubt we *could* find it. Nabil and Taaft have been up and over the mound all night, and even though they can see the hole in the fence, they can't find a path."

"So . . . only a student can see it?"

"That's what we think. Only an adolescent, and only before they get the Call."

THE CAGE

A series of punishment cells lines the third floor of the staff building. The amenities are poor: a hard, spiteful pallet leaves space only for a chamber pot that needs to be lifted out of the way whenever the door opens.

"Well," says Megan through the grille, "you finally made it to the Cage. You're wasting your time if you think you can beat my record."

"You're not supposed to visit! You'll end up in here yourself!" Nessa can't see her friend's face, but knows there's a grin on it.

"I'd slip some chocolate through here, but it's two years since I've seen any."

"You're talking about the bar from my granny I was saving?" says Nessa. "The one that went missing from my locker?"

"That's the one. I didn't mean to take it. I just woke up one night and it was smeared all over my face."

They both laugh at the idea of this. It never happened of course. The bar *did* go missing, but their chief suspect is Nicole.

"I'm glad you came, Megan. I wanted . . . I wanted to say sorry for running. I didn't think Conor would go after you too."

"Your running was the whole point, you silly whore!"

"I know. But he's capable . . . of anything and—"

"And nothing! By the shit-filled cauldron of shit! This is all because he wants you, you know?"

Nessa did.

"Couldn't you just bat your eyelashes at him until he gets Called? Or write him a wee poem?"

"Would you? Would *you* bat your eyelashes?"

"Of course not! I'm going to eat his liver. I'd eat it now if you put it in front of me."

"Okay, then. Bring me that chocolate and we'll do a swap."

It shouldn't be funny, but for once it is she who makes Megan laugh, and Nessa remembers the sense of humor she used to have—or thought she did—back when she knew nothing of the Grey Land and her parents spent all of their love and inventiveness to keep her that way.

After Megan leaves, she wraps her arms around her knees and thinks about her parents, and poor Dómhnall, her brother. He has no Testimony, of course, having died in the Grey Land. But somewhere in the library there will be a report on the state of his body and she has never dared to read it. She wonders now if her parents did, if this explains her mam's fragility.

The day progresses and she watches the light from the window move down the length of her pallet. The mourning bells ring and she wonders who was lost. And she obsesses over food, although less than a third of her three-day sentence has passed.

But mostly she thinks of Anto. She thinks of the sheet with which he covered his entire body and how he had begged her, actually *begged* her, not to look at him. And the distress on his face! And the terrible loping gait as he fled.

He saved her life and she was too out of it to thank him or even to say how happy she was to see him.

The imaginary world she thought dead has come back to torment her and it's twice as strong as it ever was. She fights it heroically. She curses the poets and all the poison they wrote that won't now come out of her veins. But night has fallen, and after Nabil has done his rounds and called in, "You still there, brave one?" she uses her strong fingers to force open the rusty window and fill the room with freezing air.

She has never done this in winter before. She has never done it on an empty stomach or forced her way headfirst and upside down out over a three-story drop where the wind batters her face and numbs her fingers before her hips have so much as left the building.

No moon shines on her efforts and nobody will see her if she falls. And it is only now the full folly of her venture becomes obvious. Her arms hold her entire weight on the narrowest of windowsills and she has no way of getting herself back inside.

Her memory has lied to her. She expected to find the drain-pipe waiting just outside, and yes, yes, it's there, but a full foot and a half from where she imagined it, and already she is tiring.

Don't panic! Don't panic! And to be fair to her, not panicking is a talent Nessa has in spades. She wedges her knees in the window and walks her hands two agonizing steps to the left.

She has one chance, one tiny chance of avoiding, at the very least, broken bones that will never heal by the time her Call comes. It's insane, but this is what she does: She allows her weak legs to slide from the window. Just as she's about to topple over into the abyss, she pushes with them for what little they're worth. Meanwhile her arms push too, splaying out and clawing at the empty air until they find the pipe and her whole body twists around and slams into the wall.

She ignores the shock. She ignores the pain and the terrifying, stomach-dropping lurch as several of the rivets holding the pipe to the wall come away at once and tinkle down three stories.

But she's still clinging on by the time her vision has cleared.

I should go back in now, she thinks. But it's just not physically possible. As it is, it's a miracle she even makes it to the ground, scraped bloody and speckled with bruises.

She falls to her knees, heaving for breath and shaking like a dying leaf. It wasn't fun this time. The only thrill she felt was one of fear. All she wants now is to turn herself in and take her punishment. Nobody has ever been stupid enough to escape from the Cage before.

But when her breath comes back Nessa remembers that she's only a few windows away from Anto's room and that this was the whole point. Candles flicker inside and it looks for all the world like something out of a Christmas movie with Nessa as Scrooge, staring longingly through the glass. Not that she can see anything with the curtains drawn. Before she knows it, she finds herself knocking.

Anto's face appears, squinting into the dark, and then confusion crosses it only to be chased off by despair.

"You have to let me in," she says through chattering teeth.

"But you're in the Cage!"

"Or maybe I'm a ghost. Look, I just want to see you."

The window is almost too stiff for his right hand, but it's the only one he'll use, pushing it between the curtains and straining until it opens a crack. Then she can add her strength to his—which isn't a whole lot at this point. He even has to drag her through, when she gets caught halfway. Pretty undignified all round.

But he has carpet on the floor and warmth, by the Cauldron! Warmth enough that when she finds her bottom on the ground and her back to the wall, her eyelids are too heavy to keep open.

"They'll come looking for you," he whispers. He has wrapped a dressing gown around himself, but it's not heavy enough or long enough to hide his misshapen left side completely. So he leans away too. "They check every two hours at night."

She blinks awake. "They do?"

"Sure. You've never been in the Cage before, but think about it. What if someone came back from a Call and needed help? They *have* to check."

Nessa raises her head to find he is sitting on the bed, as far from her as the room will allow. She wonders if he wants her gone. He's trembling more than she is, his face is flushed in the candlelight, and those once-beautiful eyes are sunk in shadow.

"Will you grow your hair back now, Anto?"

"I'm sorry?"

"I'd love if you'd grow it back. Long enough to braid again."

He has no answer to that. Nor does he know what to do when she uses the very last of her strength to pull herself upright, although her hands are nearly as useless now as her legs. It's only three steps until she's standing in front of him.

"They'll find you. Nessa . . ."

She bends over and kisses him. He ducks away, but it's all right, because she knows why and she has a fix for that. She reaches under the fold of the dressing gown and takes hold of his massive left arm.

"Please, Nessa. Oh, God, I don't want you to . . ."

Other than the fact that it's twice as big as it should be, it feels normal. If he overreacts now, he could kill her with it. He could rip her head off or punch bricks out of the wall. Why *did* the Sídhe do this to him? What were they planning on turning him into? Whatever it was, their work was interrupted when the Grey Land spat him back.

He doesn't resist as she pulls it free and places it over her shoulders. She is sitting beside him now. She can feel the warmth of the arm, feel its massive pulse.

"I'm a monster," he says.

"I could go to sleep right here" is her only reply. And it's true. She has always imagined this moment. Their first kiss since poor Tommy's death opened their eyes to each other. She thought there would be excitement and passion and the ripping away of clothing. That sort of thing. But what she feels now is comfort. As though she has finally taken off those too-tight shoes she'd forced herself to wear. The ones nobody else noticed or liked.

And he too is finally beginning to relax, the pulse slowing and his breathing approaching normality.

"I know it was you," he says. "With the poetry."

"Bet you couldn't read it."

"There may be few Irish speakers left in Dublin, but even we know how to use libraries."

She is grinning hard enough to hurt. He continues, "I thought you were crazy. And I was right about that, wasn't I, Nessa?"

"You were."

"I wanted to tell you to stop."

"Why didn't you?"

He doesn't answer. His cheek now leaning against her forehead feels damp.

"I came back here for you, Nessa," he says eventually. "And yet . . . I couldn't bear for you to see me."

"I know all that."

Then they both jump as a knock comes at the door. "Can I come in? It's Nabil."

Anto springs to his feet. "I . . . I can't open the door, sir. I . . . I have no clothes on."

"Oh," Nabil replies, deeply embarrassed. "Because, uh . . . because I'm not here for you."

Nabil takes her away and she thinks he must be furious. He hushes her and half drags her up the stairs, as though he's racing for the last bin collection with a particularly vile sack of garbage. But he apologizes as soon as the door to her cell slams shut behind her.

"Look," he says, "once I've confirmed nobody saw us, we will forget this whole thing."

"We . . . will?"

"You are incredible," he says. He hunts around for a good Sídhe word, but there isn't one, so he has to content himself with English. "Like, um . . . like the acrobat, yes? At the circus?" And he grins, his dark face as handsome as a movie star's, despite the scars. "He's a nice boy, that Anto, but I don't think you will try this again, will you?"

She laughs and shakes her head. She feels suddenly amazing. Giddy and clean.

"Close the window," he tells her. "Then get some sleep. You know you'll have nothing but water for two more days."

And both of their smiles disappear at once, for the Grey Land is never very far away.

THE WOUND

Two doors down from where Anto sits on a bed with Nessa, another girl, eighteen years old, stands naked before the full-length mirror in her room. This is Melanie, the college's female veteran. According to the doctors, who have also seen her without her clothing, she'll be lucky to reach her twentieth birthday.

This is because of the hole in her chest—and, yes, it is literally a hole. With the help of the mirror, Melanie can see right through the fist-sized gap to the patched blue curtains behind her. She calls it her "wound," but no blood seeps from the edges. Instead the skin around the sides is so smooth and perfect that she might as well have been born with it.

And yet, the pain when it happened! By Crom! She staggers with the memory of it, pawing at the frame of the mirror for support.

Breathing hard, she thinks of the dour Dr. Moore. He got it wrong when he swore the wound would kill her. And he's wrong too in thinking she'll have to endure it the rest of her life, reminded every time she lies down and sees her T-shirt fall into the hollow between her breasts. A cure exists, and Melanie knows exactly what she has to do to get it.

"Be strong," she tells herself. It's really very simple.

But the wait is driving her mad. In particular the secrecy and the loneliness of the whole thing. Melanie wasn't meant to be by herself. What a beautiful girl she was! Everybody wanted the attention of those startling blue eyes. And how they admired that pert chin of hers, held aloft over the elegant neck of a ballerina. She used to have Bart Dundon kiss her right there, so that the tingles ran over her entire body. Every day until the Sídhe took him.

But who can she talk to now?

Five of her class survived the Call. A few of them got in contact with her after. Sleazy Eamon, totally unscathed! No holes in him! And Anne Boring Asshole Shevlin. Gods! Not even if she were the last person on the planet!

Melanie also has invites from support groups. From the best therapists in the country, who have given their whole lives to helping people just like her. Except that . . . except that most of the survivors *aren't* like Melanie, are they? And that's the terrible part. She needs the help on offer, but can't avail herself of it. She needs somebody, anybody, to talk to. She's like the boy in the legend who kept King Lowrey's secret so well he began to die of it.

"How long must I wait?" she asks the mirror in Sídhe.

As a survivor, she doesn't need to speak that language anymore. But many like her are more comfortable in it than English, and since they have no choice but to marry each other, the primary schools of the country are filling with tiny tots whose innocent mouths spout the long-dead language of their distant ancestors, which also happens to be the living, never-changing tongue of the enemy. Some day, she thinks, we will be them, a greater victory for the Sídhe than if they kill us all.

She hears knocking on a door farther up the corridor. A low voice asks, "Can I come in? It's Nabil." And, after a pause: "I'm not here for you."

Melanie is curious enough that if she weren't naked, if her . . . her *wound* weren't on display, she'd be out of her room like a shot. She grabs for her clothing anyway, in case the Frenchman should come to her too. It's not that he won't know what happened to her—it's in her Testimony, after all, and no lies on her part would have obscured the doctors' report. But she shudders at the thought of Nabil's eyes—anybody's eyes—lingering on it.

Melanie did lie in her Testimony though. Her story also has a hole, but this one is big enough to swallow the world.

By the time she has covered her wound in three layers of T-shirts and a dressing gown, strange shuffling footsteps fill the hall. She opens the door a crack, but is too late to see who went past. However, she is not the only one looking on. Her fellow veteran, Anto, quickly retreats when he sees Melanie there.

"Interesting," she mutters to herself.

Like her, he came back to the college after his Call without so much as a break. He's as good-looking for a boy as Melanie is for a girl. And he too has been horribly altered by the hands of the Sídhe. What if, she wonders—she can't help it—what if he shares the same secret she does? The idea makes her rickety heart pound dangerously fast. If he does, he won't be allowed to discuss it with anybody. Nor is Melanie of course. Most of the time she won't even permit her thoughts to wander there for fear she will blurt it out over dinner with the staff. What a shock that would be to them all! Oh, Crom! By the Cauldron!

But she could be careful, couldn't she? She could sound him out.

Back to the mirror to comb her golden hair—it's no longer short, but she keeps it in a bob these days. There'll be time enough after she's cured to set it free. She tightens the belt of her dressing gown to ensure its folds can't fall into the hollow in her chest, or the matching one at the back. Then, excited for the first time since her Call, she is face to face with her fellow veteran.

"Melanie?"

"You're good," she says, and her face forms itself into the impish grin that once served as her trademark. "It's about time we talked."

"It is?" Anto's face is flushed for some reason, and while they have exchanged a few words before now at meetings with a very frustrated Ms. Breen, he seems happier than he was then. And Melanie wonders if it's because of her. Imagine the lucky boy to be visited by a beauty in the night! Her grin widens. How she has missed this!

But maybe it's not her, after all, because he pleads exhaustion and makes as if to close the door.

"Anto, you look less tired than I've seen you since your Call. Anyway, I just want a few minutes of your time, and I swear by the Cauldron I'll leave you be."

He backs away before her and, while he's a bit young for her taste, she can't help thinking that after this, when it's all over and they're both cured and back to normal, maybe something could happen between them. Certainly Bart Dundon never had such a solid chin!

They stand looking at each other in the warmth of the room, their faces in shadow, because the only light here is from a single candle.

"What did Nabil want?"

He ducks his head and she doesn't push it, any more than she would want to be pushed when it comes to his turn to ask questions. There is definitely something different about him though. In Ms. Breen's office he hid himself away behind a pile of books and the Turkey kept saying, "Look, Anthony, you were the one who insisted on coming back to serve here."

"I have to be here!"

"Right, right. But if you're not comfortable to share your experiences with the students . . ."

"I . . . If they see me. I . . ."

Melanie understood completely! Anto had a "wound" of his own and it was a far uglier thing than hers apparently. She would have run off to a cabin in the woods if that were her! She would have thrown herself off a cliff, allowing that monstrous arm to drag her down under the sea. But all he did was hide it under a bedsheet when he came to the meetings.

"Listen, Anthony"—Ms. Breen was practically gritting her teeth—"survivors are supposed to be . . . morale boosters, as well as instructors in their own right. But it's not going to work if you hide yourself away all the time."

"I'll . . . I'll do it," he said. "Let me stay. Just let me stay."

In spite of this promise, he has yet to show his face at any of the classes as far as Melanie knows, although rumors are flying that he made an unannounced appearance at a hunt of all things!

"I have a question for you," says Melanie now.

He nods, and she notices that he's facing her straight on this evening, not turning his right side toward her so as to hide his deformity. *Is that because he knows he can trust me?*

"Why, Anto?" she says. "Why did you tell the Turkey that you *had* to be here?"

The question startles him and Melanie grins at his reaction and even more as the words come tumbling out of his mouth, "I . . . I can't talk about that."

"Good," she says.

"Good?"

"Me neither. About why I have to be here, that is."

"Oh."

"I can't talk about it," she continues, watching his every reaction, "because I took an oath."

"An oath?"

"I took an oath *on the Cauldron*." It's something students at the college swear by every day, along with taking Crom's name in vain, or Danú's or Lugh's. But they don't know, any of them, that Dagda's Cauldron, with its ability to cure any hurt, is a real thing and that she herself has seen it. They don't know that the Sídhe will heal you with it in exchange for certain . . . services.

She waits for a tiny nod from him, for his mouth to crease into a secret smile, but all she sees is confusion and her voice is far angrier than she means it to be when she says, "You'd better start pulling your weight with the students or you're out of here! And I for one won't be sorry." And out she goes, pulling the door shut behind her before he can see her tears.

It doesn't matter, she tells herself, a hand over the wound in her chest. Soon she will be whole again. The Sídhe never break a promise: It's the one thing both the legends and the Testimonies agree on.

But it doesn't stop her from sobbing on her bed, because she doesn't want to be alone in this, to be the only monster. To betray her own kind.

You could run now, she thinks. *Go to Nabil, to the Turkey, to anyone. You could confess.*

Instead she whispers, "It won't be long, it won't be long . . ."

And she's right. Only a few weeks remain.

HUMILIATION ENDS

And so this is it: the last ever meeting of the Round Table. Once Conor had nine soldiers to call upon. You are the elite, he told them. The future of Ireland because you are stronger and so much more dangerous than the cannon fodder who share our dorms.

However, Tony, Keith, Rodney, Chuckwu, and Cahal are gone. More than half the gang. Year 5's only survivor so far is one of the very weaklings he warned them against.

Conor still has his old chair at the head of the class, but nobody else can be bothered to sit. They won't be here that long.

Bruggers's face is beetroot red as he hammers the desk in front of him. "And those girls! A bunch of little girls has beaten you, Conor! Again and a-bloody-gain! By Dagda's Cauldron! *Girls!*"

Bruggers doesn't care that he is saying these things in front of Liz Sweeney, who flattens him on the mats every time they meet. She raises no protest, she, who only a few days ago worshipped Conor as though he were Lugh in the sky. She hasn't said much of anything since she chased Clip-Clop up the mound a week before.

Only Fiver and Sherry remain loyal. The runt of the litter and the girl who wants to be Conor's consolation prize.

"Go on then," Conor says at last. "Go on, the lot of you." Even now he might win them back by smashing Bruggers in the nose, by making him weep and beg. But it is the king's own loss of faith that matters to him now. He has always known that he would be one of the Call's survivors. He even dreams about the event itself, the ultimate challenge that will confirm him in his greatness.

Except he no longer believes it. What Bruggers says is true. If Conor and his nine knights cannot overcome a red-haired freak from Donegal and a cripple, surely the Sídhe will swallow him whole.

He watches them leave: Liz Sweeney in a daze; Sherry, casting glances like the kicked puppy she is; Bruggers and Fiver disappointed that he made no effort to win back their loyalty.

Clip-Clop is getting out of the Cage today. He's been counting down the hours because he has decided to kill her. This will mean the end of his own life— the country has no resources for murderers. But he doesn't care. He can't live with this idea of himself as a failure or with the thought of her scorn when he lowered himself so far for her sake.

Everyone will know soon enough that she rejected him. Just as they already know about his failure to make her and her friends pay in the forest, and the fact that he ran from Anto, of all people.

Conor doesn't rush things. Even now he fantasizes that he is more predator than prey. So for the next few days he watches her. He goes to the library and pretends to read Testimonies, but he has cleared out a hole in the shelves so that he can see through them to the door of the girls' toilets.

His opportunity comes sooner than expected. He hears her uneven footsteps on the worn and faded carpet, and he's on his feet with a large glass paperweight in his fist even as she pushes open the swing door. He wants to kill her quickly and with the minimum of bloodshed, because there is still a small chance that in the labyrinth of the library he might get away with it.

He's in through the door like the avenging angel he is, but Nessa is always faster than he expects, so that when he swings the paperweight, she gets an arm up.

He's strong though! Oh, how strong he is, especially now that he is dispensing justice! He smashes through her awkward block, and while she has saved her own life, still he strikes hard enough to leave her dazed and utterly helpless.

It's an incredible feeling for him. Never has he been so powerful, so much in charge of anybody. *This,* he thinks, *is why I was born.*

And then the paperweight hits the floor in a shower of glass, and the mess is covered by the empty tracksuit that falls on top of it.

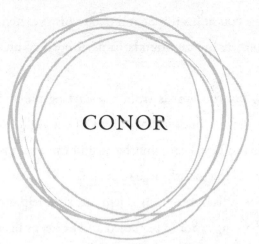

CONOR

Conor laughs when he realizes what has happened. The swirls of faint grey light above hypnotize him with their beauty. In the distance, tornadoes rip through the hills and every plant, from the slicegrass at his feet to the smother trees out to his left, represents the very challenge of which he has dreamed his whole life.

"Oh, thank you!" he says. A great king does not need to believe in gods, but Conor knows now that the Call has saved him from a pointless murder. His losses of the past few weeks are suddenly irrelevant, because this is the only test that anybody in the country cares about. And *he* is ready to face it.

The Sídhe always come to the place where their victims first appear. But Conor, perfectly calm, takes a minute to pick out a route for himself. Then he starts to jog, gambling, as anybody must, that he is running away from the pursuit, rather than toward it. He skips over the slicegrass and, with a cheeky grin, sidesteps the grab of a spider tree.

The air cuts at his throat and makes his eyes itch. The stench of vomit on the breeze offends him with every breath, and yet he feels amazing.

A few hundred yards from his starting point, he hears the first of the horns coming far off and to the right. And now his heart begins to beat faster, but he steadies it with proper breathing and resists the foolish urge to sprint.

A voice calls out to him, "Help me, sir! Help me!"

But the king is not to be fooled and he keeps his eyes focused on the route ahead of him, ducking under the death nettles that hang from boulders; trampling a herd of tiny, screaming men; veering left when a cloud that might be ash or a swarm of bloodsuckers hovers above some nearby trees. He is Mr. Hickey's perfect pupil, and Nabil's and Taaft's. No student before him has absorbed his lessons so deeply that they have become part of his very flesh, and either the Sídhe will never catch him, or they will rue the day that they did.

The horn sounds again, much closer than before. But how can that be? Surely the Sídhe can't run that fast without exhausting themselves? He would have read about it in the Testimonies.

Conor jogs out from between the trunks of some mighty smother trees, to find himself on a flat mucky plain, and now the horn is sounding from his left and the ground beneath his feet shudders as though a herd is thundering toward him—as indeed it is! Conor can see it already, and he feels his first doubts. Because this time the enemy have horses!

As with the "dogs," they have molded men and women, by stretching their heads and necks, by increasing their bulk and size until they stand on all fours as high as Conor's head. Each bears a laughing Sídhe on its back, twirling weighted nets of human hair above their heads as they charge toward him.

Conor is not stupid enough to run. Instead he stands as though frozen to the spot with terror until they are almost upon him. The first net swings toward him, and that's when he explodes into action, leaping to one side, yanking at the woven hair to sweep the surprised rider from his mount.

"Oh, well played, thief!" the Sídhe cries, until Conor smashes his face with the heel of one foot. Other riders are regrouping and gathering their nets, but the riderless "horse," her long face twisted into hatred, charges him straight away. She will crush him; she will rend his flesh with her teeth.

But great King Conor grabs up his victim's net. He tangles the human fists that make up her hooves and then, as she finds her feet again, he leaps onto her back, screaming directly into her ears: "I'm your master now, you dirty bitch! Ride! Ride! Or by Crom you'll wish for the pain of your making all over again!" And he pulls back hard enough on her hair to rip out a bloody clump of scalp. She panics, pelting across the plain, while the grinning Sídhe cavalry rushes on in pursuit. How ironic, he thinks, for the master of the Round Table to meet actual knights! He laughs, and if anything convinces the "horse" that he is now her master, it is this.

How fast she runs! Quicker than any real horse. The Sídhe have molded her back into a comfortable, natural saddle, but Conor has never ridden before and he spends most of the trip across the plain gripping her neck, never more than a heartbeat from a deadly fall. He glances behind him and sees the rest of the merry band following on after him, their calls of encouragement and laughter swallowed by the wind.

Up ahead, brown hills rise to the height of small houses. A horn sounds again and he wonders, *Is it coming from in front of me? Should I try to turn?* And then it's too late, for the hills are full of holes, and from these dozens of beautiful Sídhe warriors come slithering out, cries of joy filling the air. Conor's "horse" shouts, "I brought him right here!" And suddenly he's flying from her back.

A warrior breaks his fall with her body. She had a spear. Now it is his, a weapon with which he has trained again and again. Although none bore such fine carvings, such a sharp tip of bone!

"I am the best," he shouts at them. And they applaud, they actually applaud!

Then they come running for him, and Conor makes good on his boast.

He stabs and parries. He leaves his spear in one Sídhe's body, while punching the next hard enough to rock her head back. Her weapon becomes his. Its butt shatters a skull. Its shaft sweeps the legs of attackers. Its point drinks again and again.

Never has Boyle Survival College, or any school in all of Ireland, produced such a perfect warrior as Conor. Even as their bodies pile up around him, the Sídhe are cheering him on. "You are a joy," says one prince with his last breath. And Conor knows it's true, as he kills and kills again, his grin as large as any of theirs.

He loses track of time, but soon he finds himself on top of one of those hills in which they live, and their attacks have come to an end. More of them have arrived from all over, and they stand cheerfully on the bodies of their own dead, as though on grass.

"Why aren't you fighting?" he shouts. His voice is hoarse. His limbs are lead weights and he has clothed his nakedness in a layer of dried blood thick enough that it feels like armor to him. He thinks that he is but moments from collapse and wonders how much time has passed, if he has survived long enough to be sent home. But then he thinks, *Why would I want to go home? I belong here!* And it's true. He has never felt so alive. He would fight and kill forever if he could.

The crowd in front of him parts for the arrival of a man wearing a crown of gleaming bone over shining hair. He is as large and strong as Nabil and his face seems to glow, like that of a god or the saint in a stained-glass window. He has the great square jaw and shoulders of a hero, with rings of metal straining to hold together around his fierce biceps. But what really draws Conor's attention is the extraordinary garment that covers his chest. It actually ripples as he moves, always catching the best light, hugging the marble muscles of his body.

"Let us speak," he cries, "hero to hero."

Conor feels his chest swell and he nods through his exhaustion.

"Come up then, lord."

The Sídhe prince smiles a perfectly human smile. He makes a show of grounding his spear before striding up to the top of the hill.

"I am named Dagda."

"After the god? The one with the Cauldron?"

"I see you have heard of me. Good. It will make this easier." He surveys the carnage. "Great work, my child. I would be proud to have one such as you in my service."

Conor grins, thinking to himself that a king serves no one. But he knows how to be polite and nods. A worse smell than usual tickles his nostrils. It began with Dagda's arrival. He sees why when he studies the man's clothing, and he gasps, for the hem of each sleeve is a set of human lips—a whole human mouth, in fact, panting in distress around the Sídhe's wrists, while a tiny trail of what might be vomit drips away to the ground.

Even as he watches, a pair of miserable eyes opens to stare back at him.

"Lovely, is it not?" says Dagda. "I could make you one, if you like."

"I . . . It looks a little cruel," says Conor. "I don't like cruelty."

"Oh, I think you do. I think you like it *very* much. But where you live, amid such constant beauty, those who appreciate suffering must pretend otherwise even to themselves. But tell me this at least: You think my garment is clever?"

And Conor has to accept that it is. The way the skin changes color from brown to green, pulsing gently in its agony. Its body heat too must keep the Sídhe lord warm at all times.

"Listen, thief, you need not die here today. Give me your oath of fealty and I will send you back to the Many-Colored Land unaltered and alive."

"*You* should be the one to give me your oath!" says Conor. "I will be a king in my own right one day, and I will finish the job our ancestors started. I will finish you!"

The Sídhe grins joyfully. "Oh, you bring me such pleasure! Let us fight then, you and I! Let us fight, and the loser will serve the victor."

"You cannot serve me as a corpse!"

"And yet I cannot die! You know of the Cauldron, do you not? You know it's real? We put in our dead and they crawl forth eager for battle again. All of these people"—he waves an elegant arm—"have lived here since the beginning."

"They . . . they have? I mean, I've heard the legends . . . but . . . but . . ."

"What do you think keeps us young?" His grin grows wider. "So, we will fight, you and I? And even if you lose, I will make you king! You have my word, and we *always* keep our word. You know that about us."

What can Conor say to such a noble offer? He can't lose any fight today anyway, for they fear him as the men of Connaught feared Cú Chulainn in his fury. And even if the impossible does happen. Even if he loses, Dagda has promised to make him king!

"Very well!" he says grandly, and clasps arms with the Sídhe.

"That was not a clever way to begin the fight," Dagda says.

"Begin? But we haven't begun yet, we . . ."

The Sídhe has his hands on Conor's elbows, and just like that he begins to squeeze. The pain is the most intense the boy has ever known. So bad that it drives him to his knees, his eyes roll in his skull, and he dislocates his own jaw in his efforts to scream. And the Sídhe pinches off the arms like lengths of putty, before grabbing Conor by the knees and working the same horrible miracle.

"Swear to me," says his new lord. "Swear to me if you ever wish to be whole again. Swear by the Cauldron that will keep you young forever. Or I will make a garment of you."

Conor swears. What choice does he have? He swears. But first, because he is the strongest of all his peers, he overcomes the pain long enough to say: "I want something!" His voice emerges as a scream; he can't help it. "I want something first."

When the Sídhe learns of his demand, he laughs—how he laughs! And Dagda promises, he swears, to grant Conor his dearest wish.

FALSE TESTIMONY

Nessa struggles to sit up in the library bathroom. She's not sure what has happened. Other than Conor hit her in the head with something and was then Called.

This is the first time in her life she has wanted somebody to die at the Sídhe's hands. It's an unworthy, horrible thought, but it's there, and the blood in her hair and the nausea in her belly keep pushing it to the front of her mind.

And then he's back. Has it been three minutes already? He stands in front of her, naked, but without a single wound on his body. He lacks even the scars that everybody has after years of rough and dangerous play under the supervision of the world's best killers.

And then she gasps, still too dazed to be afraid of the boy who twice now has planned her death. "Your arms," she cries. "Your . . . your legs."

Conor is in even more shock than she is, his nakedness of no concern to him. His head bobs down, as though on a string, and he lets out a whimper of his own. For these limbs are not his. He has a right leg and a left leg, but one looks African, one maybe Asian. His arms too are different sizes. One is certainly Caucasian, but hair grows more thickly on it than anywhere else on the boy's body.

"What happened?" she asks, all enmity forgotten.

He opens his mouth as if to answer, but then shakes his head and, making no effort to retrieve his fallen clothing, stumbles out and off into the library.

An hour later, Nabil has caught Conor and has herded him into Ms. Breen's study.

She knows about the broken paperweight and wonders what his intentions were toward Nessa.

Any of Ms. Breen's students could beat her up, the head of the college. But rarely has she feared to be alone with one before. And yet, here she is.

"Can you tell me about it?" she asks.

Within the week, Conor will be required to testify before a swarm of expert interrogators and all of his experiences will be made public. But whenever she can, for those whose minds haven't been destroyed by their visit to the Grey Land, Ms. Breen likes to get their fresh first impressions.

Conor won't be supplying any. He hangs his head, as though guilty, and then says, "I'd like to stay. As . . . as a veteran maybe."

"No" is all she says, and he doesn't push it, or ask why.

"I'll live in Boyle then. It's only a few miles away."

"Why, Conor? Boyle is dying. Why not go home to Tipperary? Cashel, wasn't it? Your parents are still there."

He shrugs and then screws up his face. He's been in her office many times, this one. He has sat in front of her, legs spread wide, his chin jutting, and every sentence out of his mouth constructed with care. But not today. He's like her mother in the worst throes of her dementia. But eventually he finds the words. "I still have friends here. To . . . I worry about them. Liz Sweeney. Fiver." Another shrug.

"All right, young man, I can't stop you if you want to live in Boyle, but I'm not having you visit the college, right? And your friends won't be getting out to you either!"

"I just need to be close to . . . I just need to be close."

She nods. He relaxes, and she takes that as an opportunity to hit him with: "What happened to your hands, child? Why are they different colors?"

"He . . . I mean, they, captured me."

"Obviously."

"It . . . it was a joke to them."

"But they let you live?"

He jumps, as though caught in the girls' bathroom with a weapon in his hand.

"Why?" she pushes. "Why did they let you live?"

And he leaps to his feet, and trips, because they're not really his feet at all. "They didn't let me live!" he cries. "They didn't!

I got away! I bested them all and I got away! By the Caul—" He stops, hyperventilating, and again Ms. Breen fears for her life. But finally he straightens and his eyes seem to harden.

"Are you all right?" she asks him, and in reply she receives the same sort of nod she might have gotten before he was Called.

"We do what we have to to survive," he says.

"For the Nation to survive," she corrects him.

He makes no answer.

Ms. Breen is relieved to watch him go. She doesn't realize that she will see him again very soon.

FAIRY KILLER

It's only been a few weeks since Conor left the college, and Nessa can't quite get over how relieved she feels. And all for the price of two measly stitches in her scalp! Rain pelts the glass as Nicole deals cards to Megan, Marya, Aoife, and herself for a hand of Twenty-Five. Other students lounge around on sofas, goggle-eyed at ancient magazines full of bizarre *celebrities*. "By Crom, she's like something the Sídhe got hold of!" And over everything, the crackling radio struggles from one thirty-year-old hit to the next. Who has the resources these days to make new music? To record it? To store it?

But Nessa doesn't care. Her belly is pleasantly full and an old-fashioned fire roars in the grate, with boys taking turns to pile on the wood. She stifles a yawn, thinking of Anto, who sat at the top table for the first time this evening, ignoring the stares at his deformity. But he did meet the eyes of one girl. He did smile, and Nessa grinned right back.

Now she follows suit on a two of hearts, while Megan flings up her hands and snorts, "Who invented this stupid game?" Then it's Aoife's turn, and she hesitates.

The blonde girl hasn't spoken much since Squeaky Emma was Called, so even Megan is patient as she breaks the biggest taboo of them all.

"What . . . what will you girls do if you survive?" she says.

Nicole looks away, embarrassed for her. Marya covers her mouth and nobody dares answer.

"It's just . . . it's just I think the State'd make me marry some guy. And I'm not . . . you know, I'm not cut out for it."

"Men aren't worth it," says Megan, winking at Nessa, who fights and fights against the idiot grin that her face wants to make.

But Aoife takes the comment seriously. "I don't hate men. I adored my stepdad. It's . . . it's the, uh, the act itself. You know what I mean? It's . . . it seems so vile."

"Oh, yeah," says Nicole. "Agreed. Vile is the word. So disgusting I doubt I could do it more than five times a night. As for ten? He'd have to be Crom-twisted gorgeous."

Marya laughs, all shock and delight, until even Aoife joins in. And slowly, the group cooperates in getting her away from the horrifically unlucky subject of "after."

But then Megan of all people digs it up again in the middle of a particularly bad hand.

"I don't care if I don't make it," she says, and Nessa feels a chill on her heart. "I mean it. The country is done for, and we all know that's the truth. Aoife is right. Even the survivors have nothing to look forward to except decline and old crones with tightened assholes in charge of everything."

Marya, however, is a true believer and surprises them all by smacking the table with her little fist. "So why bother?" she hisses. "Nobody can make you stay in a survival college if you don't want to. Why not enjoy the rest of your worthless life? You don't have to put up with all the training."

"Oh, I want the training," Megan says, glaring right back at her. "Because the Sídhe did this. They're the ones who ruined everything. Everything! My parents are weeping wrecks. I'll never travel in a plane or climb Everest or whatever Crom-cursed crap everybody had that we don't. But there's something I can do. Something I want more than living forever or flying into space. I want to kill a fairy." She uses the English word for the Sídhe, while both spit and spite fly from her lips. "I want to kill as many of them as I can, but even one would make my life worthwhile. Even one!"

The whole common room has fallen silent at Megan's outburst. Her eyes travel around the table, meeting their gazes one by one. Marya stands abruptly, then circles around to where Megan sits and hugs her hard. "Me too!" she declares. "Me too. I want to be a Fairy Killer." And Nessa, though she never allows herself any show of passion, wishes she had been the one to hug her best and only friend. It's Megan who supports and tolerates Nessa, who gives total loyalty for no other reason, it seems, than that they travel on the same bus.

It's not too late though. Nobody is stopping Nessa from hugging her right this minute.

Yet habit pins her to her chair.

Slowly, wordlessly, they all take up the cards again. Round after round, with Nessa keeping score on a scrap of paper and the rain beginning to weaken, until eight o'clock comes around and Marya insists on tuning the common room's ancient radio to the news station. "I want the lists," she says, and everybody lets her have her way, so that they catch the very first part of the broadcast. The announcer burbles on about how great the survival of the Nation is going today: the achievements, the government appointments, and so on.

"And now," she declares proudly, "the list of today's survivors. We had ten today! From all over the country. So, in order of their return, we have O'Donnell, Charlie. McDade, Elaine—"

Megan grins. "Two Donegal names to start! We are the best!"

Nessa holds up a palm for the high five that must inevitably follow.

But it doesn't. Because Megan is gone, and it will be exactly three minutes and four seconds before any of them see her again.

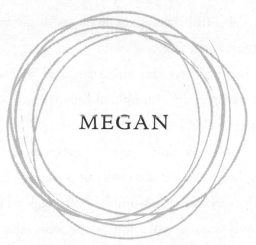

MEGAN

S odden rock walls rise to either side of Megan, but not so far away that she can't reach out and touch them. She is terrified. All her brave talk of a few moments before is worth less now than a breath of the heavy stinking air at the bottom of the canyon in which she finds herself. She pants, trying desperately to make herself move.

"Stupid wee bitch," she tells herself, and her voice echoes from the dripping walls. Then she all but leaps out of her skin when a horn sounds. "Crom twist you!" she shouts, outraged at her own cowardice. Then she turns. She turns and runs *toward* the place where the sound came from.

A rock has appeared in her fist and she has no memory of picking it up. All she knows is the voice in her head, Sergeant Taaft's, screaming at her to run, to run for her life. And then she is around the corner, smacking into a woman so beautiful that in the last century she would have launched a hundred stupid magazines.

"How delightful!" the Sídhe manages to say before Megan makes a cavern of her face.

"One for me," says the girl, struggling to keep her food down. She stumbles on, triumph and nausea and terror all still fighting for control of her belly.

The canyon splits into a dozen passages, each barely wide enough for her to run along without scraping shoulders and elbows with every step. She stumbles over rough rocks and slides on Lugh only knows what foul excretions. She follows the echoes of laughter, gripping her pathetic weapon, praying to her mother's God that she'll take one more Sídhe, just one, down with her.

And then, somehow, the hunt has passed her by. The laughter grows fainter, trailing off in the direction from which she herself has come.

She has been in the Grey Land less than twenty minutes and already she has thrown off the pursuit. She stands confused, trying to deal with the bizarre idea that she might not have to die. "Thank you, God," she whispers, and finds herself trembling, uncontrollably. Did she really smash in somebody's skull? Now the vomit comes, and the force of it is enough to push a stream of tears from her eyes too.

But, yes, why shouldn't she live? She deserves it more than Conor and a whole lot of others. She has dropped her stone, but she retrieves it and grips it hard, blood and all. "It's more of the same if any of you stand in my way," she growls.

And off she goes again, through the endless maze of rock, before they realize their mistake.

The geography of the Grey Land makes little sense to Megan. The canyon walls at some points widen, while at others they close in around her. That seems normal enough. What puzzles her is the way the materials of which the walls are made change from one type of stone to another, when surely if water or weather had formed these passages, the rocks would have eroded at different speeds? And why are there no plants growing here?

And then, without warning, she hits a dead end.

Megan doubles back, running a full two hundred yards in the wrong direction before she can find another viable passage. But again, although the walls of this one are made of what appears to be millions of pebbles crammed together, it too ends in the same place. And then, just as she is trying for a third passage, she hears the hunting horn.

They're coming back. They're coming back for her and she wants to weep with rage.

"I could lead you out!"

She turns to find a creature standing less than a couple feet behind her. It hunches low like an ape. One of its long clawed arms constantly touches the earth around it as though unsure of its reality, while the other is used to hide its face, so that its Sídhe words, though comprehensible, are muffled. The spines of a porcupine cover the rest of its body, but so thick are they clumped, and so inappropriately placed, that the creature impales itself with every movement.

Megan tightens her grip on the rock. "Why would you help me?" The Testimonies are full of warnings against trusting the monsters of the Grey Land. Half the beasts adore their Sídhe creators, while the rest crave human meat.

"Carry my message back with you to Ireland. That is all I ask. My only price."

The horn sounds again and the creature jumps, cutting itself some more. "Tell Red Hugh not to go to Kinsale. Do you understand me? He's not to go. The English have it surrounded. This is the last favor I'll ever do him. The last!"

"All right. I'll pass your message along." Megan follows the creature as it leads her back toward the horns. She would have agreed to anything to save herself, but is puzzled why it thinks she can bring a message to a man who died hundreds of years ago, for who else can the recipient be but Red Hugh O'Donnell? She has only heard of him at all through an accident of birth, since he too came from Donegal. Yet somehow this tiny connection makes the monster's offer of help more real to her.

Then the voices of her enemies cry out in excitement over some clue she has left behind. Their proximity drives all thoughts of the mystery from her mind.

"This way!" says her monster, ducking down a side passage. But it's too late! It's too late! The first of the Sídhe is right ahead of her, a spear in his hand, a great grin on his face. "She is here!" he cries. "She is hiding with a traitor!"

She throws her rock with every iota of force in her body, aiming for the head. It catches him in the chest with a crunch of bone, but already other excited footsteps are coming along behind him.

She sprints after the guide, who may, or may not, be leading her into a trap, but what difference can it make now?

The walls widen out, and stone gives way to packed earth riddled with holes. She sees many of the spiny creatures here, and the sight of her sends them into a panic as they desperately cover their faces and leap into their burrows. And Megan has no choice, none at all, but to follow her ally into what she supposes to be its own lair. Soil falls on her head near the entrance; a death trap, she thinks, but it turns to harder clay farther in.

She's praying again, praying that none of the creatures will betray her, and that by the time the Sídhe have figured out which one of the hundred holes is hers, she will be back at home.

But it's hopeless, of course it is! And her plight gets worse, because no more than six feet into the burrow, her supposed friend comes to a stop.

"Keep going!" she says to it.

"This is my home," it replies mournfully. "We traitors are allowed to dig no deeper than this. Nor can we. Only rock lies ahead." Megan wants to weep. To cut herself beating at the monster's spiny body. "They might not find us though!" it says. "They might not!"

Then the poor grey light at the entrance to the hole disappears.

"Hello, thief," says a beautiful voice.

Megan freezes.

"Listen," it says, "most of the day remains for us to play, you and I. Almost all of it. Imagine what I shall do to you. And as you suffer, little one, as you suffer, think on this: The place where you gather to train, the place where you found our sister in the rock? We will kill all of your tribe who remain there. A dozen days of your time, perhaps a score. And we will come for them. I tell you this because it is a happy final thought for you . . ."

The man who is speaking pokes his head in, reaching blindly with his deadly hands. But Megan has hands too and, before he knows what has hit him, she has taken his eyeballs so that he falls back in confusion and the other Sídhe call out in admiration of her clever attack.

She has no time to waste basking in their praise, however. To the protests of the terrified monster behind her, she caves in the loose soil at the entrance to the burrow.

"We'll smother," it cries.

"No, we won't. Unfortunately. They'll dig me out long before that." There is no escape from the Grey Land now but death, and it can be quick or it can be terrible beyond all imagining. "Give me one of your spines."

"Why?"

"Just give it to me. *Please!*" And the desperation in her voice must have convinced it, because in no time at all she has one in her hand and she begins stabbing at the skin of her wrists.

The digging has begun outside, and the laughter. And the taunting.

"Your time has come, thief!"

She cuts deeper, tears streaming from her eyes. The spines are all but useless.

"How beautiful you will be when we are done with you! And then you will die!"

"Oh, yeah?" she screams at them. "Oh, yeah? Well, I had fourteen years of life in the Many-Colored Land. Do you hear me? I had the wind on my face, and by Danú's tits it smelled sweet. And everything was green and alive and lovely. And the sun shines there; can you imagine it? Can you see the streams full of fish? The heavy orchards? You can't. You never will, but every one of my ancestors had that. Every one for two thousand years! While your only pleasures are jealousy and blood!"

A great wailing sound comes from beyond the earth wall.

"You will stop, thief! You will stop this!"

"Bees!" cries Megan. "I sat outside when the whins were all golden flowers and the bees flew among them! And the sounds that you will never, never hear, you empty fools. The birds in the morning. The foxes barking at night under the glory of the stars. I had it all and I'll take all of it to my grave. And taste! Strawberries picked in our garden. By the Cauldron!"

"I'll shut her up!" says one of them now.

He catches poor Megan by surprise as his hand shoots through the remaining thin layer of soil and pulls her right out of her burrow. "I'll shut her up," he says again.

It's strange, because in all the Testimonies the Sídhe are described as joyful. But a dozen of them around her are sobbing.

He continues to hold her by the neck, while blood runs down her wrist from the cuts she made.

Megan manages a smile. "I hope you live forever." She grins. "*Here.*"

And then her captor reaches across with his elegant, free hand, and covers her mouth.

LAMENT

Megan returns. Dead. Her eyes wide. But no other expression can be identified on her face, because her nose and mouth have been erased as though smudged out by the hands of a child on a chalkboard.

"She suffocated," somebody says. "She must have been mocking them; you know how she is."

Nessa's vision blurs. She is hyperventilating, as though she is the one in danger of suffocation, whose mouth is to be sealed. She has imprisoned her emotions for four years, but now they will have their way with her.

A chair crashes to the ground and so does she.

Hands lift her. Nessa shrugs them off and there's a scream, like that of a wild, desperate animal.

"Nessa! Don't! Wait!"

The rain is freezing on her face and she doesn't know how she got outside. Beyond the college buildings is only blackness and mud. She scrambles through it on all fours, scraping her skin on the trunks of trees, with wails pushing themselves randomly from her raw throat.

It is impossible in such conditions, on such a moonless night, for anybody to navigate the forest. But Nessa's path is unerring, though her legs keep betraying her and her hands are soon cut to ribbons. Eventually—she knows nothing of time now, knows nothing at all—those same hands are pulling her upright against a chain-link fence. Here, here in this *presence*, enough of her mind comes back to her to ask a simple favor: "Take me," she begs. Megan's wrists had been all bloody. She must have tried to kill herself. She must have failed. The pain she suffered! Oh, Crom! "Take me!"

Nobody answers and she screams her demand again as rain streams over her face and makes a sodden wreckage of her tracksuit.

But then she remembers the path. She remembers the *door* in the cliff. She pulls herself around, looking for the spot. Ms. Breen has had the fence repaired of course. And it's supposed to be guarded at all times. But Nessa knows that it will have been broken again, that the guards will be huddling out of the rain in their hut. She will find her way inside. The door will recognize her emptiness and admit her. It must do.

Nausea! She had forgotten the nausea. Like a fist in the belly. Instead of welcoming her, she is pushed away. Nessa's journey here has stolen every last scrap of strength and all she has left is the pitiful pleading of a child.

"Please . . . I need her . . . Please . . . I have no other friends . . ." She has treated the whole world with disdain and this is her reward.

"There she is!" cries a voice. "Pull her away."

A blanket materializes about her shoulders.

"I hate this place, by Crom. Let's get her back."

An impossibly strong arm lifts her onto a boy's shoulders. He smells familiar. And there are girls' voices, arguing excitedly. "I swear, Nicole," says Aoife, "I'm trying. It was easy to find the mound, it drew us right here, but I think we're lost now."

"It's this way," Marya says, flighty Marya! And she adds, "Don't worry, Nessa, pet. We've got you. We've got you."

Nessa does not leave her bed the next day. Nobody can make her. Nor can they force open her jaws to give her food.

"I don't understand," somebody says. "You've fought so hard to live. What if they Call you now? Do you . . . ?" Do you want to end up like *her*, they might be saying.

Whoever it is, they are right. Nessa's Call is not so very far away, and however much pain she is in now, it will all shrink to insignificance the instant she sets foot in the Grey Land.

But in the end, what pulls her back is the poetry.

On what might be the third or the fourth day, somebody has the bright idea of digging out her books and shoving them into her hands. She flicks idly through them and that smooth face of hers, once so impassive, twists into the ugliness of a sneer. What is this? What is any of this? Page after page of *nonsense*.

"I loved a maid who—" *Useless! Useless!* She rips it out.

"How lovely your shod feet—" *Empty crap!*

"Sweet girl, I hear your song and—" Another page torn and crumpled and flung away. She'll burn it; she'll burn all of it and everyone! How did she waste her life on this, on any of this? Spoiled men and women balked in their lust? For the first time in days laughter fills the empty dorm. But it is not a gentle sound.

And then her eyes fall on a few blurry lines, marked with what might be the tears of another owner.

> *Your blood flowed out of you*
> *And I didn't try to clean it*
> *But drank it from my palms*

The words startle her. They remind her of Megan's poor wrists and they have no place surely in a collection of love poetry! Which might explain why she has never read past the first few lines before.

"Lament for Art Ó Laoghaire," the title says, and it is not suitable for the young. Not suitable for anybody really, this ferocious screed of outrage, of fury, of pain. Untranslatable, its rolling Gaelic syllables echo in the bones and the teeth. It is a ghost. It is a curse. It is the last great cry for justice of a murdered culture before the darkness came to take it away, and Nessa swallows every word of it from start to finish.

She goes back to the beginning to read it again, aloud, as it must be read, her voice shattered like that of a hag, her bloodshot eyes wide with rage.

After the third reading she drops the book and falls immediately asleep on top of it, smearing the pages of the Lament and staining her skin with its old ink.

———————

It is Ms. Breen herself who shakes her awake.

"I'm hoping, child, you'll take some food? If not—"

"Yes," the girl interrupts. "I want it. Megan would want me to have it."

The head of the college feared she would have to send the girl home to her parents for a while. Or worse, to the hospital to be force-fed. It wouldn't be the first time such a thing has happened. Now, however, she smiles. "Listen," she says, "I've made the announcement to the rest of the students already. It's . . . it's about Megan. In a way it's horrible, but . . . but it's amazing too."

"Tell me."

"You saw the blood on her wrists?"

A nod is all Nessa can manage, her newfound strength suddenly dipping again.

"Megan wasn't trying to kill herself. She . . . she had a message for us. She knew she would die. She knew she would be sent back and she . . . she cut a warning for us into her own skin."

"The Sídhe can't read," breathed Nessa.

"As far as we know. And probably not in English anyway."

"Megan always preferred it," Nessa manages through a catch in her throat. "What . . . what did it say?"

"Just three words. *Our school next*. They're coming for our college. Any day now. They want to wipe us out the way they did the schools in Bangor and Mallow. I thought . . . I thought we should maybe evacuate, but—"

"No!" Nessa sits up violently. "No! We stay here! We kill them all! We're trained! We'll cut the lot of them, we'll—"

She's still weak enough that even Ms. Breen can push her back onto her pillows. "Yes, child. That's exactly what Nabil wants to do. Exactly. We're the only college to have prior warning. We have drafted in extra instructors from around the country. All our food will be brought in from outside and so on. Don't worry. There's even a cordon of soldiers from the regular army around the mound. Not that they do much these days but guard our biodiesel and the like. But they have guns, and if the Sídhe come here, they will suffer for it."

And Nessa nods. "I want to see Anto," she says.

"I'm not sure that's appropriate . . ."

But for a little while everybody will treat Nessa like a delicate piece of glass and she can do anything she wants.

A week goes by. Nessa still cries a lot for Megan. She doesn't hide it from Anto, nor does she conceal the laughter that happens from time to time. And she makes sure to tell him she'll miss him when they part for the night, each to their own bed.

"No more poetry for me?" he asks her one evening.

"There's only one poem now," she answers, "and it's not for you. At least, I hope not."

As for her other friends, she has yet to master the art of hugging them, but Aoife, Marya, and Nicole all have reason to know of her gratitude.

In spite of these changes, Nessa trains harder than ever, eating every available scrap of food for strength, clearing her mind before each sparring session. When she hits the mat, she doesn't need to think before rolling out of the way or yanking opponents by the ankles so that they tumble down to join her.

It doesn't matter. Nessa has far, far less time to prepare than she needs. The same goes for most of her class. Of the original sixty who came here as fresh-faced Year 1s, a higher proportion than ever before will be dead by Christmas. It's going to be a bloodbath.

THE STORM

It is the twenty-first of December and bullets of rain spray against Melanie's window. Beyond, ancient trees cower before a wind that, in spite of its strength, can't seem to break up the freezing fingers of mist rising to waist height about the buildings of the college.

It's finally happening, she thinks, and she has to control her breathing like the doctors taught her or the hole in her chest will kill her. This time tomorrow night, she will be beautiful again. She will be whole, because the Sídhe always keep their word.

She sets off across the parking lot with the windup flashlight she inherited from her grandfather.

They meet in the kitchens, and for the first time she sees those who will be working with her. She wants to weep, for what better sign could there be of her own evil than the identity of her allies? Horner was on guard duty for the kitchens. Now the blood of his only friend stains his hands, and his teeth too, if she's not mistaken.

Then there's the survivor from Year 5—Conor his name is. "I got most of the dogs," he says. He's breathing hard, failing to hide his glee. "Are any of *them* here yet?"

Melanie knows what he means by "them" and her pulse quickens dangerously. *How?* she wonders *How did I end up here?* But she has seen the Grey Land and seen their power too. The Cauldron and all the rest. Everybody at the school will die no matter what she does. The only question is whether she will be joining them. And what would be the point of that?

Sweat runs down her face and Horner licks the last of the blood from his lips. Then the door from the refectory opens and she thinks it's another conspirator. Instead it turns out to be Frankenstein. Horner grins, producing a knife, and Melanie has a crazy notion of throwing herself at the ex–special forces soldier to save the life of this wasted old man.

"Wait!" Conor warns the soldier. "He's with us. You are, aren't you, Frankenstein?"

The old man nods. His whole body seems to pulse in the light of Melanie's flashlight.

"I want what I was promised," says Conor. "I still have a lot of friends here. I won't enjoy hurting them, so you'd better keep your word."

Frankenstein is swelling before their eyes. His voice is harsher, hoarser, more muffled than ever. "We always keep . . . our word . . . you will . . . have what . . ."

He explodes. Pieces of flesh spatter across the kitchen and Melanie can't resist a gasp when something warm and slimy hits her on the cheek.

Impossibly, Frankenstein, now a mass of blood and viscera, still lives. He shakes himself like a dog before wiping his face. Underneath lie the features of an angel. Of a Sídhe.

"I used the flesh of a thief," the newcomer explains, "to stay here in the Many-Colored Land. From this moment on, the world of our exile will call me back."

"You'll get smaller?" Melanie says, overcoming her disgust. She has seen far worse than this in the Grey Land. "Is that it? You'll shrink to nothing? But surely . . . I mean . . . It will happen fast, like it did in Bangor, won't it?"

"Not as swiftly as before. Our worlds circle each other like motes in a pool. Far away sometimes. But when they draw close, as now, our grip grows strong and bargains with such as you may open doors."

Melanie opens her mouth to ask what he means about opening doors, but the bloody prince cuts her off. He wants to know if they have each kept their part of the bargain. And so Horner shows his knife and Conor repeats his boast about killing the dogs.

When the handsome grin turns to focus on her again, Melanie removes a shaking hand from her pocket and produces the keys she stole some weeks before and copied. They belong to a shed behind the college and she has no idea why her part in the murder of her own people lies in procuring them. But the Sídhe is more delighted with her than with either of the killers.

"You will be whole again, sweet thief, and while we will allow you no children, you may live out your natural span." She shudders, feeling tears pricking at the corners of her eyes.

The shed, it turns out, has a steel door and is full of priceless fuel. A few more human men and women, strangers to her, slosh it generously all along the ground floor of the student dorms, hiding their faces from each other, or openly weeping as they work. For some reason, nobody upstairs awakens and none of the guards comes to investigate the flashlight beam.

By the time they have finished, the Sídhe lord is a head shorter than Melanie, but still as perfectly proportioned as a Greek statue and delighted by everything he sees.

"Are . . . are you going to light it now?" Melanie asks him.

"Not yet, sweet thief," he answers. But he doesn't say what he is waiting for.

"And what about me?" Conor asks. "I don't see this getting me what *I* want."

"We always keep our word," the Sídhe replies. "The power of a promise is all that keeps our two worlds together."

———

Fifty soldiers guard the mound.

They waste vast quantities of fuel to keep spotlights trained on the little hill, and have spent the last few days cutting down the surrounding trees to provide themselves with a clear field of fire. Not that they expect anything to come out of there. Mainly they have been told to keep the kids away, the ones who are always coming back, for whatever reasons.

Private Shields can't understand what the students see in the Fairy Fort. He is one of the very few young men and women who have not only survived the Call but have been judged safe enough afterward to wield weapons in the defense of fuel convoys and warehouses and whatever other resources the Nation has left. Only he knows how close he has come on several occasions to turning the barrel of his gun the wrong way. Or how he smashes all the furniture when he argues with his wife, until their small daughters plead with him to stop.

But he's trying. Every day he's trying and making progress.

"What are you staring at?"

It's Rebecca—Private Madigan. Barely twenty-five and already the mother of three. Even then she had to fight to be allowed to join up without having any more.

"Staring?" he asks. Like many of the young, they still speak in Sídhe among themselves.

"You're staring at the mound."

It's hard to see it through the curtain of rain, luminescent in the glare of the spotlights, but eventually he finds an answer for her.

"The color's wrong," he says. "I know . . . I know that's just the . . . the *night*. The rain or whatever. You know."

They watch it together for a moment. Neither can feel the mound's presence as the students do, but their eyes begin to play tricks on them.

"I think," says Private Shields, "I think I'm having one of my flashbacks." He points a shaking finger out from under the flap of the tent. "Is that . . . is that *slicegrass* growing there?"

"By all the gods," says Rebecca, "I think you're right. I think it's happening."

"What?" he asks. "What's happening?"

He has no idea she's been holding a dagger this whole time until she slides it into his kidneys. By then she has her hand over his mouth and she whispers in his ear. "Yes, it definitely looks like slicegrass to me. There's a spider tree behind it. See?" She lowers him to the ground and needs now to kill the rest of the sentries, but she's too slow. Humanlike figures are pushing themselves out of the earth all over the mound, as though climbing from a stormy sea onto the deck of a boat.

On the other side of the hill, a gun barks out and one of the figures jerks and falls forward, still half immersed.

Time to fight, Rebecca thinks. She wants what she's been promised. Wants it more desperately than anything in the world. And so she sprays the nearby tents with an antique semiautomatic, reloads and single-shots the sergeant, who barely has time to say, "Private Madigan, what are—"

Several of her comrades have made it out of their tents with weapons loaded. Most aim for the figures on the hill, but a few shots come her way too until she throws herself flat and feels the air above her head humming with death.

She curses and reloads, her hands as steady as ancient boulders. But there's no need to fire a second burst, for a few of the Sídhe have made it off the slopes now to run riot among the soldiers. The most beautiful woman Rebecca has seen since her Call taps a man once on the neck. He falls, grabbing at his melted windpipe, while her other hand sinks through the captain's head as though it were jelly. Rebecca feels like she is flying. Like she is a goddess. Only once before in her twenty-five years has she felt so alive. Only once.

Now a dozen Sídhe—no, a score of them!—are dancing naked among the humans, until finally the first of them, the young woman, is standing over Rebecca.

"We have promised," she says. "We have promised to allow you eternal life in the Grey Land."

"Thank you," Rebecca says, her voice barely audible above the fizzing rain.

"Wait here then," the princess says. "Until the killing is done."

"I'm not staying here!"

The Sídhe's grin widens. "Come then, sister. Join us!"

And Private Madigan's heart leaps. She has tears in her eyes and a knife in her hands as they run off toward the college.

Ms. Breen runs into Conor on the ground floor of the staff corridor.

"What . . . Conor? What are you doing here?"

He grins. "It's all right. I'm one of you. Honestly! Even me! And it's happening. It's happening tonight. They're already arriving."

She glances nervously toward the bedrooms, each with a veteran, or a highly trained instructor.

"Oh," Conor says; he's holding a can of kerosene and he waves it about gaily. "Don't worry. They're not supposed to wake up. It'd take an earthquake, it—"

Ms. Breen has no idea what he's talking about. She has just come home from the bedside of a dying friend and finally, finally it hits her that something is deeply wrong here. She begins to back away, her palms sweaty against the wall of the corridor. This is a mistake. Conor narrows his eyes, sending a chill through her. He's very large for a fourteen-year-old. Man-sized really, and muscled like the great athlete he is. And she has just given herself away.

Her time runs out. He drops the can and the liquid spatters everywhere. He pulls her away from the wall and flings her back again. "Oh, I get it now," he says, shaking his head in disappointment. "Another mess I'm supposed to clean up. This will give me no pleasure, by Crom, no pleasure at all." He cocks his right fist. "I was never one of the kids who mocked you behind your back."

He doubles her over with a punch. Ms. Breen coughs, having no wind with which to shout for help. "Even though you were so ugly. Like something the Sídhe spent an hour working on!" Her glasses crunch under his boots, and without them she is patting desperately at the wall, as if it's the mat in the gym and she's asking for mercy. "What? You think you can *surrender*? To me? The future king of all Ireland?" He grins ruefully. But only until her fingers find the fire alarm she was looking for.

In the stories it is often church bells that awaken dreamers from a fairy's spell. This alarm is far louder than any of those. It is insistent, impatient, and brutal beyond words.

Nabil and Taaft leap apart, their decades of training urging them to untangle limbs and surge from the bed.

"Get off me, get off, you Arab shit!"

"I am a Frenchman, you whore. French!"

The door shatters and a beautiful child stands on the far side, its eyes huge, its mouth fixed in a grin.

Nabil stands helpless as the alarm continues to scream at him. Why, he wonders, is the boy's head so small? Why is he naked? And how did the door break down like that?

As though it's all a dream, a small hand stretches out—

Then a book flies past Nabil's shoulder and smacks the boy right between the eyes, so that he tumbles backward into the corridor, where, already, an army of tiny figures gathers.

"That's not a child, you stupid frog!"

And suddenly a shiver passes through the Frenchman's body, as he recognizes those large eyes from a hundred illustrations. And such is his shock that all he can think to say is "You threw my Koran at it?"

"I knew you were an Arab!"

He has no time to reply to her deliberate ignorance, because the chest-high figures are reaching toward him and he remembers what he has been telling the students for years: *Don't let them get their hands on you! Never the hands!*

He jumps back, but Taaft . . . Taaft is not as confused as he is. She has made a morning star for herself, swinging the strap of a metal canteen to crack the first Sídhe across the nose. It laughs at the pain, but falls and trips those that follow. And finally, Nabil has recovered enough to join in. His feet are deadly. He smacks a girl in the abdomen.

"By God!" he cries. "They weigh as much as adults!"

Taaft screams as a hand brushes her own and leaves a dent in it. "I'm all right," she cries. "Keep them out, keep them out!" She breaks a tiny neck. He cracks a little skull. They have made a pile of bodies that is impeding the others behind it, although the corridor is crawling with them.

But then a human, an actual human, is standing at the door in a soldier's uniform. She points an ancient Steyr AUG rifle into the room. "Time to die," she says with a grin. There's no cover for the instructors, no cover at all.

An almighty crash comes from the corridor and the soldier foolishly looks away from her targets. Two Sídhe seem to fly at her, to strike her full in the face. As she goes down, more bodies fly over her. Nabil hears bones crunching. He sees blood spatter the walls. And then Anto comes past swinging that huge arm of his, smashing the enemy like a bag of grapes until they flee before him.

The boy pauses at the door, his face a mask of Sídhe blood.

"I thought you didn't like to kill." Taaft always was great at diplomacy. "You wouldn't hurt a fly."

All Anto says in reply is "Can't you smell it?"

"The blood?"

"The burning. They're burning the student dorms." And off he runs.

Nessa wakes, the alarm so loud it hurts and the stench of smoke heavy on the air. Her main concern is the hand reaching for her face.

Unlike Nabil, unlike almost everybody, Nessa never freezes in surprise. She grabs the wrist, twists once, and rolls out onto the floor.

"Get up!" she cries to wake her friends, but screams are drowning her out. She crawls on all fours to stay under the smoke that rolls in from the direction of the stairs. It's glowing out there, as fire spreads through sloshes of kerosene deposited by gangs of human traitors.

The sound of laughter fills the room, along with the slap of small feet on the floorboards.

Nessa finds Nicole with four dents in her forehead where fingers pushed into it. She hears Marya curse in the name of the Cauldron, but the sound is cut off all too quickly.

Then Aoife falls to the ground right in front of Nessa. Other girls used to mock her for her sloth, but of all of them, Aoife is the only one to think of throwing a sheet over her attacker. It's so, so simple! The terrible hands can't touch her skin, and as the creature fought to free itself, she must have leaped on top of it, bringing it to the ground.

It struggles though. As strong as a full-grown human until Nessa's powerful fist rams into the side of its head.

"We have to go for the window," Nessa says. "We can drop out onto the bushes . . ." They may break their legs, but it's a chance, isn't it?

Three other girls are still resisting the invaders with their superb training, but already flames have entered the room, and, though they don't know it yet, even the attic has been doused with fuel and the roof is fiercely burning in defiance of the weather.

They crawl from bed to bed as the last of their comrades die, as the floorboards above them weaken and the Sídhe get smaller.

One of the enemy cries, "She's missing! She got away!" And Nessa thinks, *You're wrong! Two of us are getting away!*

"We have an agreement," the Sídhe insists, and several of them run through the smoke as though in a panic.

The window is no more than six feet away and already open, with poor Rachel from Year 3 lying dead beneath it.

"I want you to go first," Aoife whispers.

"No! It has to be you. It—"

A roar comes from behind them. A human voice raised in outrage and horror.

Anto is there, coughing and hacking with the smoke. He needs to get down! To get under it! He could die!

But he scatters the Sídhe.

"Go," Nessa says to Aoife. "He's here for me. Get to the window. Now! Now!"

Aoife lurches forward. Then a support falls, caving in half the ceiling. And Nessa is right beneath it.

Anto staggers, blinded by the smoke, hacking his lungs up.

He prepares his cursed arm for a swing as another figure stumbles toward him, but stops in time when he recognizes Aoife's voice.

"You've got to get her out. Nessa! She's going to burn to death! She's burning!"

She's under a bed apparently, which itself lies under a flaming beam of wood. And for the first time since his Call Anto thanks all the gods and the Cauldron and the Sídhe themselves for the horror they have worked upon his body. Because nothing else they could have done to him would have made him better suited to rescue the girl he loves. No other human, no group of humans, could shift such a weight.

He screams as burning wood chars his skin. He hacks and coughs. He is mere minutes away from collapse with the smoke, but when he finally throws off the beam, relief fills him, for the bed didn't take the full weight of it. He and Aoife push the mattress aside . . .

But instead of Nessa, all they find are empty pajamas.

He stares at the clothes in horror. He'll stay there and die there, except Aoife drags him away and shoves him face-first out the window. She tumbles down after him to lie in the bushes.

Above them, the whole first floor is now ablaze.

In three minutes and four seconds, Nessa will return to it, either dead or alive. The flames will consume whatever's left.

NESSA

Nessa has always intended to survive her Call, regardless of what anybody else thinks. But now, lying on her back with the silver spirals above her head, and air that burns worse than the smoke she just left behind, she knows she is going to die.

In three minutes and four seconds, flames will be eating the bed that was protecting her from the burning ceiling. The floor will char with heat intense enough to cook her in the time it takes to blink. Here or there, she is dead. Her parents will sink from fear of loss into its certainty, and Anto . . . Anto will have nobody to leave secrets beneath his pillow; to drag him to Donegal and garden with him in the shadow of Mount Errigal.

Nessa is not given to self-pity, but now it threatens to smother her, and not even the sound of a hunting horn can shift it.

She finds herself lying on a small flat area at the top of a slope so steep that in parts it resembles a cliff. A stream runs down the face of it, leaving acidic muck in its wake all the way down to the bottom. Nessa ignores it. She also ignores the wrist-thick worms with human faces that emerge from the mud to taste her skin. *Is she edible?* they wonder nervously. *Is she bait to trap them?*

The horn sounds again, closer now, and Nessa struggles with herself until the part that never surrenders finally gains dominance. She's already thinking of standing up when the footsteps come pounding toward her and, in a heartbeat, a gang of Sídhe stands about her in a semicircle.

"Why doesn't it run?" one asks.

"Its legs," a woman says. She wears a cloak of human skin, decorated with startling patterns of bone. "We should fix them for her. Make them like an ostrich's and she would give us more sport than this!"

The woman bends down, and only now does the girl remember that avoiding the Sídhe is more than just a matter of life or death: It's about agony too; about the outrages they work on human flesh and bone before sending the remains home as a souvenir for the friends and parents. Far better to face the fire than whatever they have planned for her!

But before the hands can touch her, another Sídhe arrives, out of breath and laughing.

"No, my friends!" he cries. "Not this one! This one is not ours to kill! We have made a promise to one of the thieves that only he may end her life. Not us! He will do so with bare hands and we shall make him king of all the Milesians!"

Nessa sits up. "Who is this? Who are you talking about? Conor? You have made a deal with . . ."

The newcomer is the most handsome man she has ever seen. His face is kind and full of humor as he kicks her in the side hard enough to knock her over onto her stomach. He laughs, and the huge worms slither away in terror.

Now Nessa has a view of the swamp at the bottom of the hill. Beyond it lie thousands and thousands of tents. Grey banners fly over them while hordes of tiny figures mill around the one spot of color she can see: a vibrant green blob that shines and sparkles.

"We can't kill her," the newcomer says, "but we *can* play, yes? We can twist her any shape we like so long as she can live an hour in the Many-Colored Land. Let us make her a spider! The thief king can break her legs off one by one!"

"No!" a woman insists. "Her legs should be plaited into her arms. We can bend her spine so that she makes a perfect ring! We will bring her with us on the invasion. It will raise morale when we roll her among the tents."

Nessa's limbs turn liquid with terror. Oh, Crom! Far, far better to find her own death! So, with one hard jerk of her arms, she shoots herself forward and over the lip of the slope. She expects to tumble down that sheer hill, breaking bones all the way, but there is far too much muck for that, and instead she slides over the water-slicked surface faster than an Olympic toboggan-ist, while cries of joy and applause and the sounding of hunting horns ring out behind her.

A mass of hungry spider trees lie in wait at the bottom of the slope. They like rivers and other marshy areas, but they enjoy human flesh more. They snatch at her as she hurtles past, each attempt scratching her skin and slowing her down. By the time she comes to a stop, three separate plants grip at one limb each, tightening and squeezing like pythons.

"Crom take you all!" she cries "Lugh curse you! Dagda reject you!"

She rips at the nearest with her teeth. The sap tastes like blood, but the thought of what the Sídhe have planned for her, and Conor after them, keeps her snarling and snapping until she can rip an arm free.

The horn is sounding and her enemies, who have tumbled bravely after her, are no more than a hundred paces behind.

And yet, when at last Nessa finds her feet, she must pause. The camp of the Sídhe army lies only a few hundred strides away and it's huge. There are baggage "animals" and lumbering war monsters of tortured human flesh. But it is the glowing spot of color she saw from the top of the slope that draws her eyes. It hangs in the air above the army and its shape is that of a door— the same door she saw in the Fairy Fort in the forest. The *exact* same.

Sídhe soldiers, by the thousand, are building a mound of earth and stone. By the rate they're going, it will be high enough to reach that glowing portal in less than a day.

But then fingers are pointing from the camp, and with cries of delight dozens of figures come running toward her. Meanwhile, behind her, her pursuers have freed themselves from their own spider bushes and those terrible hands can't be more than a minute from taking her.

———————

A massive rhododendron saves the lives of Aoife and Anto, despite a thick trunk at its heart that bounces them toward the sparser foliage on the edges.

The boy is coughing and weeping. "She's gone," he says. "Oh, God, she's gone!" and Aoife hugs him like she wishes she was hugged when Emma was stolen.

Aoife is terribly aware of the mound off to the west. The feeling is stronger than it's ever been, and for some strange reason the image of a huge door keeps appearing in her mind. It's about to open, she thinks, and she wonders if that means her Call is imminent.

But she can't think about that now, because they are in a terribly dangerous place. Fire spits from the windows above them and something strange is happening in the old parking lot. Hundreds of people are gathering there, adults and children alike. No! *Not* children. She shivers when she finally understands what she's looking at. Belly-high Sídhe are herding the population of Boyle ahead of them and forcing them to kneel on the soaking, cracked concrete.

Before them all stands a tall, muscular human boy, proud and powerful: Conor.

Behind Nessa, the stream feeds into a small lake.

She staggers into the water as the Sídhe rush toward her. It stings every cut and bruise on her body, but despite her legs, Nessa is as strong a swimmer as any in her class, and she makes it to the far bank before the resident monster can do more than shout curses after her. It catches a few of the Sídhe though, forcing the rest of the hunters to run around the banks with spider trees slowing them all the way.

She has gained herself a few minutes. No more. And nowhere does she see any trees with branches thicker than a finger—not a single one. Nessa has always bet big on the ability to make crutches here, but instead her only chance now is to find a place to hide.

So she gets down on her hands and knees to stay out of the line of sight, and she clamps down hard on the urge to cough that grows stronger with every breath of the foul air.

In front of her lies a great flat bog of spider bushes and other grass-type plants. But a strange path runs through all of it, covered with thumb-high clumps of moss and nothing else.

Nessa wants to avoid such open ground, but before she can move a Sídhe girl comes running along it, her face full of laughter, her blonde hair and cloak of human skin flying out behind her. Nessa scrambles around for a rock—any kind of weapon at all!

She won't need it. The Sídhe steps on one of the lumps of moss, and suddenly she's gone, replaced by a hole in the ground. There's the sound of a large splash and a scream. Silence returns to the bog.

Nessa crawls forward. She avoids all the other clumps of moss and comes right up to the lip of the hole. It stretches down, three times her own height, to a pool of bubbling liquid, probably acid because the body of the Sídhe below looks like it's *digesting*.

Small lumps, or sticks maybe, line the inside walls of the pit—perfect handholds and footholds if she wants them. And of course she does! This could be the perfect hiding place!

She climbs in, gagging on the fetid stench of rotting flesh. The Sídhe might never see this hole in the vastness of the bog. But if they do, if they bring their "dogs" or whatever, and climb down to get her, she need only drop into the acid below to kill herself. It will be a horrible, horrible death, but she might not have to avail of it and it can't be any worse than what the Sídhe will do to her, or the flames back home for that matter.

At least I'm fighting, she thinks, looking at the digesting mess below her. *And I've caused this one's death already.*

The sticks in the walls of the pit turn out to be bone of some kind. It chafes at the soles of her feet. She ignores that pain and climbs all the way down until she is no more than a few steps above the dead Sídhe, so that a casual glance from above might not spot her.

The stench is beyond appalling, as the body beneath her continues to bubble and dissolve in the faint silver light of the Grey Land.

Beads of moisture are forming on the surfaces around her. Her hands become slick and, like her feet, they too are chafing. The sticks she thought of as bone more closely resemble teeth. And the shape of the wall is beginning to change, curving inward at the top, with the teeth up there now pointing down. Above her, the hole looks smaller.

"What?" she whispers to the monster whose throat she now occupies. "You don't want me to leave?" It's more like something Megan would have said.

Except Megan would never be this frightened.

"You see," a Sídhe woman says, her head at Conor's hip, "we have made you king of this place." She waves at the locals, on hands and knees in the parking lot. "They all acknowledge it. All these thieves here pledge their loyalty to you."

"On pain of death," Conor says.

"Yes," she agrees. "That is kingship. On pain of death, the weak kneel to the strong and proclaim their love. You have the right now to declare an end to the treaty in this tiny part of the Many-Colored Land."

"And then what?" he asks. But he can't keep the grin off his face, because it's all happening now. Exactly as they promised.

Ms. Breen, battered and bleeding, lies in front of him, having sworn an oath to serve him. Other teachers are here. Some of the instructors even, unable to resist the agony of a Sídhe hand sunk deep into their backs, caressing their organs and threatening to squeeze. He wishes *he* could do that. He wishes he had asked for that power, but it's too late now. "You'll go into the rest of Ireland, won't you? You'll make other kings?"

"We need no others," she says. "The other tribes we destroyed were mere . . . training for us. This is where our exile will end! Here! When our army arrives, we will expand your kingdom. The Gate will open and those who pass through will not grow smaller, but may live and die here! That's what the end of the unjust treaty means. And all the remaining thieves will be yours to rule so long as they bear no children."

Conor thinks back to his Call. To when the Sídhe lord pinched off his arms and legs. The memory shudders through his body, but he also remembers the moments that followed it, and they are in a way the proudest of his life. For he overcame the pain to demand revenge.

"You promised," he says now, "that I would be the one to kill Nessa. Give me that and I will revoke the treaty. *Not* before."

"It must be revoked tonight," she says.

"Then you'd better bring her by tonight. Otherwise the treaty stays."

It's the first time he's ever seen one of the creatures lose their grin, and she's no longer beautiful in its absence, for it has left deep, deep lines behind it in her cheeks and at the corners of her eyes. Like scars. "We cannot control what a thief will do. She may be in that burning hall above us. She may kill herself as so many do before we can play with them."

Conor's chest swells, enjoying her discomfort. "For your sake, she'd better be alive. An oath is an oath. I played my part. I killed the dogs and then strangled two of my friends with my own hands." Liz Sweeney got away from him, but Bruggers . . . Sad to kill a friend. Nevertheless, Conor smiles in satisfaction over a job well done. He'll strangle Nessa too, he thinks. Her white neck was all but designed for it.

He keeps imagining the look there'll be on her face! He'll make her apologize first. He'll make her swear her love. And then he'll do it anyway, yes, he will.

"Bring Nessa to me and I will revoke the treaty."

Nessa is hanging on for her life. It may be a whole hour she's been clinging here, but in the Grey Land who can say? Her arms, her powerful arms, wobble with exhaustion, and her hands are slick with blood, as the teeth slowly, slowly grind into them.

She has decided she doesn't want to die like this, all alone. She wants to see Donegal one more time. She wants to apologize to her parents for how cold she has been with them. And for them to say sorry for their lack of faith in her chances.

They were right of course.

She longs to hug Anto. And she's never seen Megan's grave and wonders if anybody ever visits it with flowers. As for children, that would be nice. They could fill her little cottage while, outside, chickens Anto will never let her eat peck their way through the grain.

She wants all of it. All!

Instead, it's to be acid if she can't hold on, fire if she can. There won't be enough of her left to fill a teacup and everyone will say how they knew she'd never make it, but wasn't it sweet the way she kept trying anyway? Really, *very* touching.

She slips again, curses, spits at the walls in front of her. Prays to her mam's God for her mam's happiness, that she might find peace. Nessa is in almost total darkness now, for in the time she has hung here, the hole above has shrunk to the size of her hand.

"Masster!" a voice cries. "Masster!"

"Oh, good dog! Great dog!" And then a laugh and a shout. "The thief! My dog has found her!"

Feeble light pours in, and above Nessa three beautiful faces stare into the gloom. A resonant male voice calls, "The stomach will not free you, thief. The only reason it has not shaken you off the wall is that it still feeds on my dear, sweet friend. Come! She would want us to have our fun with you! We will drop you a rope! We will pull you free! And after we will take our companion's remains to the Cauldron."

She looks up, to see him above her. The Sídhe all look alike to her, with their glittering skin and large eyes; with their elegance and beauty. Even their hair is all the same color in the pallid grey light. But this one wears a circlet of bone at his forehead and he is much less delicate than the rest: a Hercules with a strange rippling costume that emphasizes the hugeness of his torso.

"Crom take you all!" Nessa spits. "I'd rather die here than at your hands."

"I swear," he says. "I swear we will not kill you."

"Oh! Oh, that's right. You have promised that pleasure to Conor."

"Exactly!" He beams. "Come, take the rope. We will make you truly beautiful, so that your people will gasp to see you."

Nessa ignores the kind offers of help that grow ever more insistent. Her hands and the soles of her feet are in agony, constantly shifting position in search of a comfort that isn't there. Below her, the Sídhe woman is a horror of bubbling bones.

But the presence of the enemy has filled the girl with defiance. She loves their obvious discomfort over the fact that they must break their word to that traitor Conor. She loves it! As time passes, as every joint in her body feels like it's popping out of its socket, as her feet shred, as the foul air savages her throat, she grins a grin every bit as vicious and joyful as theirs.

"You'll never last," the hero pleads with her. "Hours remain!"

"Oh, I'll last!" she cries. "I'll last! And nobody will know it, because I was Called from a burning room and the flames will take me the moment I return! But they were wrong about me.

Everybody was, for I will have survived the Grey Land, and Crom take the polio and the doubters! Crom twist you all!"

"A fire?" the man says. His great brow creases, and Nessa laughs.

"No matter what happens," she says, "you have broken your word. You are liars, no different to us Irish. You are liars and oath-breakers."

A terrible wail breaks out among them, and it sounds as though there are hundreds of them there now, crowding around the pit.

"You must come out," says the man. He leans dangerously forward. "You cannot do this. Do you understand? This cannot be!"

His hands are on the edge of the pit. The sleeves around his wrists are each formed from a human mouth, breathing in distress.

"It doesn't matter." In spite of her pain, Nessa relishes the words. If she must die, nothing can be better than causing these monsters such anguish. "It's not like you can stop me going back to where I came from."

"No," he agrees, "we cannot keep you from the fire. But we can change you! We can change you just enough to prevent it harming you."

Nessa is near the ends of her strength. Ready almost to drop. To let the acid take her while they cry despair over a stupid broken oath. But the princeling above has stirred her interest.

"You can make me"—there is no Sídhe word for this, so she has to invent one—"fireproof? You could do that? Of course you can!" She grins. "But I think I'll just wait here. I'm tired. I'm letting go."

"No!" he shouts. "I beg you, no!"

"You will just twist me anyway."

"Twisting?! Why do you say such a thing? We will make you *beautiful!* You will be a jewel in living flesh!"

Nessa has had enough. She's so weary, in such pain, that the acid mess below her has come to resemble the softest mattress in the world. She struggles to speak.

"Fireproof me then," she says. "And promise you will do me no further harm."

"We never harm! What we do is—"

"Oh, for Crom's sake! You will do nothing that *I* consider harm. Understand me? Do you understand?"

The smile of the hero slips, but he nods solemnly and Nessa knows he will keep his promise. They're so famous for it she wonders why nobody has ever taken advantage of it before. And why do they care so much anyway?

A rope dangles in front of her face, made, she doesn't doubt, of human skin. It doesn't stop her pushing torn hands into the loops they have tied in it so they can lift her up and out. It is only when the Sídhe have taken hold of her arms that she realizes she could have asked for more than just fire protection. She could have demanded health. Strong legs! Anything! But it's too late.

The enemy are standing all around her, hundreds of them and their "dogs." In the distance, the door in the sky is still glowing green. It is brighter than ever now, and the mound they were building is high enough to reach it. A great host fills the plain around it, and she recognizes it for what it is: an invasion force.

"That's right," says the Sídhe hero. "I, Dagda, thank you! For if you had killed yourself below, we would never be able to return to our country, and your people might have survived. By saving yourself, thief, you have killed them. All we need now is for your king to renounce the treaty, and why would he break his promise to us if we have kept ours?"

"I . . . I don't understand," she says.

His grin is back, more powerful than ever. All of the Sídhe are laughing at her.

"I will prepare you for the fire," he says now. "And the pain will be memorable."

He's not wrong.

THE FIRE

Everything is burning. Everything, that is, except Nessa. It doesn't look that way, because the flames dance along her skin and play in her short hair. She breathes out, and that too is fire.

She should laugh, but the Sídhe were no more generous than they had to be, and she hasn't a scrap of strength left in her body. Her palms and feet are still torn, and they hamper her efforts to drag her feeble legs around to the parts of the floor that might just still support her weight.

Burning drapes rage outside the dorm. Windows crack like shotguns going off one after another. On the same stairs she used to skid down on her way to a run, paint now bubbles in the heat, and smoke bends her over in a coughing fit that threatens to shoot her lungs right out of her body.

In the end, Nessa slides down the last few steps on her belly and crawls out the main entrance.

This part of the building has burned the longest and little more than a shell of it remains, held together by scraps of iron and the memories of all the students who have lived and died there.

One fire remains, taller than she is, composed of burning timbers fallen from the upper floors. She barely notices it, but when five Sídhe come running toward her, no higher than her hips, they shy away from the fury of its heat.

"You must come," they urge her. "You must come to him now."

"Or what?" she says, each word a spew of flames from her lips. She can see how desperate they are to make her move, but they have promised her to another and they keep their distance.

The last of the fire she absorbed leaves her skin and her breathing returns to normal, no longer full of flames. Rest is all she can think of. She longs to lie down. But unfinished business remains. And here it comes: Conor strides from the direction of the parking lot, his face furious. He knocks aside the Sídhe, as they beg him, "Revoke the treaty now! Just do it now! Then you can have her! You can have an eternity with her if you want!"

"Come here!" he orders Nessa.

She doesn't move, swaying gently in the tremendous heat of the burning timbers at her back. Her whole body glows with it. She is lovelier than any Sídhe, than Danú herself! His fury shrivels and blows away.

Why? he thinks. *Why did I ask them to let me kill her? Of all the things, of all the things!*

She stands helpless before him. Stunned, he thinks, to see him here in his glory, the king that Ireland has always needed.

And, like a king, he must take charge now, pushing through the boiling air, until, at last, his hands tremble on that slender, lovely throat of hers. It's delicious! He could crush it like a sparrow. Except he can't. And yet he must. What choice have the Sídhe left him?

"Kiss me," she says.

"What?"

"Kiss me first. Just once."

Conor has always wanted her to beg, hasn't he? To apologize. To desire him. And what is a kiss if not all of these things at once?

She leans her long neck back. He can't help it, his lips lead him on, bending forward and down. She wraps her powerful arms around him. Draws him close.

And drops back into the fire.

THE GIANT'S FIST

Somewhere, a door slams shut.

Aoife no longer feels the presence of the mound. Turn her around a few times and she won't even remember where it was. All of the Sídhe shriek with the horror of their loss.

It's enough to wake Anto out of his misery. He screams like a wild beast and charges into the parking lot. Human prisoners scatter before him, but the mourning Sídhe have only ever lived for vengeance, and here now is a worthy target of their hatred.

At least thirty child-sized men and women run in from all angles. Anto meets them with a giant's fist. He sends the first flying into three others, scattering them like skittles. The next he smashes flat, and the sound is the most sickening thing that Aoife has ever heard.

But soon they are all around him, little hands reaching for his ankles, knowing that if they can cripple him, they will swarm him like ants.

Anto doesn't seem to care, but Aoife is terrified for him. She comes in from behind, trying to keep his back clear. She punches a tiny man in the face, but another manages to touch her hand and the pain is enough to bring tears to her eyes. She stumbles back, finding that three more of them have appeared to separate her from Anto's desperate fight.

"It was I who killed your lover, thief," says a tiny woman. Her silken hair flutters like a flag in the breeze. "Her heart lay in my palm, a trembling bird. And then—"

And then the Sídhe woman's head explodes.

Crack, crack, crack! Three more enemies fall with unexplained holes in their bodies and Aoife witnesses a sight so strange that even after this night she will remember it for as long as she lives: Nabil and Taaft—both stark naked apart from boots—are striding across the parking lot. They have armed themselves with the late Private Madigan's weapons, and every bullet finds a target.

In their own world the Sídhe give their lives joyfully, or so the Testimonies say, again and again. But the slamming of the door, the loss of the mound, or whatever that was, seems to have taken the fight out of them. They scatter before the gunfire.

By morning, even the townsfolk are hunting them—a dozen rat-sized people fleeing into the undergrowth. And it is only then that Aoife finds Nessa. She is still alive, by Crom! Like the princess in a story. She sleeps amid a pile of ash, her arms wrapped tenderly around a charred skeleton, a sweet smile on her face.

Of all the buildings, only the gym has escaped damage. In better times, the entire population of the college would squeeze in here to watch a movie on the roll-down screen. Nobody has to squeeze now. Barely fifty chairs hold the survivors from the night before.

Anto intercepts her before she can pass through the double doors. "Nessa!" he cries, torn between outrage and concern. "You're supposed to be in the medical tent!"

Aoife dragged her there as the Red Cross were still setting it up. Before handing Nessa over to the medics, Aoife said, "Don't tell anybody about Conor, you hear me?"

"But . . . Testimony."

"Yes, your Testimony must be honest, I know that. But it ends when the Three Minutes are up, doesn't it? It's about the Grey Land; they don't need to know what comes after that. Your parents don't need to know it."

Maybe Aoife's right. A survivor's Testimony is something that follows them around the rest of their lives, and while nobody will sympathize with Conor, Nessa knows how it might look. Wrong. Vicious. Unnecessary. People don't see women as killers, even now, even after all of this!

Perhaps in time she will feel regret for what she's done, or shame. But not yet. *Not ever!*

"Nessa!" Anto says again. She must have been daydreaming, for she finds herself sliding down the wall until he grabs her with his normal-sized right arm.

"Let me take you back."

"No. I'm staying here." And by "here," she means nestled into the warmth of his body, close enough to sense the beating of his heart, forcing him to bring his larger arm into play just to keep her on her bandaged feet.

She lifts her chin, but hesitates, suddenly aware the whole hall can see them together, her weaknesses exposed.

Then she kisses him anyway. By Crom, it hurts! *Everything* hurts. Even his hair chafes where she's grabbed it with her torn palms, and the pain makes her laugh suddenly, for she never imagined a heaven like this, where even agony serves as a reminder of life, survival, victory. Every sense is screaming for her attention. The smell of him! Sweaty and sooty at once. The scratch of his unshaved chin. The tenderness of his lips and the care with which he curls his massive strength about her frame.

"Do you like farms?" she whispers.

"Farms? Why . . . I don't know. I've—"

"Say yes."

"Yes. Um. I . . . love farms?"

"Good. And Donegal?"

"It's, uh, the best place in the world?"

"Take me inside. I don't think I can walk."

Alanna Breen hobbles in last of all. Past sleeping bags and bandaged faces. Past hanging heads and slumped shoulders. The dragging of her injured leg is the only sound in the place, and with her glistening burns she knows she looks worse than anybody here.

But she owes it to the students to keep her back straight. Only six months ago, some of these were playing with dolls. Most still await the Call, God help them. These are her children, she thinks, and she shakes with a love for them that is every bit as strong as that of their parents. No wonder her reserve crumbles the moment she turns to face the crowd.

She has prepared words that won't come. Instead Alanna Breen, who has never so much as hugged a weeping pupil for comfort, is forced to walk from chair to chair, kissing each person solemnly on the forehead.

On she hobbles, from little Bronagh Glynn, to Cormac O'Malley, to Aoife and Liz Sweeney. There is pudgy Mr. Hickey with burnt bits of his own maps caught in his singed hair, a fierce grin on his face. After him, she finds Nabil and Taaft; the veteran Melanie, looking even more afraid than the others for some reason. Next she comes to the five members of Year 3 who tricked a similar number of Sídhe into getting locked in a basement. She kisses them all, as well as crotchety Ms. Flynn and Lorcan Bianconi and Mitch Cohen . . .

Ms. Breen holds her composure all along the first two rows of chairs. But then she comes to Anto and Nessa. So wrapped up are they in each other that they barely register her presence, or the fact that she has paused before them.

What's wrong? Ms. Breen asks herself. *What's wrong?*

For once the answer is "nothing." They are happy, that's all it is. They are like something transported from the world of her youth to remind her of how things used to be sometimes. How they ought to be, even now.

She starts sobbing, all dignity lost, crying for the ones who didn't make it, for twenty-five years of empty chairs in the refectory. Then everybody is at it, the whole gym filled with their drawn-out despair, until at last the school head recovers herself and shouts, "Enough! Enough!"

At last she can speak, because the truth has finally dawned on her: "We have won a battle," she cries. "Don't you understand? We have won! The Nation must survive! We *will* survive! We are winning! The Nation will survive!"

She has pressed a magic switch that has them all leaping to their feet, yelling the slogan back at her. They're still weeping as they shout, of course, but it doesn't stop them fighting through it. The Nation will survive! The Nation will survive! They scream it loud enough for the whole country to hear.

And perhaps, in the Grey Land of their exile—wherever exactly it may lie—the eternal grins of the Sídhe slip, just a little.

IMAGINE

Four years ago they believed their daughter to be doomed, and were so afraid of the suffering to come they even considered poison.

Yet here she is, beautiful and strong. She has found love. She is a hero of the Nation, whose Testimony will forever change the way people think of the Sídhe. But all she wants now are her mam and dad, as she did when she was an infant.

They feel her arms, strong as anchors, when she hugs them. Her skin against theirs is strangely smooth, like porcelain baked in a kiln.

"I can't stay long," Nessa says. "The doctors want to look at me."

"Where's Anto?" Agnes asks. "Don't we get to meet him?"

They've had a letter from her already, that she sent before she came home, so they know a little of what's gone on, but no details. And, to be honest, the details don't matter. She has returned to them, while around the country other parents are not so lucky, for even after all that has happened in Boyle, children are still being snatched away by the Call.

Nessa spends all of Christmas with them, staying in her old room, insisting on the presence of the worn-out teddies of her childhood.

But she has changed. Fergal gasps to see her rearrange the embers in the hearth with her bare hands. And he gasps again as she shows him how she can spit the fire out of her fingers after, or even her lips.

Early in the new year, she tells her parents that she has to leave again.

"The Nation must survive," she says. "I can help with that."

She sits alone on the bus, her suitcase propped up on the seat beside her so she can pretend it's Megan sitting there instead. And off she goes through the snowy roads, Agnes and Ferg waving her away, hugging each other, their pride so fierce it burns.

ACKNOWLEDGMENTS

This is a grim book, but it wasn't grim in the making, what with people from all over the world adding in energy and encouragement. My family were brilliant. Then, there was Julie Crisp, who was wiser and more generous than she had to be.

And what about the beta readers like Carol Connolly, Iain Cupples, and Doug of the McEachern clan? They gave up lots of time, didn't they? And not just for *The Call,* but for the manuscripts that came before it too! And I don't want to forget Carole Fleres, of course, who helped with earlier works. Thanks, guys, seriously.

I'm also grateful to the Ficklings—all Ficklings. Everywhere. But in particular to Rosie (aka "The First"), who pushed my work on the rest of the office; to David, who loves to phone with good news; to Caro, who gave me the run of her home and pretended not to be traumatized by my strange ways.

One day in July, I was introduced to the incredible DFB team in Oxford, and that's when I knew everything was going to be okay. Professionals every one of them, and if I were a drinker, I'd raise a glass in honor of Carolyn, Bron, Anthony, Phil, and Simon, and all the rest.

I'd need *lots* of glasses for the editing side, since so many people chipped in. But the steady hand on the helm belonged to Bella Pearson, who gathered everything together and fired brilliant suggestions into my inbox.

Others may be completely unaware of their contributions to *The Call*. They include the dead poets, Amergin, Eibhlín, and Anonymous—my apologies to you all, and my sincere respect. There's also the boarding school I attended when I was Nessa's age, Clongowes Wood College, and the ones I attended in spirit in the company of Enid Blyton. Art helped too—the swirly heroic stuff of Jim Fitzpatrick. The first *Book of Conquests* I ever picked up was the one he illustrated.

Plenty donated courage to the cause when they came to readings of early versions of this book at Boskone, LuxCon, and TitanCon. The Brotherhood Without Banners showed up every time and they have no idea how much it helped to hear them say what worked or didn't work for them.

And let's not forget the organizers of the above cons, who work so hard every year to provide people like me with such opportunities!

To all of you, my thanks for this book.

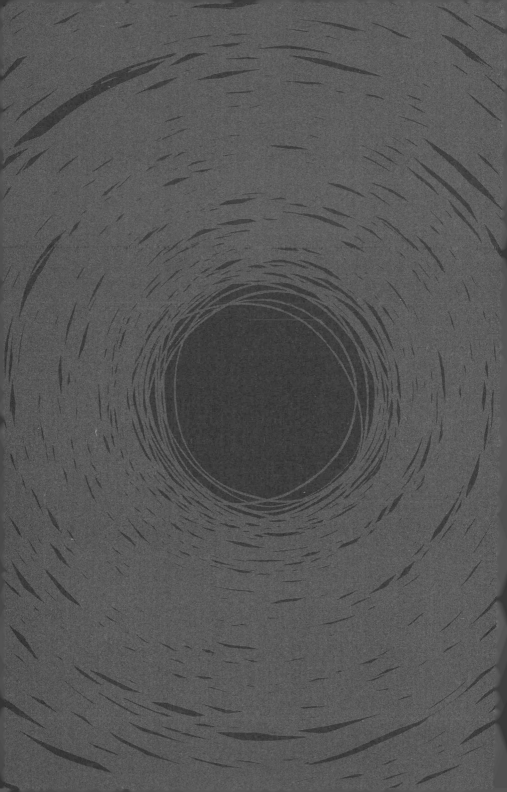